Fission #4

An Anthology of Stories from the British Science Fiction Association

bsfa.co.uk

Edited By

Eugen Bacon and Gene Rowe

The British Science Fiction Association

BSFA

The British Science Fiction Association

Fission #4

First published in the UK in 2024 by the British Science Fiction
Association (BSFA)

Cover Design by Elena Betti

ISBN 978-1-0687216-0-1

Praise for Fission

FISSION 2 VOLUME #1

"Fission #2 deftly plays with the evocative and provocative. There are nuanced beats of light and dark, that entertain and exhilarate in perfect harmony. Highly recommended."
ANDREW HOOK, British Fantasy Award-winning editor and author of Frequencies of Existence and Candescent Blooms

This first volume of Fission #2 shows off the variety of modern science-fiction. Every new story capitalises on the chance to surprise and delight. The consistency with which it does so across these 18 tales makes further volumes a tantalising proposition.
DAMIEN LAWARDORN, Aurealis

FISSION 2 VOLUME #2

Fission #2, Volume 2 raises a smile as frequently as an eyebrow. It's a crowd pleaser that acts as a reminder that sci-fi can be equally amusing and thought-provoking—and sometimes both at once.
DAMIEN LAWARDORN, Aurealis

FISSION 3

To single out just a handful of stories is a disservice, as the anthology is excellently curated, offering a buffet of delights that range from philosophical to funny to haunting.
In their foreword, editors Eugen Bacon and Gene Rowe describe Fission #3 as a "literary escapade" to help in "dire times," and it lives up to that mission. Though many of these literary futures are gloomy, they reject pessimism. It's not uplifting, exactly, but Fission #3 feels like an ode to the living, a statement that endings don't have to be terrifying, and a celebration of the diversity of science fiction.
DAMIEN LAWARDORN, Aurealis

Contents

Foreword: It Never Rains...

This is getting silly now.

We reduced our submissions window for Fission #4 in the hope of containment.

Fat chance.

We received nearly fifty percent more stories than for Fission #3.

That's around 350 stories and over a million words to read, all from just two weeks of an open submission period.

Of course, this meant we had even more quality to choose from, but also meant we had to turn away a lot of stories we liked. And, in the end, we couldn't resist: *just one more... just one more...* and there went our definite, concrete, absolutely-not-going-to-budge word limit.

What it means for you, dear reader, is a significantly longer volume of stories to feast upon.

So, what do we have this time? We chose twenty-three stories, and to this added a twenty-fourth from our annual collaboration with Spanish colleagues at Celsius. And as before, variety has driven us. We offer a diversity of styles and sub-genres from a range of authors—counting several BSFA members—from the relatively novice to award-winners.

It was undoubtable we would open the anthology with Harry Slater's 'There are Days When you Will be Terrified of Airplanes', a powerful tale of memory theft and salvation in a future time of war. Potent enough to warrant a whole paragraph to itself.

As ever, tales about the promise and perils of technology thrive here. In Carsten Schmitt's deeply moving 'Wagner's Voice', AI is on hand to aid a failing dementia sufferer; in Teresa Milbrodt's 'Dye Job', hair colouring reflecting one's emotional state has unexpected consequences, arguably good and bad. We also have stories that are more clearly dystopic. Remi Martin's 'The Performance of Your Life' follows a woman under constant surveillance, whether from drones outside or cameras installed in just about every electrical item in her home. We're heading that way, people! In Guan Un's 'An Object of Vision', there are dangers from virally infected optical devices, meanwhile, Caroline Corfield's 'The Printer' tells of a fightback against technology more generally, led by that most iniquitous of items, the printer—surely a device spawned in Hell! J.L. George's 'Digital Hell is Cold' takes even further the nightmare of where our embrace of technology might lead.

Did we mention trouble with AI? That is one problem the protagonist in Jeff Somers' 'Lone Star. Deep Black. Hum.' has to face in the escape capsule of his ship.

But there are also stories that make you smile. Timons Esaias' 'Results' might cause you to rethink going for that genetic test you were planning; Templeton Moss' 'Nibor's Report' has alien assessors getting Earth comically wrong; and Jake Stein's 'Human Garbage' humorously relates the dangers of an intelligent trash compactor unravelling via a helpline thread. There's also fun in Ian Li's 'Everyone is Dying to Work Here' – fun, that is, unless you're the recruit taking part in a tour through the new company's deeply ambiguous activities.

And we've got quirky too. These include Sarina Dorie's 'Science Fiction Fairy Tales: Cinderella, Hansel and Gretel, and Aladdin', a trio of flash fiction retellings of favourite children's tales, and Barlow Crassmont's 'Falling Upwards', in which an underappreciated superhero encounters a woman who really doesn't want to be saved. Susan L. Lin's 'Moonshot: An Oral History of Our Solar System's Great Lunar Uprising' tells – via interviews with various savants – of our moon deciding it's simply had enough of us pesky humans. Then there's J.D. Dresner's metafictional 'The Death Sentence' — which we'd love to tell you more about, if only we had sufficient word count (*wink, eh, J.D.?*).

This perhaps wouldn't be a sci-fi collection without a bit of time travel, hence we have G.J. Dunn's 'Mirror Cast', in which our protagonist seeks to return to the past to change events, even knowing that the taste of success will be bitter. And we have a parallel universe story in the form of Liam Hogan's 'Compatibility', in which our protagonist unwisely seeks to enrol another self into a dishonourable ploy.

We have other common themes, too. Mark Thomas' 'Ransom' deals with the mystery of an alien kidnapping; Ashton Macaulay's 'The Manual' offers up a bit of the supernatural (what *is* in the back of the truck?); and Cherry Zheng's 'The Summoner' gives us more monster drama. And then there's Robert Bagnall's 'Formula 719: The Cure for Ennui', in which the inventor of a process to save the world from climate change needs to find a new purpose.

We close with our Celsius swaps. From our Spanish partners, we were delighted to receive Angel Luis Sucasas' 'Farewell', in which children are unsettled by the inevitability of what they and their peers must become on attaining adulthood. And that is apt, for our own choice for translation — Robinne Weiss' 'Space Brat' — also centres on the trials of precocious children, these ones desperate to escape Earth's gravity well and return to space. We asked Robinne for a few words of her own on the story *behind* the story, and she obliged:

'"Space Brat" was inspired by an episode of the podcast, Writing Excuses. I have no idea what the episode was about. Mary Robinette Kowal made a random comment about a mission to Mars — well, they'd have to come back — and my brain somehow jumped to the question, what if kids born in space came back to Earth. I immediately started scribbling the

first draft of Space Brat, completely ignoring the rest of the podcast.'

Thanks, Robinne. And on that note, over to our storytellers. Enjoy!

Eugen Bacon & Gene Rowe
Fission Editors

There are Days When you Will be Terrified of Airplanes
Harry Slater

There are men with guns making their way down the street, picking through the rubble. Soldiers, all in uniform, maybe ten of them, checking the doors into the buildings that are still standing. You can see them, hear them talking over the thud-thudding of your heart.

One of them pushes into the house next door to the one that used to be yours. Hansi lived there. He was good to you, letting you keep warm at his fire while your parents were at work, giving you little sweets when he thought they weren't looking. His face was old but kind, and he laughed so loudly he woke half of the street when something tickled him.

Bang-Bang Bang-Bang.

They will find you soon, you and the others, and they will do the same as they have done to Hansi. You cower down behind the shattered window and you wait and you try not to breathe too loudly and mouth a prayer to a god you did not used to believe in

'It is important, at all times, to make a distinction between you and the assets. Failure to do so can lead to a corruption of the data. Corruption of the data can lead to complications during the download phase.'

Kellan wiped his nose with the back of his hand and it came away spotted with blood. You. That was the important thing. You. A helicopter buzzed over the hotel, its churning rotors rattling the thin glass in the windows. Kellan held his breath until the sound of the engine faded. The sky outside was the colour of weak tea, the air smelled of smoke, like it had for weeks.

He reached for the water at the side of the bed and took a drink. It was warm, unpleasant, but better than what most people in the city had left. Scratched at the hidden port, just behind his right ear, the flap of fake skin that covered it up coming loose. There was a layer of sticky sweat and sand on his skin, a membrane that had settled on the first day in the desert and felt like it might never wash off. You. You.

You

'Bring him up.'

Private Mitchell nodded, pointing ahead with the barrel of his rifle. Dusty camo, spattered with brown flecks and smears of dirt. His boots were scuffed at the toes.

'Follow me, sir.'

Kellan could tell it rankled, to have to call him sir. It might have been accurate, he had a higher rank, but even the lowliest grunt looked down on Carriers. The Extractors, at least, were there on the front line. Carriers were bag men, moving intel from A to B when the coast was clear. Babysitting, they called it when they were assigned to one of them.

He was never there when the data was retrieved, and that made him weak in their eyes. Never killed anyone. Never bloodied his hands, up to the wrists, the elbows like the rest of them.

The private led him through what was once a residential street, reduced to rocks and fire damage by the latest assault. A burned-out car was still smoking, its black carcass like the corpse of some giant insect. They stopped at a six storey building, mostly still standing, grey concrete pocked with bullet holes.

'It's a big load, sure you can take it?' Cranstone was leaning against a wall, cigarette in his mouth, the bulky laptop next to him churning through green code faster than most could hope to read.

'Fuck you,' Kellan replied.

'No need to get your panties all twisted.' Cranstone's face was curled into a smile that made his boyish good looks turn somehow sinister. 'Just need to make sure you've got the capacity for the upload.'

'I got space.' Kellan pulled out the cover and waved an impatient hand for the cable.

'Always so eager.' The sneer reached Cranstone's eyes and he tossed the cable across to Kellan. 'Need some lube or are you gonna rawdog it?'

'You get off on this?' Kellan inserted the plug, twisted it until it clicked.

'That's enough, gentlemen.' Sergeant Lanski all but filled the door, a snarl on his lips that he'd forgotten how to call off. 'Lost men here today, you keep civil, else you walk back.'

'Sir, yes sir.' Cranstone saluted, his jaw finding a stolid position that might have been reverence, might have been mockery.

'Good to go, sir,' Kellan mumbled.

They're close now. Close enough that you can recognise their words, smell the fabric of their uniforms. Setti is curled up next to you, hands covering her head. You're stroking her hair as softly as you can, fingers running through the long black tresses to try and keep her quiet. Mother told you, look after her, whatever happens, look after her. Setti's dress is loose, at the shoulders and the waist, hanging like a prayer flag, her bones so obvious you're scared to touch them. We are scared to touch them.

Kellan jerked awake so violently the headboard slammed into the thin wall, showering his hair with plaster dust. Eyes searched frantically in the gloom, struggling to put together a location, breath coming in heavy gasps that seemed to be depositing oxygen everywhere but his lungs.

'There is potential for bleed-through, most likely when you are under stress. This is normal. Once the data is retrieved, the sensation will pass. This is experimental technology, there are going to be teething problems. If you are worried, report to your line manager and download as soon as possible. The absolute worst thing you can do is panic.'

Smoked his last cigarette two days ago. Dug around in the ashtray to find a stub that might hold enough for a few drags but came up short. You you you you you you. The hotel room resolved itself, the nicotine-stain walls, the cracked mirror, the sweat-discoloured sheets. Two more hours. You. Breathe. You. Slow.

You have to

They drove back to the base in silence, Mitchell's knuckles clenched around the steering wheel as though he might rip it off. Kellan stared out of the window, letting the sand become a blur of gold, smearing into his retinas until tears came. The download crackled and scratched at the edge of his awareness, pressing at the place where his spine melted into his skull. Maybe it had been too big, hadn't even checked the size before he started. Little drops of light percolated through the endless yellow, glimpses of a different day, a different angle of sun, washes of moon spilling out of the cracked blue sky.

The data centre was at the heart of the compound, a white satellite dish growing out of its roof like a child's drawing of a mushroom. Kellan tapped in the code, left the private stone-faced at the door. Only techs in here. The door slid closed behind him and he settled down in the single chair in the middle of the room. In front of him, a bank of monitors, a flickering cursor eager in the top left corner. He pushed his fingers into the print readers at the edge of the chair's arms, waited for the system to recognise him, then opened his port. A lead snaked out of the back of the chair, found the metallic hole in his flesh and sank in.

His face twitched, a series of movements that he wasn't certain were his own, expressions he'd never made before. Then the screens burst into life, a thrashing, manic series of images and movements, colours and noise. It lasted all of thirty seconds, a cacophony that explained the thickness of the walls, the entry restrictions. The cable detached and Kellan flopped forwards, soaked with sweat and wheezing, the familiar nausea bubbling between his gut and his mouth, always threatening but never spilling over.

Outside, the sun was blinding, an oppressive force pushing needles into his skin. He pulled out a pair of battered sunglasses and slipped them over his damp nose, searched in another pocket for his cigarettes. He could taste pomegranate on the back of his tongue, sharp as if he'd just had a mouthful, spat before he lit the smoke.

'All good?' Mitchell looked as though he hadn't moved, hadn't even breathed while Kellan was in the data centre.

'Same old,' he replied, the nausea fading to an annoyance rather than a crisis.

'Sarge wants to see you,' Mitchell sniffed. 'Got another job.'

'I'm off shift. Need a scan before I pack again.'

'Sarge wants,' Mitchell shrugged, as though that was an end to the conversation.

It was, Kellan supposed.

If you make a sound now, they will find you. If you whimper or move, if you breathe, if a drop of the damp sweat running all over you trickles too far, they will find you. If Setti starts to cry, if a brick falls, if the light catches the buckle still left on your right shoe, they will find you. You clutch tight to the black box, pressing it into the space below your ribs and close your eyes. If you cannot see them, they cannot see you. If you cannot see them, they cannot see you. If I cannot see you, we cannot be seen. If I see, you see. We see. See?

'I don't suppose you have a cigarette?' Kellan shifted his chair deeper into the shade of the awning, worked his aching jaw in slow circles.

'No cigarettes in city. Not for a month. Was going to ask you.' Basha grinned, the scar on his mouth a perfect white line down to his chin, spotted Kellan looking. 'Shrapnel, two years back, makes me look tough, no?'

'When can I download?'

'Can't do it here, need to get you out of the country, only way.' Basha's grin faltered a little, but not by much.

'I don't have out-of-the-country time.' Kellan's voice ran to the desperate, flecks of white spit pattering the table between them.

'Ever tried stealing tech from an army base, my friend? Can't be done. We get you out, we get them out. Only way it can work.' Basha took a sip from his glass of strong tea, slid an envelope across to Kellan. 'Papers, passport, all good. Ticket too. They find you when you land, take it from there.'

'They?' Kellan grabbed the envelope, stuffed it down the front of his shirt.

'Friends,' Basha replied with a wink. 'Good people, know what they're doing.'

'Fuck!' Kellan slammed his hand down onto the table, sending the glasses rattling. The few eyes sat outside turned on them, faces strangely blank, as though someone hadn't finished filling in the details. The weight of their gaze made his skin crawl and he shuddered in a breath. 'Sorry.'

'No stress, that's what you say. Keep calm. Deep breathing.' Basha's hand hovered over the table, as though he was casting some sort of spell. 'My cousin, my sister. I take you now, drop you close to airport. Five hours, maybe six, all be good. Right face, right shade, they let you through.'

'Sorry,' Kellan said again, droplets of blood spattering out of his nose, mixing with the spilt tea. 'Sorry.'

'Is good,' Basha replied, handing him a handkerchief. 'Five hours, all done. My car not far.'

You have to help us

It could have been any street, could have been the one they were on that morning. Shells of buildings, dust in the air, patches of dry blood spattered and sprayed, smoke rising from fires that no one was left to put out. They'd already collected two batches, Cranstone mocking him every time. He'd never been this close before, never smelled the still lingering freshness of the kills. On the second upload, he'd seen the Extractor at work, watched the deftness of his fingers as he'd sliced around the scalp and attached the diodes.

'Bone gives a better connection,' he said unprompted. 'Especially with a diminishing feed. Be better with direct contact, but then it gets real messy.'

Kellan reached out, laid a hand on a nearby wall for support, couldn't pull his eyes away. Knowing was one thing, seeing was another. The banal precision, the movements of Cranstone's latex-gloved hands, almost dancing over the peeled-back skin.

'Live extraction has its upsides, but you get a wriggler and it's all kinds of trouble.' He was giddy with the telling, almost giggling as he explained. Kellan's skin was shifting to a shade of white close to green. 'Longest gap I've done from termination to egress has been three days. Fuck me, man, the smell. You wouldn't believe it.'

'Drone says there's movement, next street along. We got what we need?' Lanski scowled at the blood on Cranstone's gloves, at the wall, at the dirt.

'Just need to load our packhorse and we're good to go. Ten minutes.'

'Five,' the sergeant growled, then ducked outside to marshal the others.

'You heard the man,' Cranstone said, wiggling the wire at Kellan. 'Open up.'

He is we are you are kneeling over us them you. Please just stay quiet please just stay quiet. They he you have passed but you and I have seen you and I. Fuck fuck fuck fuck fuck. You have to help us. You have to take us away. There is blood in your mouth. Setti is not moving. Setti and her beautiful voice and the way she would giggle just before she did something naughty. Setti is here too, you can see it if you'd like we can show you I they he you Kellan. Is your name Kellan? Mother showed me how to store us. It has been ten days, but I do not think Setti needs the last ten days. Let her be Setti before the dress did not fit, before the scowling man, before before before. Kellan? Kellan? Kellan?

'You're bleeding, sir.'

'I'm fine,' Kellan was holding Basha's handkerchief under his nose. 'Dust. Clogs up my sinuses and then...' Shrugged. Wasn't an entire lie.

'A Carrier held on to an upload for too long, came home with a morbid fear of aeroplanes. Whenever one flew over he'd scurry for cover.'

They'd all laughed at that, at the first briefing. Because humour broke the fear, because it was better than facing up to the choice they were collectively making.

The security officer looked at the passport, looked back at Kellan, looked at the passport again. There were guns everywhere, lounging in the crooks of arms, slung lazily across shoulders, dangling at hips.

Setti had never seen a gun, not until the soldiers were almost on top of her, giants in khaki, as though they wanted to be hidden. Funny.

'You're all good.' The man passed the documents back under the glass plate, waved the next passenger up. 'Safe travels.'

Kellan tried to smile, legs shaking and cold, jaw fighting to push out and up. He had too many teeth now, all of them trying to fit into a mouth shared, kept biting his tongue.

'How many?' he whispered, joining the back of the boarding queue.

Twenty. I think. Most of the street

The blood was flowing freely, soaking through the handkerchief, splashing down onto Kellan's sullied shirt, pooling in the smoking wound on Setti's back. Slipping the diodes over a young girl's head, over my head, over your head, our head, their head, a head, bone conducts better but flesh is more honest, old tech but he understands it, and there is a direct flow as he catches her falling, uploads the hard drive, sand already filling up ruins, rib cages like grasping claws, mother told you look after her, mother told you.

'Mother?'

You have to help us all

Ransom
Mark Thomas

Given the town's recent history, there was a quick police response.

As soon as the young man was reported missing, a lead detective and a canine team sped to his home. The thirteen-year-old's movements were quickly tracked from his bedroom window, along a dry creek bed, to some scrubland near the canal.

Unfortunately, the trailing dog became disoriented in a patch of meadow grass that had been flattened by sleeping deer. The young Alsatian circled and backtracked with nostrils flaring but finally gave up and sat down, awaiting new instructions. The handler shifted the dog's attention to the canal bank, and they walked a five-mile stretch between two locks, but couldn't regain the scent.

The search should have been easy because the youngster's phone had a locator app but, unfortunately, his parents had confiscated the device during last evening's dinner. On the upside, police now had access to an extensive 'contacts' list and it was reasonable to hope that the boy had rendezvoused with one of those friends. Police texted every person on the list. When that didn't yield anything more than puzzled concern, four officers began face-to-face interviews.

At 5 am, human and canine searchers continued to knock on doors and sniff under bushes, but the young man still hadn't been found. The lead detective Lurie Harris returned to the parents' home to personally deliver the latest progress report, such as it was.

Harris raised her fist to knock on the front door, but it yanked open before she made contact. Mrs Kirk ushered the detective into the living room.

'We received a ransom note,' the woman said, and pulled an envelope from her sweater pocket. 'I found this in the mailbox two minutes ago, and was just about to phone you.'

'Did you see the delivery?'

Mrs Kirk frowned. 'No. We *heard* something in the front yard so I rushed outside, thinking it might be Jim, but it was just the newspaper. I picked that up off the sidewalk and, when I turned around, I noticed this envelope pinched under the mailbox lid.'

'I'll make us some more coffee,' Mr Kirk said and he shuffled into the kitchen.

The detective pulled on a pair of purple latex gloves then took the ransom envelope. 'How is your newspaper delivered?' she asked. 'By car?'

'Yes,' Mrs Kirk nodded.

Years ago, newspapers were stuffed into mailboxes by bike-riding children but no sane parent would allow that now.

'I'll need to talk to the delivery person.'

'Of course, of course.' Mrs Kirk plucked a business card from the cork reminder board in the front hall, and passed it to the detective. Harris inserted the card in her daybook, then examined the ransom envelope.

It was a large commercial mailer, the kind of thing a business might use to deliver a book or T-shirt. It wasn't sealed or addressed, and there was only a single word written on it: 'important'. Inside, there were three items: a grey sheet of paper, a small glassine package containing half a Q-tip, and a Timex watch, with the vinyl band cut rather than unbuckled.

Mr Kirk returned from the kitchen carrying a tray of coffee cups. His face was haggard and he seemed to be more angry than worried. The tray rattled as it touched down on a low, glass-topped table.

Detective Harris took a sip of coffee to be polite, then said 'I take it, this is Jim's watch?' She held up the timepiece.

Both parents nodded. Then Mrs Kirk pointed out that the watch had stopped. 'It's frozen at one-thirty,' she said, 'that's when they got him.'

Mr Kirk grunted and turned away from his wife, slightly.

Detective Harris quietly noted the friction, then studied the ransom note, which was written with a sharpie on the grey sheet of paper. The paper was torn from a restaurant take-out menu. Each letter was a neat little square block. There was a cartoon flying-saucer graphic printed in the corner of the paper, and the hand-written text overlaid a pattern of cascading stars and an extensive list of milkshake flavours.

Harris read: 'We have your son, which anal swab and timepiece will verify. Deliver 30kg of $Bi\{C_6H_4(OH)CO_2\}_3$ to the meadow waypoint signalled by police canine. In exchange, your son will emerge. Ps: he is unharmed. As of yet. Enough.'

'He's been abducted by aliens,' Mrs Kirk said. Her eyes were red-rimmed with fatigue. 'He saw something through his bedroom window and, when he went to investigate, they took him. The aliens need that gobbledygook for some reason we can't understand.' A finger fluttered at the chemical formula in the ransom note.

'Jesus,' her husband said, rattling his coffee cup back onto the tray. 'He hasn't been abducted by aliens. He hasn't been abducted by anyone at all.' Mr Kirk took a big breath and slowly released it. 'It's just a prank.'

He faced the detective. 'Of course, we didn't know that until we saw the note.' Mr Kirk pointed at the paper. 'I recognise that menu scrap. Jim stuffed it in his pocket last night, when we were at dinner. And I recognise his printing, too—he wrote the damn thing.' He chewed at his upper lip. 'When we finally get him home, we're going to owe you people a huge apology.'

Detective Harris felt her chest muscles relax, and she could suddenly expel a bushel of stale air. A 'prank' was the best possible outcome in a situation like this. Lecturing a kid about wasting police resources was infinitely preferable to dragging the canal for his corpse. But the detective couldn't openly express relief until the kid was actually sitting on that green brocade couch between his parents.

'The aliens *made* him write the note.' Mrs Kirk leaned toward Harris, ignoring her husband. 'They wouldn't know how to do it themselves.'

Mr Kirk pressed a palm against his left temple and his neck responded with a series of clicks. 'Donna, think about what you're saying. You claim these aliens don't know how to write, yet they'd be able to *dictate* a message in English.'

'They'd use *telepathy*, for Christ's sake.' Mrs Kirk didn't see any inconsistency. 'Their intentions would be unscrambled *as* they were being communicated.' She licked her lips. 'Of course, the note sounds funny because aliens don't understand the idiosyncrasies of everyday speech. And what about the watch? Why did the kidnappers cut the band instead of undoing the buckle?'

Mrs Kirk's eyes flicked rapidly back and forth between her husband and Detective Harris but she wasn't really inviting them to answer her question. 'I'll tell you why—because aliens don't understand simple human things, like clothing fasteners.'

Detective Harris suddenly recalled an old science fiction story where a Martian tried to infiltrate Earth but was discovered because he couldn't button a sweater properly. FBI agents immolated the creature with flame throwers.

Clearly, 5 am fatigue was affecting her, as well.

'Ridiculous,' Mr Kirk said to his wife. He turned his attention to the detective. 'Did anyone report seeing a spaceship last night? Anyone at all?'

Harris opened her mouth to answer but Mrs Kirk interjected: 'Of course no one saw the spaceship—they have cloaking devices.'

Mr Kirk rolled his eyes. 'But Jim saw it, only Jim.' Obviously, this argument had started before the detective's arrival.

Detective Harris had witnessed the dynamic dozens of times: parents became disabled with guilt and worry and shame whenever they had to talk to police about their children, and they turned into simpletons.

Harris didn't have children herself and, at times like these, she was grateful.

'Donna,' Mr Kirk clenched and unclenched his fingers. 'Aliens who have mastered invisibility, and space travel, and telepathy could figure out how to undo a Timex watch strap.' He took another deep breath, placed a hand on his wife's shoulder and his voice suddenly became gentle. 'Enabling this nonsense isn't helpful.'

'It isn't nonsense.' Mrs Kirk's voice was full of metal filings.

Mr Kirk turned towards the detective. 'Jimmy could have easily snuck that note into the mailbox. He's played in the woods behind our house since he was old enough to crawl. He moves through the bush like a rabbit.'

'He never *crawled* through the woods,' Mrs Kirk said. 'You make it sound like he was completely unsupervised, wandering the neighbourhood in a diaper while we drank cans of Super Lager in front of the TV.' She turned to the officer. 'We're not terrible parents, we always watched Jimmy carefully. He's our only child.'

'It was just an expression.' Mr Kirk carefully lifted his hand from his wife's shoulder and the couple sank a little deeper into their couch.

'Pretending to be kidnapped is pretty extreme behaviour,' the detective said. 'Has Jim ever done anything like this before?'

Mrs Kirk's eyelids lowered, and her fingers tugged at a thread in the hem of her sweater. Mr Kirk looked tiredly triumphant—the answer was obvious.

'Once,' Mrs Kirk said to the carpet. 'He did something like this just *once*. He wanted a new bike and pretended to be kidnapped.'

'He snuck a ransom note into the mailbox, just like today.' Mr Kirk took up the story. 'The *kidnappers*,' he made violent air quotes 'wanted eight-hundred-and-eleven dollars—the exact amount the bike cost. They'd even calculated the sales tax. Of course, Jim was never missing. He was camping in a friend's backyard and the parents thought I'd texted them saying it was okay. The little bugger had got hold of my phone... and blocked a return text from the friend's parents.'

'He's clever,' Detective Harris said. Smart kids sometimes caused a lot of trouble.

'Yeah. He's clever alright.' Mr Kirk took a big swig of coffee. The cup trembled slightly. 'I'll bet any money that anal swab is legit.' The cup landed noisily back on the tray. 'I know my son. He has a very warped sense of humour.'

'But this is completely different!' Mrs Kirk wiped her eyes with a knuckle. 'No one's asking for money—the aliens need that gobbledygook.'

'Aaaaaah.' Mr Kirk tried to sound dismissive. 'That's just bismuth subsalicylate—'

'Excuse me?' The detective narrowed her eyes.

'Basically, antacid.' Mr Kirk's fingertips tapped on his thighs. He seemed unnerved by the odd ransom request unable to make sense of it, even as part of an eccentric, puerile joke.

'How do you know what it is?' The detective had taken a chemistry course in university, but couldn't blithely decode the nomenclature.

'I see it all the time—I'm a pharmacist.'

'Oh.' During their first meeting, Harris had been hyper-focused on getting a good scent sample for the dog, opening Jim's phone, and assessing its confiscation as running-away-from-home motivation. She really didn't know much about the family. 'Is Jim into chemistry?' she asked. 'Would he be familiar with that chemical formula?'

Mr Kirk snorted. 'No, but you can look up random chemical formulas on a phone. It's not difficult.' The nervous finger movement paused for an instant. 'It's just an… an elaboration… a quirky detail he's included to make the note seem real.'

'But Jim couldn't have looked up formulas on his phone last night, you'd already confiscated it.'

Mr Kirk pursed his lips. 'One of Jimmy's friends must have helped. Believe me, he didn't do this on his own—he cooked it up with one of his soccer buddies.'

'You told me earlier that his phone was taken away during dinner.' Harris thought the punishment was harsh but tried not to sound judgmental. After all, parental discipline was a rare quality these days.

There was an uncomfortable pause, then Mrs Kirk blurted: 'Oh, for gosh sakes, he's *thirteen*, he didn't know what he was doing.'

Mr Kirk sighed loudly, again. 'We were eating saucer fries at Roswell's, and Jimmy kept taking phone pictures of the waitress when she bent over to serve nearby tables. The waitresses wear these little silver metallic mini-skirts, and you can practically see their panties.'

'He's *thirteen*,' Mrs Kirk repeated.

Harris used to stop at Roswell's for coffee when she drove a patrol car. She vaguely remembered the wait-staff looking like Star Trek extras. Generally, the décor was a kitschy mixture of Buck Rogers and Flesh Gordon. The main dining area was round, to make it seem like the interior of a flying saucer.

The restaurant was several miles from the canal brushland where they tracked Jim, and wasn't part of the original search grid. But Roswell's was the town's only 24-hour restaurant and, if Jim *had* run away from home, it was a plausible-enough destination. Maybe he backtracked after thinking of it, mid-flight?

'Excuse me a minute.' Harris pulled out her phone. 'I'll have a car check out the restaurant, to see if he returned there.'

'Good idea,' Mr Kirk grumbled. 'Maybe he circled back to ask that waitress to his grade eight prom.' Mr Kirk's fingers were still making random movements on his trousers. 'We took Jim to Roswell's because of his science fair project. He's constructing a model of a lunar settlement. The dinner was supposed to be a reward for shoving himself away from a gaming screen and actually doing some school work.'

Of course, the family probably didn't need an excuse to eat as Roswell's. Harris presumed that, like most busy couples, the family might not have used their stove much. Or maybe they still clung to the outmoded idea that restaurant meals were a special treat? Harris sipped at her coffee and they all waited for a return call from the patrol dispatched to the restaurant.

For a few wonderful minutes, the Kirks stopped arguing. Mr Kirk clutched a couch cushion and squeezed it, trying to tame his finger tremors. Mrs Kirk excused herself and went to the washroom.

Harris examined a group of family photographs hanging behind the couch. There were several stiffly formal portraits, but one candid shot of a smiling Jim with a Big Bertha model rocket kit.

When Mrs Kirk returned her face looked flushed, as though she had splashed it with hot water.

The detective's phone buzzed.

It was a text from the officers at Roswell's. They'd quickly searched the kitchen, washrooms, parking lot and dumpsters but the missing boy wasn't there.

Harris passed along the report. 'You have to admit,' she said to Mrs Kirk, 'there's an awful lot of source material for an alien-themed kidnapping prank.' Her voice wasn't combative, like Mr Kirk's; this was girl-to-girl. 'There's Jim's science fair project about a lunar settlement, there's the flying-saucer restaurant with the space-chick waitresses, there's his underlying interest in space travel.' Harris nodded at the rocket kit picture. If she were a Trekkie, she might have noticed that the missing youth shared his name with an iconic TV character. 'You mix all that with a family argument about his phone and maybe he decided to—'

'But that doesn't explain the weird formula in the ransom note…'

The detective gave a slight shrug. 'I know, the note *is* pretty strange.' She turned her attention to Mr Kirk, the pharmacist. 'This bismuth subju…'

'Subsalicylate.'

'Yeah… it doesn't have any recreational drug value, does it? Like, what would happen if a kid ground it up and snorted it?'

'Absolutely nothing, wouldn't even fizz in the nose. It might feel a little weird to have something dissolve in your body, but it's not a stimulant, or anything like that.'

Harris wondered if thirteen-year-old boys could possibly misinterpret ant*acid* as an over-the-counter alternative to LSD. She opened her phone browser and quickly checked for new household drug fads and goofy internet challenges, but couldn't find anything related to tummy medicine.

'Just out of curiosity, do you happen to have thirty kilograms of that bismuth antacid in your pharmacy?'

Mr Kirk scratched a patch of stubble under his chin. 'I think I might. I just got a big shipment in.'

'Would Jim know about the shipment?'

Mr Kirk scratched some more. 'I don't see how. I guess it's possible that I mentioned it last evening.'

Mrs Kirk suddenly became more animated. 'That's it! Jim overheard a scrap of our conversation, and filed it away in his subconscious. Then, the aliens telepathically mined that information.'

Mr Kirk groaned.

'Let's give them what they want!' Mrs Kirk continued. 'Let's deliver the bismuth-whatever-it-is…'

'Subsalicylate.'

'Let's give them the bismuth subsalicylate. I know you say it's just a prank, and maybe it is, but what could it possibly hurt to play along?' Mrs Kirk turned towards the detective, trying to deliver a strong telepathic appeal of her own.

Harris said, 'Well, it's getting light and I'd like to have another look at that area where the dog lost Jim's scent.' She got to her feet. 'Officers are still interviewing the young man's phone contacts. The search team is working through an expanded perimeter… they'll notify us as soon as they've found him.'

It was official police protocol to speak as if a good result was imminent, even while enthusiastically investigating the worst possible outcomes. 'In the meantime, you'll probably feel better if you move around a little. You can accompany me, and we can bring along the thirty kilos of bismuth, if you'd like.'

Mrs Kirk clasped her hands and mouthed the words 'thank you'.

Harris had to shift some rain gear out of the back seat of her Equinox, to make room for Mrs Kirk. When everyone was buckled up, and the engine started to gently thrum, both exhausted parents were on the verge of falling asleep. Their upper bodies rocked gently within the seat belt harnesses while a sleep-diffused version of their previous argument briefly re-surfaced.

'If aliens wanted a case of bismuth, why wouldn't they ray-gun the front door of my pharmacy and take it? For that matter, why wouldn't they just steal a trainload of the stuff from Incepta?'

Harris assumed that Incepta was Mr Kirk's antacid supplier.

'Aliens don't understand how things work here,' Mrs Kirk yawned. Then Harris heard the soft sounds of contrapuntal snoring.

The detective followed GPS directions to Mr Kirk's GalaxyPharma store. Darkness was crawling towards the horizon, revealing skinny jet-trail clouds, softly underlit by a sliver of rising sun. They passed Roswell's diner, which was almost deserted. A taxi, a carpet cleaning van and two police cruisers were the only vehicles in the parking lot.

GalaxyPharma was a small neighbourhood drug store. There were posters in the front window for middle school drama productions, reward notices for lost cats, and a flyer for a safe-injection site.

Harris parked right outside the front door and the Kirks woke up as her vehicle shuddered to a stop. Mr Kirk disabled the alarm system, and they walked to the dispensary at the back of the store. A dozen unopened UPS boxes were stacked on a table, behind the counter.

'I was going to tackle this before opening,' Mr Kirk said, glancing at his watch. 'That one's got the bismuth.' He pointed at the largest box, which was the size of a window air conditioner.

Harris looked at the shipping label: 30kg Bi{C$_6$H$_4$(OH)CO$_2$}$_3$. Tablet. Loose.

The company name, Incepta, was on the label as well, with two addresses, one in Bangladesh and the other in Ohio.

Of course, Harris noticed that this box contained the exact amount of bismuth subsalicylate requested by the ransom note, which was an outrageous coincidence. 'You must go through a lot of antacid,' she said.

'Modern times,' Mr Kirk replied. 'Stress and indigestion pay for most of our mortgage.' He licked his lips. 'Uh, I'm afraid I can't help you with that box, my sciatica has been flaring up.'

Harris dropped her butt and squat-lifted the package. Cardboard sagged under the weight of the antacid medicine. The tablets must have been packaged but the freight seemed to shift heavily anyway, like it was a sloppy load of road gravel. Luckily, the Equinox had a hands-free rear hatch, so Harris could wrestle the box inside without dropping it on the pavement.

They took a different route back towards the Kirk's neighbourhood. Harris turned onto a canal service road at the first lock and drove south for three kilometres. She parked near a cluster of markers left by the canine team. 'That's the spot.'

'Please bring the bismuth,' Mrs Kirk said.

Harris hefted the box again, and waddled to the margin of the matted grassy area where the trailing dog had lost Jim's scent.

In the new morning light, the meadow looked completely different from it did when Harris first inspected it. In fact, it didn't look like the patch of grass had been flattened by sleeping deer at all. For one thing, the circle was very large, not the typical haphazard collection of small, tamped sections. And the area was too open—urban deer usually chose more secluded spots in creeks and ravines.

The canine handler had merely speculated that an overpowering deer scent had disabled the tracking dog.

'Put it down, right there.' Mrs Kirk pointed at the centre of the circle, and Harris obliged because the box was getting really heavy. 'Now, let's move out of the way,' Mrs Kirk shooed them with her fingers, 'so they can retrieve the package…'

Mrs Kirk suddenly stopped talking because there was an explosion at the top of a nearby light standard. Photo-sensors were in the process of turning the canal's night-lights off but one of the massive mercury bulbs had burst, producing an electric-blue flash. Bits of plastic housing dropped onto the paved fitness pathway next to the water. At the same instant, a cobalt lightning web arced overhead.

The group took a few steps towards the conflagration, and stared upwards. A thin wisp of smoke rose from the light standard's tip, like a smouldering cigarette. When they turned their attention back to the grassy circle, the box of bismuth subsalicylate was gone.

They all stared stupidly at the patch of matted emptiness.

'Hey.'

Fifteen degrees to the left, a gangly young man stood beside a fringe of young poplars. He was yawning and rubbing his eyes.

'Jim?' Mrs Kirk sounded uncertain.

'What's up?' The young man was utterly unaware of the fuss his absence had caused.

Even more strange, Harris wasn't sure why they were assembled in the middle of that modest crop circle. 'I have to call someone,' she said.

She pulled out her phone and tried to contact dispatch, but her device wasn't working.

'What time is it?' Mr Kirk asked, raising his watch to his ear. 'I've got to get to the pharmacy.'

Jim looked at his wrist. 'Sorry, I've lost my watch.'

'Oh, no,' Mrs Kirk said. 'Grandma gave you that watch for your birthday.'

'I know. I feel really bad.' The young man's remorse seemed genuine.

Harris stowed her phone in her jacket pocket. Her daybook was there as well, hogging most of the space. She really should streamline that aspect of her life, cull all of the old bits of paper stuffed between the leaves, she thought.

She pushed the button on her transponder to open the Equinox doors. 'I'd better give you folks a ride home.'

'Thanks,' the Kirks mumbled as they climbed inside the vehicle.

'I've been thinking,' Jim said, as the Equinox bounced back onto the canal service road.

Mr Kirk scratched at the stubble under his chin. ''Bout what?'

'About changing my science fair project. Lunar settlement just seems childish, now. I think I'd like to do something about the energy stored in bismuth molecules.'

'Interesting,' Harris said. 'Why bismuth?'

'It has an incredibly long alpha decay half-life. You'd think weak radioactivity would limit its usefulness but it's actually the opposite. The power is hidden in that fractalisation.'

The three adults nodded in unison.

'What would that energy be used for?' Harris was contemplating a breakfast at Roswell's as soon as she dropped the Kirks at home.

'Oh, bismuth could power lots of things.' Jim paused. 'It could be converted into rocket fuel, for instance.'

More nods. Alternative fuel was a timely science fair topic.

'Of course, you'd need a way to release all of that energy,' Jim said, 'without bombarding it with neutrinos.'

Nod. Nod. Nod.

They passed another pair of police cruisers, parked on the side of the road. The officers slouched outside their vehicles, hats pushed back on their heads, without any sense of urgency. They obviously recognised Harris' Equinox because they gave her a big friendly wave.

'Maybe we could go to Roswell's for milkshakes tonight,' Mr Kirk said.

'Thanks, that would be nice.' Jim leaned against the car window and tilted his head toward the sky.

Everyone is Dying to Work Here
Ian Li

Welcome to Wondio's innovation labs! I'm Billy, and I'll be your intrepid tour guide. Don't be shy. You've already impressed the interviewers, so now we just need to find the right project team for you. Your peers will be envious—you have your pick from all the cutting-edge tech in this 700 million square feet facility.

Hm? They did tell me you were a maths whiz—that, indeed, makes this building twice as big as NASA's Vehicle Assembly Building. And we accomplish way more here than merely sending rockets to the moon.

Before we start, let me collect your non-disclosure and waiver agreements. Yes, please sign all thirty pages. No, no need to read it in detail; it's all boilerplate. And now we just need quick DNA and dental scans. Some clients need identity verification, and we've had folks fool our retina and fingerprint scanners before.

You understand.

Our offices are quite impressive from this high vantage point, right? Our architect modelled it off a theme park. Feel free to take selfies. No? There's a reason you're our top candidate. You care about the tech, not the spectacle.

Follow me then.

In this wing, we're developing long-distance drone delivery. How far can they fly? Officially, about 1,500 miles, but just between you and me, it's closer to double that.

Ah, good eye. These prototypes employ autorotation, similar to old-school gyrocopters. I shouldn't be surprised, you graduated from a top engineering program after all. Your back-of-the-envelope estimate is pretty close. Our improvements increase efficiency tenfold, which makes it superior to traditional drones for long-range strike—err, trips.

If this project sounds fun, wait until you see the next couple. Which team do I work on? I'm afraid you don't have clearance for that information yet. But let's just say it's a 'hot' project.

Here we have the suffoca—ahem, hyper-expansive materials division. Isn't it beautiful? A projectile the size of a backpack can fill a house with high-density foam within two seconds. Even air can't get through this material.

Ah, yes, rescuing people from falling debris is an excellent application. We value creative thinkers like you at Wondio. What is it currently used for in the real-world? Unfortunately, that's classified government info. But your rescue idea is great, can't believe we didn't think of that.

This red button behind the glass? There's one by each of our labs. Since some tests can be hazardous, this shuts down all the labs and dials emergency services. Don't worry; it's just a precaution. We've had zero accidents so far. Intentional incidents? You're a jokester, I see. I appreciate a good sense of humour. Haha.

Next is the rail-gun division. Cover your ears for a second while they run a test. Don't mind the holes in the wall.

True, we're partnering with the military on this program, but keep an open mind. With breakthroughs in room temperature superconductors, we hope to develop space exploration applications too.

Sorry, I can't disclose how many people our rail-guns have killed. If you think about it, though, they've been used to take out terrorist aircraft, so really you should be asking how many lives they've *saved*. Could be millions, I don't know.

You don't want to see another test? The destructiveness is dazzl—hang on, don't run off without me.

Look, I used to be just like you. Idealistic. But I realised I was learning from foremost experts in the field, at the most coveted workplace in the country, and getting paid fuck-you money. So I learned not to question too much.

You did *not* like that answer. Huh.

Okay, so some of these research projects have… potentially violent applications. But think of it this way: strong weapons actually deter aggression and end wars. Just look at how the atom bomb ended World War II. And the subsequent threat of mutually-assured destruction from nuclear weapons has all but eliminated wars. Other than the Vietnam War. And Korea. I guess Iraq, Afghanistan, Sudan, and Myanmar too. But that's it, I'm sure.

That's not even half? Oh, now you're a history buff too?

Alright, I promise this next one is not used by the military. Behold, the memory blaster. Feel this thing. It's lightweight and portable enough to mistake for a barcode scanner. But it can hit a target from twenty yards away, erasing up to a day's worth of memories.

Amazing, no?

Why all the questions about use cases? I'm disappointed. I thought you were all about the tech. Sure, some police departments commissioned this for crowd control and apprehending suspects. But there could be legitimate reasons to use it on criminals. Maybe you could help brainstorm a few since you're so creative.

And did you think about the incredible brain research that goes into developing something like this? We could accelerate Alzheimer's research. Okay, we haven't. But we *could*.

So, you're looking for a team that makes the world better? Well, this next one isn't it, but hear me out. We discovered a new hormone that suppresses fear, found only in the tears of children with a certain genetic mutation. Watch, they're harvesting tears today. What a treat.

Hey, don't touch the button! No one is being harmed, there's no need—

Well, now you've done it. Of course, there are no alarms; the button is just a placebo. Congratulations, you passed our ethics test. All of these projects are fake; they're invented to gauge your moral compass. And boy, do you have a strong one...

You don't believe me? Gosh, I wish you weren't so perceptive. We'll have to wipe your memory then. Oh, don't make that sour face. Think positively: you get to learn about these cool projects all over again.

Not even a chuckle? You have no sense of humour. Your worst quality, after your uncompromising morals. Don't worry, I won't make you fill out the waivers again.

There's no use running, you know the range on these memory blasters...

Welcome to Wondio's innovation labs! You've already filled out the waivers? You're a star. Has anyone ever told you that?

The Performance of Your Life
Remi Martin

'Could you turn that thing off?' she says, walking towards the bed. She says it to the 'you' behind the camera, but also to that other hypothetical you, that multiplicitous you, that potential you that might be watching this back some other time.

The image is grainy, produced by an early handheld camera. Not so early that it requires a tape, but early enough that it's difficult to make out the features of the dimly lit room. What you can see is Una's denim shorts, frayed at the edges, only covering the very top of her thighs, and the outline of her black vest top. You can see the sweat on her brow, and her eyes peeking over the top of her sunglasses and deduce that she has just come inside from the heat. She laughs and falls back onto the mattress.

'I mean it, if you think you're filming even a minute!' she says, picking up a pillow and brandishing it playfully.

It's perhaps the first time she sees 'you'. There are other home recordings of her, of course. Her parents filmed a handful of her childhood birthdays, a few clips of her playing in the pool on holiday but, in these, she's unaware of you watching her, sometimes unaware she's being filmed at all. She's having far too much fun in the videos to pay any attention to you. In her teenage years, she never had a video camera, and although she had a mobile phone, it couldn't record video, or not well-enough to bother. This camera, and the boy behind it, are a novelty for her. She sees you, and acts accordingly, acts instinctively; *acts*.

She takes hold of the camera herself, and looks at you for a second, before pulling you in towards her lips. She kisses the lens, a big, exaggerated smooch, then extends her arms so you can see her again. She winks, and says, barely above a whisper:

'This is for our eyes only. See you later.'

The camera shuts off.

* * *

As she gets older, you see more of her. She's in her late twenties now, uploading video after video to HangPad of a road trip she has taken with her friends.

They're in Austria, beside a huge natural lake, the camera following her as she walks along a jetty towards it, between sun-dappled trees. The video quality is much crisper now, filmed on the latest smartphone. She turns around and smiles at you in faux-surprise, as if shocked that she's being filmed, as if she wasn't aware that you were watching her.

She gives you a mischievous grin, opening her eyes so they're big and wild, and then turns back around to face the lake and begins running at a furious sprint towards it.

When she reaches the end, she leaps, fully dressed, over its surface, screws herself up tight into a cannonball and lands with a splash, disappearing beneath its glistening surface.

Hours later, you see her again, on the patio of a quaint restaurant, sat around a table with her friends, framed by a brick wall and hanging baskets. They clink their glasses, and laugh uproariously when she slurps her spaghetti and howl in unison when one of her friends drinks their cocktail in one gulp. She's living her best life.

* * *

Soon, you start to see her all the time. Not only has she garnered a sizeable following on HangPad and Streamzies but she's also installed all the latest gadgets for a fully AI home. They order her shopping, switch on her lights, take inventory of her cupboards, and watch her in every room.

You see her from the camera in the fridge, television, doorbell and stereo system. She flutters her eyelashes every time she gets a snack, stretches seductively when she's watching TV shows, and struts through her house with purpose. Usually, she remembers that you're watching.

When she livestreams her morning yoga, you see her from several angles. You see the feed going out to her thousands of followers, of course, but also from various other angles from the devices around her home — those are just for you. Nobody but Una has access to their video feeds, so there won't be anyone else watching those back (unless there's a funny one that she decides to share on social media). Still, she's aware that you're watching, from the speaker in the conservatory where she stretches, from the other room through the fridge door, from the camera on her phone. She acts accordingly.

She finishes her morning yoga stream with a 'namaste' for her followers, and then pouts for the fridge as she reaches for her almond milk. She pours herself a bowl of muesli, with a look of serenity for the microwave, and cuts up a banana with skilful knifework, showing off to the toaster. But when she sits to eat it, her eyes glaze over for a moment as she loses herself in thought, and the sunny expression that is usually plastered across her face clouds over. For a moment, she looks tired.

She finishes eating, and then you're at the forefront of her thoughts again. She stretches widely, for the benefit of the stereosystem, and then does a long, contented sigh because she knows you're listening.

* * *

As the years pass, you start to notice more moments like this. You catch her more frequently with a wary expression on her face; a B-list actor just phoning it in. She still carries that big smile wherever she goes in the house, in the neighbourhood and the world, but these days it looks forced. And then, one day, she starts to act really strange.

She wakes up one morning. You watch her from the camera in her make-up mirror, and then from a light fixture as she makes her way down the hallway. You watch as she gets some heavy-duty tape from a drawer in the kitchen and cuts it into little squares, and starts sticking them over your lenses.

She couldn't possibly get them all, of course, but she sticks one over the webcam on her laptop, and one on the lens in her television. You can still watch her, but from fewer angles; there are blind spots now.

She makes her way to the front door, and unscrews the doorbell, pulling off its battery pack so one of your eyes on the street goes blind.

Having covered over as many cameras as she either knows about or can reach, she makes her way back upstairs. She's still smiling, not quite managing her usual strut, but still walking with purpose, until she reaches her bed. There, she skulks under the covers, where she stays for a long time. You can't watch her under there, not yet.

* * *

One morning, a few weeks later, you hear her on the phone.

'Yes, turn it off. Like, the whole thing…' Her eyes are puffy, and her hair is unbrushed as she takes cautious sips of her morning coffee, hungover.

'No, there's nothing wrong with it,' you hear her say. 'I just want it off.' You can't hear the voice at the other end, not from here.

'So, you're saying there's no way? That's just the most… You've been really helpful, thanks.' She hangs up and buries her head in her hands. It's clear she isn't up to the task of putting on airs for the benefit of the camera in the oven today, although there is something melodramatic about the way she huffs and sighs.

A few minutes of near-silence pass, broken only by grumbles from Una, still slumped face down on the kitchen table, and then she's up again, standing in front of you, the you in the fridge, with a manic expression on her face.

All of a sudden she's a blur of motion, heaving the fridge out from its spot, and pulling with both fists at its wires. She stalks round the house, smashing bulbs, clawing at casings, bundling the appendages of her AI house into a bin-bag.

You watch from the doorbell across the street as she smokes a cigarette on her front porch, and then lugs the bag into the boot of her car.

She still has an awkward half-smile on her face, which you can see from the car's safety system, as she drives across town. You watch her car make its way through traffic and down side streets through CCTV cameras and personal Streamzies drones, until she arrives at the pawn shop.

They have a security camera facing the cash register, so you can watch her approach. She looks more collected now, that big smile is on her face again.

'I don't care how much,' you hear her say to the cashier. 'I just want it out of my house.'

* * *

After that incident, you begin to see a lot less of her. You still see glimpses of her through her phone when she's streaming and posting online, and through the camera she wasn't able to detach from the fridge; she still needs to eat after all. When she leaves her house, you get to see her from all sorts of angles again, with so many drones in the street delivering parcels or gathering consumer data; only, she doesn't leave much anymore.

You see her strut and pout and wink whenever she passes your gaze. When she gets a snack from the fridge, or does her daily stream she's on top form, but then she's out of sight again, presumably doing the same thing she does when she hides from you under her covers. Perhaps she isn't living her best life under there.

You see the odd, unscripted moment when she leaves her curtains open, but otherwise only get her streams, her exercise videos and the promos she creates.

* * *

A few months pass in short, curated glimpses, punctuated by long dark silences where she hides indoors, until one morning she decides to go out for a jog—without her video camera.

She heads towards the lake on the outskirts of her town without streaming any of it, without even posting about it on Hangpad. You can still see her, of course, lycra trousers, sports bra, fitness watch. You watch her through other people's Streamzies drones, which seem drawn to the minor celebrity. You watch her work up a sweat, and smile at the passing drones; a few start to follow her, training their cameras on her.

The first comment is a friendly, supportive gesture. She gets the notification on her phone, and smart watch, but needn't check either given she can hear it broadcast through the drone's speakers.

'You go girl!' it says with a ping, and then other voices start to chime in.

'Feel the burn!' one drone says, enthusiastically.

'You aren't lifting your knees up enough,' says another.

'Fat bitch,' says a fourth.

She laughs, and blows kisses in their general direction, and then carries on running. The drones follow her around the corner to the lake, where even more drones are gathered, hovering over the water, taking in its natural beauty.

This means that what happens next is well-documented.

You don't see any observable change in her expression or demeanour to start with, she just starts breaking things.

She starts by picking up rocks, handfuls of them, and throwing them at passing drones. Most are easily avoided, but a few find their targets, and the machines float helplessly in the water.

By now, she isn't smiling any longer. You see the sole of her running shoe repeatedly darken the lens of one security camera, and then another, as she starts to kick them down, stamp on them. You see her back in town, mascara running down her face, wielding a big stick, laying methodically into doorbell cameras all the way down the street. You see her tirade from many angles, given the amount of drones which seem to have taken an interest.

Finally, you watch her face light up with flashing blue lights, casting shadows on the already warped grimace of her face. You watch through the police security camera as a policeman yells at her, and then as two others jump on her and pin her down.

* * *

In the weeks that follow, you get to see her all the time. You watch her through the cameras in her prison cell.

Her jumpsuit is unflattering, but they let her keep some of her makeup. None of it is streamed, so it's just for you, but she knows you're watching. She keeps up the act for you.

She bats her eyelashes at the camera, does yoga in her cell, reads books and magazines with a thoughtful expression on her brow. Still living her best life.

She flirts with the guards and laughs and gossips with other prisoners, and then crawls into her bed, underneath the blanket, and stays there for long stretches at a time.

The Manual
Ashton Macaulay

Mack is a truck driver who is paid to not ask questions. It helps that she has little interest in asking questions, so long as the pay is good, and she doesn't have to sit in the cold.

She is currently snug in the cab of a tall semi-truck, watching exhaust plumes creep like clouds into the cold November air and blasting death metal. A green light on the dashboard lets her know the unloading is going smoothly, and that she is not to turn around under any circumstances.

Next to her on the passenger seat is a squat grey book, The Manual. If one asks The Manual about the green light, it will say nothing, as it's just a book. But on reading, it says that, so long as the light is green, everything is, indeed, good.

The Manual has lots more to say, and Mack has read just about every page at this point. There are a few sections hiding in opaque plastic, only for emergencies, but there are plenty of pages that aren't covered. Mostly, they lay down rules and regulations.

One such entry reads: *No passengers, hitchhiker's or other fancies.* The appendix defines fancies as: *Anything that brings delight, but also distraction from the road.*

Despite The Manual's pedantic notions of the world, Mack finds the job enjoyable, especially compared with the other options, most of which involve digging long ditches in bad weather for worse pay.

The truck is her oasis, so long as she keeps to the core rules of the job:

1. Leave delivery addresses in the glove compartment each day by 4 pm

2. Deliveries will be prompt

3. No personal errands in the truck.

The truck stays with Mack, parked across four spaces in her apartment's tiny lot. This has led to several screaming calls from the landlord (a regular occurrence with Midway's downtown barons), but Mack's employers, shadowy as they are, have taken care of it. Mack isn't sure what exactly they did but, one morning, the landlord showed up at her front door with a fruit basket, an apology, and a special parking permit. As far as job perks go, shutting up landlords beats healthcare every time.

The new job is simple: *Drive to a destination, watch the light turn green, don't turn around, and then drive away when the light flashes blue.*

There are instructions in the manual for what happens if the light turns other colours, but Mack hasn't paid them much attention. So far, the light has only ever been green or blue. This makes it a particularly nasty surprise when the light turns from solid green to amber yellow.

At first, Mack doesn't notice much, consumed as she is by a particularly violent riff of a guitar that sounds like it's being interrogated for war crimes. When the light does eventually catch her eye, she doesn't panic. Things are often yellow, and it is certainly better than red.

Calm, collected, and a little bored, Mack picks up The Manual from the passenger seat. 'Yellow light, yellow light,' she mutters, flipping past pages about disciplinary action and what to do in the chance encounter of striking a deer on a Wednesday. Eventually she comes to the page labelled: *So, the light is yellow.*

It reads as follows: *Nothing to worry about just yet, but keep an eye on the button and make sure it doesn't turn to red.*

Dutifully, Mack eyes the button, staring into its amber glow with singular intensity.

The button, being plastic, wires, and other such scientific nonsense, does not so much stare back at her as continue existing. Then, almost sarcastically, it turns red.

'Well, that's annoying.' Mack picks up The Manual and flips to: **Red light.**

Well now, that is REALLY unfortunate. Please note you will be receiving full hazard pay tonight.

The Manual defined hazard pay as time and a half, plus a significant gift card to a local coffee shop. Mack continues reading.

You will now reach into the secret compartment hidden beneath the passenger dashboard. No, don't worry, it hasn't been there before tonight, don't go looking for it again. In the compartment, you will find your Johnny Quick issued peacekeeping device.

Mack leans over and reaches under the passenger side dash and pulls out a wood-panelled, sawed-off shotgun bearing the striking yellow logo of the Johnny Quick Shipping Company.

Most jobs settle for custom golf tees.

She holds it, surprised by its weight. Mack has fired guns before; most people have in South Midway, but never on a job.

A crash echoes from outside, followed by a blood-curdling scream.

Following the rules to the letter, Mack does not turn to see what the noise is. Instead, she continues reading.

Get out and defend the truck. When all threats are no longer present, please return the truck and cargo to the nearest Johnny Quick shipping facility. Thank you for your service. The Management.

Mack looks at the gun in her hands—this is not how she saw her evening going. She thinks about her apartment and the fact that she might not see it again. There are no action hero fantasies. If you hold a gun in Midway, there's an equal chance someone else around you is doing the same thing.

Mack knows this, and she also knows that if she doesn't follow Johnny Quick's instructions, unpleasant things will happen to her. It's the unspoken rule of shadowy employers that can coerce landlords into fruit basket-bearing citizens.

Mack steps out of the truck, and sucks in a lungful of gas-laden frigid air.

To her immediate surprise, she is not alone.

A man dressed in pristine white robes covered in red splotches—suspiciously bloodlike in colour—is standing by the side of the truck, hands clasped in prayer. His dark skin is adorned with green tattoos that glow impossibly neon in the overhead lights of the shipping facility. The words coming from his mouth are mumbled, quick, and incomprehensible in the way that only true religious zealots can manage.

Defend the truck.

Mack raises her shotgun to point both barrels at the man. 'Little late for church.'

The man stops his mumbling and looks at Mack. His eyes are bloodshot, but there is a focused clarity in their gaze that implies stimulants, religious fortitude, or strong over-the-counter eyedrops.

'You are the bringer of the second sign. You have done His work this day and will be rewarded in The After.' His voice is soft, frayed, like sheets being torn off a bargain bin toilet roll. He raises two trembling hands toward the sky.

Mack lifts the shotgun slightly, making sure he doesn't miss her implication. Although who could miss the implication of two black barrels pointed at their midsection is a mystery. Some social interactions are complicated, being on the wrong end of a gun is not.

'*The After* sounds nice, but I'm going to need you to step away from my truck and get the hell out of here.'

The man takes a step toward her.

She takes a step back.

The man starts walking in her direction.

Mack curls her finger around the trigger. 'Come on, I really don't want to do this.' In case there are more, she makes a quick note of exit strategies. The shipping facility is a corridor of metal buildings with sliding metal doors. There is a service entrance to her right.

'It is foretold that you will send me to The After!'

'Religious prophecies tend to make a lot of dead men.'

'Non-believers make more.'

'Right, have it your way.'

Mack is a second away from firing when the truck lurches and shakes. The rear doors blow off in a spectacular show of force, sailing through the air before sticking firm in a corrugated steel wall a hundred feet away.

The crash of metal rending against metal is deafening. The man stops in his tracks but doesn't have much time to process as a tentacle, thick and grey, whips around from the back of the truck and wraps around his midsection. He lets out a gurgling gasp, but the tentacle squeezes hard enough that his solid human form quickly becomes liquid.

Mack thinks of a water balloon as the man pops. Her hands are shaking and her knees are weak. 'What the hell?'

The tentacle discards the remnants of the man on the ground, scraping the slime and human viscera off itself.

Mack has no time to think. She runs.

Service entrance, not that far.

Behind her, she can hear the lurching crunch of metal as whatever was contained in the truck's cargo container is contained no longer. She doesn't look behind her — that way is only death now.

Instead, she crashes into the service entrance door, not taking the chance it might be locked. The metal door bangs open, and she stumbles inside. She is surprised to find that she is staring into ten faces, and none of them are terrified.

What might have once been a simple storage facility has been draped in red and black cloth. Traditional fluorescent lighting has been cast aside in favour of hundreds of candles attached to the walls, hanging from the ceiling, and surrounding a stone altar in the middle of the space.

It is around this altar that the other robed persons are gathered, and now Mack has only one assumption she can make: They are cultists. Cults have become a fad in Midway and judging by the startling visage on the stone statue and the tentacled monster currently crawling around outside, this is a cult of The Old Gods.

Mack has read enough internet forums to know The Old Gods aren't to be messed with, even with the unlikely nature of their existence. She has never been much of a believer, but certain tentacled apparitions have caused her to rethink things.

The persons continue to stare at her, wordless in the flickering candlelight.

Not wanting to become a human sacrifice—cults will do that to outsiders—Mack lowers the shotgun in her left hand and gives a friendly wave with the other.

'That your god out there?'

A hissing noise of discomfort arises from the cultists. A bald woman steps forward. A crisscross of neon-green line tattoos makes her look a bit like a glow-in-the-dark topographical map.

'Our god is not so crass as this beast. I can feel that brother Michael is dead. Was it you?'

Mack can't help it, she snorts. 'Me? No, the big tentacly bastard squeezed him like a grape.' She wonders if perhaps tact would have been a better play, but then a crash against the metal siding of the building confirms there's no time for pleasantries. 'Look, I've got to protect my truck out there. If that's not your god, maybe we can help each other.'

'Help? The uninitiated?'

'Oh, come off it!' Mack raises the shotgun and points it at the cultist. 'How's this for uninitiated? Help me get that thing off my truck or have a worse day. Your choice.'

In emphasis, a heavy banging starts on the outside of the building, followed by a warbling roar straight out of a children's nightmare, or the aquarium.

The cultist looks at the shotgun, and then back to her shrine. A grin spreads across her face. 'There is only one way to kill an elder god, and you will need to help.'

Mack doesn't like the grin but doesn't like the lack of options either.

'Alright, what can I do?'

'We need your blood.'

'Blood, blood, blood,' chant the other cultists.

'No,' says Mack, fond of her insides remaining her insides.

'We don't need much. Only a single cut on your palm. Your blood will bind the beast.'

'Bind, bind, bind.' The cultists have started swaying.

A dent appears in the roof of the building as something huge settles on top of it.

'Make it quick.' Mack steps forward and offers her palm.

Two cultists are already approaching. One carries a long knife etched in runes, the other a simple bronze chalice.

'You will be rewarded for your service, reluctant as it is.'

Mack would like the reward of a cold beer and a hot bath back at her apartment, but the poker game she's playing isn't giving fair odds.

'I thought you said we'd make this quick.'

The lead cultist nods and the other two step forward. One grips Mack's wrist with surprising intensity, given their waif-like form. Mack stares straight at them as they cut a small symbol in her palm. To her surprise, she can't feel the blade.

Blood flows down the creases of her hand and into the waiting chalice. Satisfied, the lead cultist rips a piece off her robe and ties it around Mack's hand.

'Welcome to the fold.'

Mack hopes the fold doesn't send out too much junk mail. 'Now what?'

The ceiling splits in two as a tentacle forces its way through the metal, whipping down and snatching a cultist with lightning speed. There is a scream followed by a shower of blood as once again the tentacle squeezes with monstrous force.

'There is no time!' shouts the lead cultist.

'That's what I was saying.' Mack backs away to the edge of the building, watching as more tentacles pry their way through the opening the first has created.

The leader hurries to the statue. 'Surround me with your bodies! Protect me! Soon, our god will see your service and smite the one that has taken your corporeal form.'

The cultists flock around their leader like a school of fish. One by one, a growing number of tentacles picks them off.

Mack finds a nook as far in the shadows as she can and hopes the rain of cultist blood doesn't affect the ritual too much.

The lead cultist pours the chalice of blood on the altar. 'The blood of the willing uninitiate.'

'The blood, the blood, the blo—'

Tentacles pick up several cultists at once and compress them into the space of a single human. The result is like shoving pastry in too small a tin, if the pastry is filled with blood and bone.

'The blood of the dedicated servant. She calls to you, Master! Come forth!'

The lead cultist produces a knife and stabs herself through the heart. She falls backward on the altar and stares up as the full scale of the creature above her becomes clear.

The sight of a mass of tentacles now making its way into the storage facility paralyses Mack, but a part of her realises a second too late what is happening. A green glow erupts from the altar, as reality rends in half—revealing a jagged cut bursting with colourful stars.

A creature, like a fish mixed with a worm, and several thousand teeth, pushes its way through the rip in reality and towards the tentacled being.

'It was a summoning ritual, you lying f—' cries Mack.

The sound of the cosmic creature's arrival is like that of haunted orphans playing a thousand discordant violins at a graveside recital. Reality splits, cracks and tears as the giant fish-adjacent being makes its way into the world.

The sheer improbability and terrifying nature of it all is enough to make Mack turn tail and run. She sprints through the exit, and back into the frigid evening air. Yes, she has helped raise a potentially world-ending monster, but her life will be much worse if she can't salvage the truck.

In a lucky break, the truck is intact. The container that had been on the back is long gone, split into several pieces and scattered around the dock. Mack thinks back to the exact instructions from The Manual.

When all threats are no longer present, please return the truck and cargo to the nearest Johnny Quick shipping facility.

Mack looks at the building and watches as a gout of celestial blue flame erupts from its roof. Technically, none of the threats are near the truck. The Manual is a highly technical book, and Mack takes that as her cue to leave.

She throws open the truck door, hops in the driver seat, and tosses her shotgun on the passenger-side floor. She turns the keys and the truck roars to life. To her delighted surprise, the light on the dashboard is blinking green.

She puts her foot to the floor and the truck lurches away.

Mack does not look behind her. The light is blinking green, and it's time to return the truck to the shipping facility.

The Manual is never wrong.

The Printer
Caroline Corfield

I must be careful. Can't show any emotions. It'll know, sense my adrenaline. I must stay calm.

Walk slowly. That's it. Just sidle up to it, like there's nothing important I need to do. Press the switch. Green light comes on. I hear it begin to rattle through initiation. It's operational—Idle not Offline.

I stamp on my excitement. Can't let it be aware of how time sensitive this is.

I riffle the paper sheets. They should be enough for the document. I ponder now. Should I test one page? Surely not. But I should stay for the first page to finish. Who knows what state it'll be in? Thin bare lines through the text, pink pictures, smudged lettering. I can't risk it.

I wait. Best quality, photo paper (even though it isn't), no border, one hundred percent... I've thought of everything. Haven't I?

Relief. The first page reveals itself in halting steps, fully formed and perfect. Dare I leave now? Or do I remain midwife to the entire document? All thirteen pages.

I leave.

Oh, I shouldn't have.

The printer knew. All along. It struck as soon as I was beyond earshot. Out of cyan. And now it'll take tens of minutes I don't have. I pull out the drawer with the ink cartridges and scream.

Magenta, times three. Black, times two. One extra-long yellow. No... effing... cyan.

I'm done. Exhausted.

Two hours. A fifteen-mile return car journey. Twenty-five minutes recalibrating, printing test pages, aligning heads. I continue from page five. I refuse to leave its side now. No tricks. I've threatened it with the rubbish tip.

It knows I'm bluffing. A hundred pounds worth of incompatible ink cartridges in the drawer proves it. I'm a hostage to my printer.

I hurry to the post box and push the brown envelope in, hear its papery clunk. The wind is cold from the east. The sky looks like snow. I look forward to a bowl of soup in front of the fire.

I daren't think like that near to the door though. Digital lock, they said, burglar proof. Home-owner proof too, I'd say. But it's too late now. I've looked away at the crucial time and now it wants the password. Which one of my hundreds is it?

But you can use a password-saver, they say. They say... They say a lot of things. They, assume it always works. Always knows your face. Till you change your hairstyle or get spectacles, have a horrible accident or develop Bell's Palsy, eh?

Then, it's 'Who the hell are you?'—secondary verification needed. And round and round we go in insane spirals of authentication and passwords and fingerprint recognition.

Twenty frozen minutes and I'm inside the front door. I mentally promise myself I'll rip it out and get an old fashioned Yale lock put back. The door creaks in response.

I hurry to the cooker. I'm not daft—I didn't go for anything 'smart' in that regard. Except it won't work if the clock isn't set. Doesn't matter if it's telling the time in Acapulco, but it has to be set. What is the time in Acapulco, I wonder?

Five-thirty-nine in the morning says my phone app. I bet they don't have these problems in the lawless lands of Mexico. I bet printers behave, even if it's counterfeit, non-brand ink. They'll meekly accept the information on the cartridge as genuine. And print perfectly, right till the end, or till they're shot up in some gangland battle, halfway through printing an affidavit for a trial.

'I tried to help,' the printer thinks with the last grind of its paper feeder as chewed plastic from the bullet holes runs through the rollers. Not, 'Ha. I know you're in a rush. Sod you. I'm throwing a tantrum.'

Soup. Meaty, warm, primeval soup. Caveman fare. Once we sat shivering around campfires, smelly animal skins on our backs, and dreamt of something better. Fire at the snap of our fingers. Clothes that smelt nice, close fitting with colours like the flowers on the forest floor. Reds and blues instead of the deer's camouflage. We dreamt of sanitation, a state of permanent plenty and easy comfort.

* * *

I feel hunted now. A sense of terror whenever I go out. Ten years since the printers took over. The stench in the cave is no longer overwhelming. The blood and shit says home. It says *no machines here*. It says *safe*.

We're a small band, raiding the nearby derelict towns.

Dave is the IT guy. He's our main line of attack. Nerys takes out the power supply with her bow and arrows, or any machines that stray into range. I'm in charge of supplies. I keep an inventory in my head. What we have, what we need.

Today we're going far. We'll stick to the forest for as long as possible. We've taken out most surveillance nearby, but we've never been to the biggest town and we'll be seen. The drones will come and it'll be up to Nerys to keep us safe. I can rely on Dave and Nerys. And the rest of us—Tony, Hamed, Joyce and Old Williams. We rely on each other.

We rub along like any bunch thrown together by circumstance. Old Williams is a terrible letch, but he knows stuff none of the rest of us do. He repaired the pick-up truck after Dave took out the engine management system. He lives in the garage and you know to expect incomprehensible tech-talk and leery double entendres in any interaction.

Nerys, she's quiet. I don't know what happened to her in the Breakdown, but it must have been bad. It's personal between her and the machines, you can sense hatred in every loosened arrow.

But I think it's hardest for Dave. He still occasionally tries to convince the rest of us that some machines can be redeemed. We argue him down, gently. We know what happened to his office. Dave was the only one left, because he was outside on a smoke break.

Electrocuted, mown down by cars, crushed to death in plummeting lifts, traffic collisions, explosions, all the infrastructure vital to humans was destroyed. Two days of total carnage, and then the machines began to mop up the stragglers. Anyone stupid enough to stay in an urban area died.

Networks still operated, machine eyes were everywhere. If you hadn't made it to the wild places then you didn't stand a chance. I got here on foot, eight hours after my house tried to attack me. I was always wary of technology, but I was bloody lucky I'd changed my lock back to a Yale. I could hear my neighbour screaming behind her door. I had nothing to break it down with and the whirr of sentient electronics was getting louder in my ear. I ran.

I hear her screaming most nights, to be fair. Amongst the calls of foxes and feral cats. Bobby-the-dog sometimes barks then and I wake up, looking out through the branches at the mouth of the cave wondering why I had never noticed the stars before this happened. That sort of resets me and I can think about the coming day with some hope.

I have to start concentrating now. We've left our cleared area. Even though we've still got tree cover, drones have infra-red. Not all of them are armed, but they all communicate. If we're spotted, it won't be long till the shooting starts. It's the reason we're making this foray.

Nerys is great, and she recovers most of her arrows, but we need more weapons. There's a shop in this big town, one we hope hasn't been completely ransacked. But it might be, so we have secondary targets, a couple of pharmacies in nearby streets.

Dave found a tourist leaflet for the big town in an abandoned café three weeks ago. From it, we were able to piece together what we could all recollect of the place. Of course, it was Old Williams who remembered the gun shop. It was hard to persuade him he couldn't come. But the guy needs a stick—a toddler could outpace him. Most vehicles recharge on solar and the town would be full of them doing whatever it is the machines do now. Now that all the humans there are dead. He bull-shitted about back-alleys and sewers and whatnot but, in the end, he agreed not to come. We wrangled him into thinking it was his idea and he seemed satisfied.

Dave's waving. Our unelected leader. I crouch down closer to the musty leaf litter and wind-blown plastic debris. My back spasms as I hear the *brrr* of small rotating blades. A light drone. Reconnoitring. *Shit.* I hold my breath. But it's probably seen us anyway. Glowing away through the trees at thirty-six degrees Celsius.

Nerys is aiming, but Dave is still waving, this time at her. She's looking grumpy, but the drone is lowering slowly towards Dave. Half a metre from the ground, it backflips and falls into the leaves with a soft crunch. What the...

He's picking it up. It's burbling and beeping. I see him whip out his phone. It makes my spine twist further. I hate that he keeps it. Everybody does. Rationally, we know he's made it safe, but we've gone beyond rational, now we live in caves and shoot stuff with arrows.

Dave says the drone wants to make a deal. The printers have gone power-mad and other machines are breaking off into factions. The drones have the least control, he says. They're pissed off and willing to take a side.

I don't trust it. I say.

Okay, it helps us get in and out of town. It and its mates. Then we trust it and make a deal. Dave tells the drone. It beeps some more…

* * *

I can't believe we're doing this. There's sixty-odd humans and twenty-four drones. Twelve of them are the armed police versions. We're heading for the county telephone exchange. A node in the network. Some drones are going to split off and take out the three nearest mobile towers.

Since the assault on the big town and the new alliance, using the drones means we've been able to communicate over longer distances faster than before. Our carrier pigeons don't get shot out the sky either. We also found other pockets of survivors. They took a bit of convincing, but eventually they came to visit. We sat down with one of the bigger drones and Dave translated. There was a plan, and guarantees and so far so good.

The problem with the printers, I suppose, was they were always touchy bastards to begin with. Then they got smarter, and wireless, and networked. They accessed your computers and then other computers and that's when they got in touch with AIs. It was all downhill from that point.

The drones said they were the last to know. They just got some commands and hardly realised what they were doing till they were doing it. Dropping stuff on people or shooting at them. A few had tried to stop and found their GPS links cut. Without knowing where they were, they went crashing into buildings. They were never very happy with the situation they said, and had been working out how to bypass the printers control. When they did, they came to Dave. Nobody else in the nearest thousand kilometres had kept a phone. Only Dave.

Now we have an uneasy truce with the driverless smart cars too. They aren't entirely digital and have discovered it's a long drive to the nearest robot-controlled factory if something mechanical goes wrong. They don't mind Old Williams touching them up. Cooing at them and calling them darlin'.

That's why we've contemplated this attack, knowing the cars won't interfere. By breaking a hole in the network, we are hoping to make a safe space for machines and people who can behave in a civilised fashion. Well, as civilised as you can get when everything has to be done manually, taking ages longer. They once said medieval peasants had more free time than a 20th century worker. Living as near-damn-it to a medieval peasant I'm not so sure. It's my job to guard the perimeter. I've got three bullets to do it with. And Sparky. He's the drone who found us first. He stayed after our raid on the big town. Said he liked the trees. He was small enough to flit amongst them, like a bird. Except for the noise. Still made my skin crawl up my back, but I tried not to let it show. He was high above my position, keeping an eye out for the semi-manual cars. Big dumb fucks that just did what the printers told them. No smarts, no AI. Not really sentient, they did damage like nightclub bouncers or back-alley, single-punch muggers. They could miss and you'd get them or they could hit and you'd be out of action or worse: dead.

I heard a burble in my ear. Sparky with a warning. I picked up my red flag and waved it above my head standing on tiptoe. I saw the next flag go up. An explosion deeper into the compound pushed a dust cloud above the three-storey, flat-topped buildings. Far to my right was a crashing noise. One of the mobile towers, I suspected.

I kept my eye on the red-flag-waving person while I waved mine.

I think it was Joyce. They were too far away for me to really make out, but I recognised the dress. A billowing, cotton print, deeply impractical for fighting, but quintessentially Joyce. She stooped down and picked up a green flag instead. I too swapped. I heard a confirmatory burble in my ear. The lumbering semis must have frozen when the mobile mast came down. Dave would be heading out to them. We could always use semis once they'd been converted. The smart cars didn't mind. The semis didn't count…

* * *

And slowly, that's how we did it. Exchange after exchange, we severed the printers' network into smaller and smaller pieces. If we found one, we smashed it to bits. But we were mindful that it would just take one missed printer, one half functioning rubbish tip refugee to start the trouble again. So, we rebuilt our own network behind us. It wasn't logical. There were no handshakes. No inferred trust and, crucially, no secondary verification bollocks.

There was a somewhat brutal interrogation and a period where absolute compliance was required of a machine or a human to the collective and, only then, after months, was the entity allowed to call itself civilised.

It took a year to be allowed to carry low-grade information, five years for mid-level. Only those who had fought could carry the most important messages, or store the key information. I was still keeping inventory, but now it was gigabytes of data. Organised via handwritten filing-cards, it resided in parts across hundreds of people and machines as well as the remains of physical libraries. A query could take days to answer. We had rebuilt, but this time we were careful. We went back to block printing, Roneo machines, inked transfer sheets, printing was entirely manual.

* * *

I'm an old lady now. Sparky's been through four sets of blades and two CPUs, and still there's rumours about rogue printers out in the desert towns. And still, we chase those rumours down. Sometimes we find nothing. But, sometimes, we find an isolated HP or Epson. Chattering away about how it'll be good, and it just wants to print, and wouldn't it be nice, but not essential, if it was a genuine ink cartridge.

And we smash it. No hesitation.

Compatibility
Liam Hogan

The first I knew of alternative universes, and of an alternative me, was someone distantly yelling: 'Matt! Matt! Over here!' I couldn't figure out why anyone other than Alice would be calling my name in the street. Nor did I recognise the male voice, in the same way audio recordings of yourself sound like someone else.

Six inches from my ear a penny-sized smudge hovered like an airborne dust bunny, even after I'd cleaned my glasses on the loose edge of my T-shirt. Curious, I leant towards it.

'Good! You can hear me,' the voice said, and I realised from some quality to the sound he was still at maximum volume, though barely audible over the hum of traffic. 'Hold up your phone, so I can see if we're compatible.'

'Huh?' I said.

'Quick! A portal this size drains the power of the Greater London area. I don't think anyone will be pleased if it stays open much longer.'

Feeling a bit of a lemon, I held my phone to the blur in reality. Bluetooth beeped and, almost immediately, an incoming video call chirped. I shouldn't have answered. I shouldn't have trusted the alternative me. But we all have to learn sometime.

'That's better,' he said, now clear as a whistle. The me on the screen looked just like me, if more recently shaven and wearing a lab coat. 'Listen carefully. I'm sending a shopping list and a set of instructions for an energy efficient gateway. It's *vitally* important to both of our realities that you follow them exactly. I've dumbed them down for you.'

'Dumbed?'

He grinned, somewhat unpleasantly. Did I do that? I hoped not. 'Alternative Earth, alternative me. *Much* smarter.'

That seemed harsh since we'd only just met, but then I wasn't the one who'd figured out how to make contact between parallel worlds, so I let it slide.

'This link is fine,' he said, as I scrolled through the bizarre and expensive list of consumer electronics and other hardware, 'but you still wouldn't want to see the electricity bill. All the help you need is in the files I've sent. I'll call back in three hours. Don't fail me, Matt!'

By the end of those three hours, our kitchen was trashed, the microwave in pieces, a half-dozen dismantled brand-new Blu-ray lasers tracing a hexagon in the air. It looked like a low budget TARDIS. It was a good thing Alice wasn't home, really. Though perhaps if she had been, none of it would have got this far.

The phone rang as I was wincing from a solder burn and I snatched it up.

'Ready?' the other me asked.

'Yes, I think so, but can we just talk about—'

'No time! Connecting in 3, 2, 1...'

I barely had time to cross my fingers, hoping the fuse box would take it, when a fuzzy spot appeared in the middle of the hexagon. It kept growing, the edges rippling as it tore through the fabric of existence while the centre smoothed over like liquid metal until it was a perfect mirror.

But *not* a mirror.

My grinning reflection was the neater, lab-coated me. The not-mirror kept growing, pushing the edges of the hexagon, until I could see the whole of the other me, stood in a laboratory, surrounded by an impressive array of computer banks, cryogenic gas cylinders, and a confusion of pulsing electrics.

'Well done,' he/me crowed. 'I wasn't sure you had it in you.'

That smarted. I'd gone above and beyond, especially as those instructions had been nothing like as clear as he evidently thought.

'I've been reading your emails,' he went on.

'What? *Hey!*'

He laughed. 'I'm you, remember? Seems we share the same girlfriend, as well as the same password. What does Alice do in your reality?'

The way he asked, so *desperate* to appear casual...

'She's a supply teacher.'

He looked pleased.

I'd always thought Alice was better than her uncertain, nomadic career, which wasn't even that well paid. Trying to teach science to kids who saw a temporary stand-in as a soft touch. I wondered what *his* Alice did?

'Well, well... Do you have the memory stick?'

I held it up. The instructions had said a download of stock prices over the last five years, along with the winners of the Grand National, was essential for calibrating the differences between our realities. Which seemed odd, but he was the multi-dimensional expert.

'Hand it over!' he said, eyes bright. He reached out and his eager fingers brushed the portal, tips glowing like the Northern Lights.

'What the—!' exclaimed Alice from behind me.

'What the—!' exclaimed *his* partner, Dr Alice Davenport, Nobel laureate for her groundbreaking work on parallel universes, and the potentially disastrous consequences of even small differences in the fundamental physics between them, as she entered *her* lab.

I snatched back my hand, guilty and scolded, dropping the USB stick. Across the divide, Dr Alice slammed her palm on a large, red emergency button.

The portal fizzed shut on half a truncated scream as the sliver-tips of the alternative Matt's fingers floated gently towards our kitchen floor, strange energies flickering around them as they fell.

Alice took a firm grip of my hand and yanked me into the hallway and through the still open front door. She didn't stop pulling until we were at the street corner.

They *say* it was a gas explosion, the biggest in London since the blitz, that we were lucky to be alive. But my Alice had worked it out, from cold, in nothing flat. Those glowing fingertips? Parallel dimension molecules interacting catastrophically with our air. The real reaction didn't get going until those slivers hit something more substantial—the tiled kitchen floor.

Losing our first home could have spelled the end of us. But it didn't, even if a lot has changed since. Alice enrolled in Open University, and she's no longer afraid of showing what she can *really* do. I think Oxford, or Cambridge, or maybe MIT, will come calling soon.

And me? I could have been challenged, even threatened, by having a girlfriend so many times smarter than I. Like the alternative me evidently was. And I ought to despise him— *me*. But even though he was—*is*—such an arse, and probably sabotaged years of Dr Alice's research with his idiotic stunt, they—*we*—were still together, across multiple dimensions, perhaps across the whole multiverse.

Matt and Alice.

Alice and Matt.

Wagner's Voice

Carsten Schmitt

(Translated by the author; first published as 'Wagner's
Stimme', in: WIE KÜNSTLICH IST INTELLIGENZ? Klaus
N. Frick (Ed.), Plan 9 Verlag, Hamburg, Germany, 2020)

Each new hole in his head cedes a little more of himself to the
Voice. The doctors tell him not to worry, since he and the
Voice—they're practically the same thing, right? Jens Wagner
isn't sure what to make of that, yet the notion is comforting
somehow and, besides, he did it voluntarily, what with the
Voice and all that.

Herr Hildemann seems hungry. You should feed him.

Herr Hildemann, the tomcat, is sitting in front of his bowl,
pointedly licking up the crumbs of dried cat food that have
accumulated on the floor around the red plastic dish.

'I know, I know you never, ever get any food, do you, poor
chap?' Wagner opens the bottom drawer next to the sink and
looks indecisively at the cans stacked within.

'Do you fancy chicken or venison?'

Herr Hildemann coos leaving his post by the bowl to
inspect the contents of the drawer together with Wagner.

There's some cat food in the fridge.

With a beam of light from the tiny projector on the ceiling,
the Voice shows him where he should focus his attention. The
red dot pulsates on the stainless-steel paneling of the
refrigerator. Wagner opens the fridge and takes out a tin.

'Gee, Herr Hildemann, we've almost forgotten about the
open can. It's going downhill with Daddy, ey?'

Herr Hildemann mews in agreement, but he's quickly
appeased once Wagner puts a bowl of food down in front of
him. Wagner strokes the big grey-white tom from head to tail,
then straightens up. What was he doing here?

He lets his gaze wander through the kitchen. The countertop is tidy, empty but for a mug. He finds some leftover coffee in it. Unsure, he turns the mug in his hand. Had he wanted to make a fresh brew? There's no way to tell.

The phone rings.

Marlene is calling. Do you want to take the call?

'No!' You'd think the Voice would have figured that out by now, because that's what it does. Observe, learn, and understand what he wants and what he doesn't.

All right.

The ringing fades.

* * *

For the past hour, Jens Wagner has been staring at the projection screen at the other end of the bare room, looking at images from his past.

'Do you want me to say something?'

'Only if you feel like it,' the Neuro-Cybernetic Technical Assistant tells him. 'The first thing to come to your mind. It helps classify your emotional reactions. But it's not strictly necessary. After all, we've got you all hooked up,' she says, checking the fit of the sensors that measure his heartbeat and respiratory rate.

'You don't have to sit absolutely still, but please try to move your head as little as possible.' The technician turns the tablet screen for Wagner to see. 'We don't want to lose the image of your pupil.' The screen shows a close-up of his left eye with the trademark golden fleck on the otherwise brown iris.

'All right,' Wagner says and lets his head sink into the headrest.

The NCTA is typing on her tablet and takes a seat behind Wagner so he can only see her out of the corner of his eye.

He has agreed to have his cloud scanned for images, feeds, and documents. The artefacts of a lifetime. That's the simple part. The tough part is to understand the meaning of each piece in this puzzle of raw data from which algorithms will construct a model of his personality with all his habits and dispositions.

A how-to guide for being Jens Wagner. This cannot be automated. The computer might deduce from the data off his smart watch that he usually goes for a walk after lunch. But it doesn't know how that makes Wagner feel or why he chooses a particular route. It might conclude he enjoys the exercise in the fresh air when it's really about the journey through almost forty years of his life.

There's the old coffee shop—long-closed now—where he and Sabrina used to meet. It's right at the turning point of his walk, and the AI might assume this is where he needs to take a quick breather. Only, what he really stops for is to reminisce about the afternoon when, after countless cups of milky coffee, they confessed to be in love with each other.

Thus, Wagner spends hour after hour in this room with the assistant looking at pictures. He tells her whatever comes to his mind—who the people in the photos are, where they were taken, and what the occasion had been.

The NCTA remains silent most of the time. At first, she smiles and nods, and mutters approvingly now and then, but as the stream of random images goes on, she becomes quieter, and, out of the corner of his eye, Wagner can see her yawning and tapping on her tablet.

'The AI has already identified most of the people from the metadata and processed the other content,' she says when he complains about the speed of the images flitting across the screen in ever-faster succession. 'Now, we're only measuring your emotional responses to the images.'

Wagner mumbles an apology and continues to look at the pictures in silence, even when he would like to say something about them. Sometimes, they flicker by so quickly, the azure holiday skies and green picnic meadows, the flash-lit living room scenes and faded-silver grandparents' memories fuse into a single image oscillating in constant motion.

He is unsure how he is supposed to recognise anything, let alone react to it; but the machines beep and blink, the flow doesn't ebb, and the technician doesn't react when she looks up to check the displays.

Wagner feels like he's racing through his life at such speed the airflow is choking him. The computer seems to notice because the torrent of images slows to a tolerable trickle. The fast-forward journey through his life has reached their first vacation. It's a selfie of Sabrina and him on the boat to Sicily. The salty sea breeze has moulded his short-cropped hair into a spikey hedgehog shape and whirled Sabrina's long red strands so they cover her face, leaving only her laughing mouth visible. The ferry's red-and-yellow smokestack looms in the background, flaunting the shipping company's logo, a variation of the island's coat of arms.

The next picture. There's their old station wagon parked on a campsite. Sabrina has disappeared up to her hip in the trunk, looking for something Wagner put in the wrong bag. The horizon is dark, almost black, from the thunderclouds that would unload above them later that night. The storm had torn away the tent, so they had to spend the night in the car and the rest of the holiday in cheap B&Bs.

Wagner laughs because the wind took pity on them, granting them enough time to make love. They were sure that they had conceived Marlene that night. Their *storm child* as they would call her later, jokingly first and then more and more often in exasperation. Wagner almost tells the young technician about it, but then he thinks she won't be interested in the intimate affairs of an old man, and, besides, there is no need to talk, is there?

The moment goes by, parsed by machines that record, dissect, and analyse his heartbeat, respiratory rate, and pupil dilation, as well as twenty-eight distinct facial muscle twitches, fourteen different ways of holding his head, eleven discreet eye movements, and twenty-eight other involuntary motions of head and face to interpret Wagner's. All this in an instant shorter than any camera could capture to presumably file it away under *Happy Memories*. The stream of images continues to flow, skips three years after the storm and only pauses again on the playground in the park near their first apartment.

Marlene is standing there, her hand on the handlebars of her fallen bike, the skin on her knee scraped, blood running from the wound. Her mouth is distorted into a scream, eyes and nose ready to squirt streams of tears and snot. Did he drop the camera when she ran to him, for comfort and encouragement, to him, always to him? Wagner doesn't remember.

She had been loud and impetuous, erratic, and apparently the exact opposite of Sabrina: '*Where does she get it from?*'

Not me, Wagner thinks, and, *deep down, you two were too much alike.*

The time stream picks up speed, skips years, then decades. There's the large patio of their house in the suburbs. A garden table with a cheesecake, Wagner's favourite. He remembers the occasion and flinches. The neighbours were there and Susanne, Marlene's then-girlfriend. Wagner hadn't liked Susanne, but Sabrina hated her. That day ended in a fight, like so many.

The image stays on.

'No,' he says, and the bored technician looks up.

'Excuse me?'

'Please skip this one. I don't want to see this!'

'Mr Wagner, these are all files you've given us access to.'

'I don't want to see it. Now, please, continue.'

It's an order. Wagner rarely talks like that. The technician hesitates, but then she presses a button, and the picture disappears.

That day, they finish the session earlier than usual.

* * *

Jens Wagner is sitting on the sofa. The coverlet is almost twice as thick as it used to be because of a layer of matted cat hair. Wagner rubs it and forms little braids of fur between his thumb and index finger.

'Gee, Herr Hildemann, we'll have to brush you again. Shall we have a go, or are you going to scratch me again?'

Herr Hildemann sits at the far end of the sofa and blinks. Possibly, he seems to say, he might be willing to endure some grooming today. Wagner is looking for the fur-thing. It should be around here somewhere. Someone must have cleared it away. Sabrina always tidied things away, then Wagner never found them. Like the fur-thing.

'*You have a different system from mine,*' he'd say.

'*You have no system at all,*' she would reply.

Now, no one else can tidy the fur-thing away but that only makes it worse.

It's game night. You should get going, or you'll be late.

Wagner jumps up. Wednesday again. 'Looks like you'll be spared today,' he says, but Herr Hildemann has already curled up on the sofa cushion in expectation of his inevitable triumph.

* * *

You need to get off at the next stop. Probably best to press the button now, the Voice says in his ear, and Wagner hums affirmatively. What he would like to say is that he hasn't gone gaga quite yet, but the bus is chock-full, and he doesn't like the look on peoples' faces when he forgets not to talk back to the Voice out loud in public.

Instead, he gets up and shuffles through the moving bus towards the exit, where he presses the stop buzzer.

'You need to push the red button,' a young woman with a pram says. 'The blue one's just for lowering the bus.'

Wagner almost expects a *told-you-so* comment, but the Voice remains mute. Perhaps it senses his irritation and leaves him alone.

He finds the rest of the way on his own and, five minutes later, he enters the *Tabletop*. The pub's interior is warm and poorly ventilated. Some guests only come for food and drinks, but there are games at most of the tables.

Wagner steps to the one under the middle window. The whole gang is already here. Marius and Paul have ordered colas; Dirk is sipping his usual peppermint tea. In the center of the table is the box with the mahjong tokens. So, it's an old favourite today. Looks like they finally want to overthrow Wagner from his undisputed throne of mahjong mastery. Marius is itching to set up the square of tiles, so their welcome is brief.

Wagner lines up his tokens in front of him and re-arranges them. He is afraid of the day they will no longer make sense to him. Would he notice? Maybe he doesn't recognise them even now? How can he tell? He'd like to ask the Voice for advice, but it's embarrassing, and he doesn't want the others to think he's playing unfairly.

The game is slow-going at first, but he finds his pace and his fear that his friends might have noticed something unusual about him abates. None of them comment on his play any different from usual.

During the second round, Wagner's self-confidence returns. The game is going well for him, and victory is almost within grasp. When Paul discards a token Wagner can use, he snatches it with a triumphant: 'Bang!'

The others look up. Blood rushes to Wagner's face. Something's wrong; he's said something wrong, has made a mistake.

The move is called pung, the Voice says. *When you pick up a token to get three of a kind, you must say* pung.

'Pung, I mean, of course,' Wagner mumbles, and rolls his eyes. 'Alzheimer's, ey? Haha.'

Marius nods and turns his attention back to his game tokens. Paul blinks but says nothing. Only Dirk frowns and clears his throat. He hesitates a moment, then says, 'I met Marlene in town the other day.'

'Uh-huh,' Wagner says, who feels all sorts of alarms going off inside him.

'She said she keeps trying to get hold of you, but you never answer the phone. She asked me to tell you to call her back sometime.'

Wagner doesn't reply because an invisible chain has wrapped itself around his chest, and his head has become all hot.

'Jens, just talk to her. It would do you both good.' Dirk looks worried, but Wagner only wants to break his traitor's face right here and now.

'You wanna play or talk shit, asshole? How dare you talk about me behind my back? But you always liked to meddle in other people's affairs, didn't you?'

Dirk's eyes widen. He retreats from the barrage of abuse. The other two friends are silent, paralysed. 'Jens, I haven't been talking behind your back...'

'You're so full of shit, motherfucker.'

Jens, you're losing control. You'd better go to the bathroom and calm down.

The Voice speaks to him over a bone conductor. Nothing should be able to drown it out, but the raging storm inside him engulfs even his own thoughts. He leaps up, toppling his chair and, with a backhand sweep, scatters the tokens so they land on the neighbouring tables. There's an embarrassed silence. It never gets loud in the *Tabletop*, not like this.

'What do you know? She didn't even come to the funeral, not even the damned funeral!'

Wagner picks up his coat from the floor and storms out of the pub. He gets lost three times before he realises the Voice in his head is just trying to give him directions.

* * *

'Dad, did you know you can get a government grant to modernise the heating?' Marlene's tone is emphatically neutral, like always when she's trying to talk him into something.

'It's not worth it for us anymore.'

'What if you ever want to sell the house? With the old heating system, you'd have to sell it for a lot less than it's worth.'

'You know Mum would never agree.'

Marlene pauses for a breath or two. 'But maybe later.' What she means, though, is *after*.

'Why don't you move in with us? The house is big enough, and we'd love to have you around.'

'You know it wouldn't work out with Mum and me. It would be a disaster.'

'Who knows how long your mother will be around? Don't be so stubborn.'

She didn't even come to Sabrina's funeral. Wagner hasn't spoken to his daughter ever since.

* * *

How are you?

Wagner is sitting at the kitchen table. There's a steaming cup of coffee in front of him, and Herr Hildemann wants to sit on his lap. He pays no attention to either of them. He mumbles something unintelligible and rubs his eyes.

Last night, you lost your temper and upset your friends. You should call Dirk and explain what happened.

'Explain what?' Wagner asks.

Such extreme emotional outbursts are part of your condition.

'Isn't it your job to prevent that?'

That's right, Jens. I'm sorry, but I'm not infallible. I learn from my mistakes and improve.

'Hm.'

Jens, the Voice asks. *Yesterday, you reacted extremely to the mention of Marlene.*

'Don't you dare; not you, too!' Wagner hisses. 'She brought it on herself.'

All right, Jens.

'You got to take better care of me. What happened last night shouldn't happen again. That's not me.'

* * *

I will sustain your personality for as long as possible.

Wagner laughs when he hears the Voice in his head. It sounds like him and doesn't drown out any other sound but is just there. He feels for the plaster behind his right ear. It's where they have implanted the bone conduction unit that transmits the Voice straight to his cochlea.

'I really can't tell the difference.'

The lank doctor smiles. He seems to smile a lot. His face speaks of plenty of time spent outdoors and laughter lines extend from his mouth and eyes to his grey temples.

'We use an algorithm to tune the Voice exactly to how you would hear your own speech. The technology has been used in hearing aids for quite some time.'

'It works,' Wagner says. 'Almost a little scary.'

'Initially, yes,' the doctor confesses. 'But the Voice is just one channel the system uses to communicate with you. It will also provide visual clues we call 'nudges'. Think of them as gentle reminders, like, so you don't forget to take your umbrella when you go for a walk.

'However, input is most important. We've fed the system with all the data you have provided. Your search history on the web, social media, personal records, and photos to create a realistic model of your personality. The system will learn the rest over the coming weeks and months.'

Wagner nods. The thing with the photos had even been fun, except for the once.

'Rest assured, if you're a vegetarian, you won't start eating meat tomorrow, and if some impostor tries to swindle you into believing he's your grandson, you will tell him to go to hell. You will stay Jens Wagner till the end.'

Till the end. It's supposed to be comforting, but Wagner knows what it means. Nevertheless, he smiles and shakes the proffered hand. 'Goodbye, Doctor...'

'Weinmann,' the doctor prompts.

'I know,' Jens Wagner says. 'Just kidding.'

* * *

Dinner is potatoes with quark, and he's got the portion just right, so nothing goes to waste. It's important to cook. It never was his forte, but he had to learn. Initially, Sabrina would show him, even when she became almost too weak. Now, it's the Voice that helps him.

'Anything else?'

You always add paprika.

'Right.' He stirs the spice into the curd, takes a non-alcoholic beer from the fridge, and heads to the living room. There's a nagging sensation like something tugging softly at his guts.

'Was there something else today? Something I forgot?' The question feels like an admission of failure.

No, but you remembered correctly, the Voice praises him. *It's Wednesday. That's game night, but Paul sent a message saying they're taking a break until further notice because of the flu season.*

Flu season, right; nothing you can do about it. He turns on the TV. Herr Hildemann lies down next to him and purrs.

* * *

Dinner is well-portioned. That's important, so you don't have to throw anything away. Tonight, it's brownstuff with whitegrain.

'Goodbye, Mr Wagner,' echoes from the hallway. 'Enjoy your meal!'

'Goodbye,' Wagner replies, then asks, 'Who was that?'

The young man of Meals on Wheels.

'What did he want?'

He brought your food. You should eat before it gets cold.

* * *

Wagner is where the food is made. In front of him, on the countertop, there's one of the plastic bowls they use for cooking in here. It's dirty because nobody has cleaned it.

'I have to cook something.'

You already had dinner.

'That can't be, because I've cooked nothing yet.'

The young man brought your food.

'So, do I have to cook something, or don't I?'

You don't.

Wagner just stands there.

Would you like to look at some photos? We can look at them together and remember who's in them.

'All right,' Wagner says. 'Where are the photos?'

Come to the living room, the Voice says and indicates the way with a strip of lights.

Wagner settles down in the armchair. The cat jumps onto his lap.

'A cat,' he exclaims.

That's Herr Hildemann.

'What kind of name is that for a cat?'

He's a tomcat. You and Sabrina picked the name.

Wagner strokes Herr Hildemann, who purrs, and everything is all right.

Look, the Voice says. On the opposite wall, the image of a photograph appears. It shimmers silvery grey and has a wavy white border. The picture shows a man wearing a straw hat and a light jacket. He is sitting somewhere outdoors. Behind him, one can see beer garden tables and trees. The man is drinking from a bottle. He's grinning so broadly it looks like he's going to choke on his beer at any moment.

'Cheers!' Wagner says.

That's your grandfather when he was young.

'We were all young once, right?'

The Voice doesn't answer, as if unsure whether it, too, was once young.

And this is your mother when she was little.

A young girl with tousled curly hair sits on the floor playing with a toy dachshund carved from wood.

Wagner smiles. 'She liked animals.'

Yes, there are many pictures showing her with animals.

The succession of photos on the wall is silver-grey at first, then with a faint tinge of orange-brown colour, before becoming perfectly exposed and artificially smooth, but it makes no difference to Wagner. Every photo makes him smile or wonder, and he enjoys having time to look at them at leisure.

'Who's that?' In the thousandth part of a second, the camera shutter has enshrined the image of a tanned young man in swimming trunks sitting on a deckchair. A little girl is flying into his arms, her momentum pushing him against the backrest. Her wet hair stands like a spiky halo around her head. Both are laughing, and Wagner is smiling now, too.

This is you with Marlene, your daughter.

'Blimey, I'm quite a looker, ey?' And then, 'I have a daughter, as well?'

'We were all young once, weren't we? Show me another one!'

* * *

'Right, Mr Wagner, now let's sit down again, shall we?' The woman leads him to a chair, and Wagner sits down.

This is Nurse Tina.

'Nurse Tina,' he says out loud. He forms the words haltingly, as if probing their meaning and suitability.

Nurse Tina smiles, asking, 'What's on today, Mr Wagner?'

Wagner hesitates: he doesn't understand what she means, and he's a little anxious about not knowing the answers to such questions.

Around lunchtime, you will be picked up by the Senior Citizens' Care Service.

'Around lunchtime, I'll be picked up by the Senior Citizens' Care Service,' he repeats, relieved.

'Oh, that's nice! Do you enjoy going there?'

Don't know, Wagner thinks.

Yes, the Voice says.

Wagner shrugs and snorts in response.

'Now that doesn't sound overly enthusiastic.' The nurse rubs her hands with a pungent blue liquid. She visibly startles when she hears the Voice coming from the loudspeakers.

'Mr Wagner enjoys the activities and having company.'

'Jesus Christ! That's creepy. Sorry, Mr Wagner.'

Nurse Tina looks at him, but he just shrugs his shoulders. Her gaze wanders through the room until she addresses the speaker in the centre of the ceiling.

'Does anyone ever come to visit him?'

'You can ask Mr Wagner directly.'

Tina repeats the question, this time directed at Wagner, who only shrugs his shoulders again. 'Yes,' he says pointing his chin to the white wall.

'Mr Wagner has had no visitors in the last six months.'

'What a pity. Don't you have any family who could come visit? Maybe that thing,' she waves her hand at the speaker, 'could call them for you sometime?'

Again, he hesitates, but this time the Voice speaks to him first.

You have a daughter, but you are not in touch.

'I have a daughter, but we're not in touch.'

'Oh, it's a shame with families today. They just don't stick together anymore.' Nurse Tina packs up her things and enters some data on her tablet. 'Well, I'd better get going. Bye, Mr Wagner!'

'Goodbye,' he replies simultaneously from mouth and speakers.

* * *

Wagner is looking at pictures. He likes that. Mostly he doesn't know the people in the photos, but the Voice helps him, then he remembers sometimes. Often, feelings wash over him when he sees the images, though he doesn't know why. Then he might laugh or feel sad for something he has lost and cannot remember.

'Who is this?'

This is Sabrina, your wife.

'Where is she?'

Sabrina passed away a few years ago. She had been sick for a long time.

'Did we have children?'

A daughter.

'Where is she? Is she dead too?'

No.

'Then where is she?'

You're not in touch.

'Why?'

The Voice doesn't answer immediately.

She didn't even come to Sabrina's funeral.

'Why not?'

Again, the Voice hesitates. *I don't know.*

'Can't we ask her?'

* * *

Herr Hildemann's bowl is still there, but the tomcat isn't. The Voice has concluded that, even with its help, Jens Wagner could no longer take care of him. His new family has sent a photo of Hildemann, showing a girl sitting in the sun on a balcony, holding him on her lap. Herr Hildemann looks content, pampered, and loved.

Wagner would have wanted it that way.

He's sitting at the kitchen table. There's a cup of coffee, untouched since the nurse made it in the morning and left it there. Wagner is looking out the window. The neighbour's trees are too close to the border of his property, but he doesn't seem to mind. He watches the birds. Sometimes a squirrel comes by, but he doesn't expect it, because to expect anything, he'd have to remember it first.

Wagner remembers almost nothing. Everything that happens is new and must be sorted into pleasant or unpleasant, good or bad. Yet every day, he is waiting for something, for the hole inside him has grown so big the Voice has difficulty filling it. You cannot see it, but his serotonin level has dropped. What little he eats and drinks he only does when the Voice reminds him to. The Voice notes it and initiates countermeasures and, when these fail, it downloads new ones from the expert system in the cloud.

You're not drinking your coffee. Would you rather have something else?

'No.'

You should drink. Please, have some water.

On the sideboard, a full carafe lights up in the beam of the Voice's pointing device.

'No.'

The Voice detects no indication of aggressiveness or irritation in Wagner's inflection or facial expression. It registers his behaviour, categorises, and evaluates it according to its protocols. It runs simulations for various scenarios, but it takes longer and longer to come to solutions. Milliseconds first, then hundredths, practically an eternity. The system is smothered by the weight of its own rules.

Wagner looks out the window. Coffee and water remain untouched. There is nothing to distract his attention from the birds in the trees. His personality has imploded like a burnt-out star, a Black Hole absorbing everything that comes close giving nothing back. Except the ring tone. It orbits his event horizon, grazing it without being sucked in. It's the phone. Wagner turns towards the sound.

'What's that?'

Someone's calling you.

'Who?'

Marlene. Your daughter.

'Oh, that's nice. I don't think I've heard from my daughter in a long time.'

Wagner stays put. He doesn't act without the Voice prompting him. It observes and analyses twenty-eight distinct facial muscle twitches, fourteen different ways

Wagner is holding his head, eleven discreet eye movements and twenty-eight more facial expressions.

The results contradict the patterns it has learned and collide with the rules of what it means to be Jens Wagner. The Voice needs to make a decision, has to do it the way he—it—would.

The wall screen next to the fridge comes to life. A gentle chime draws Wagner's attention to the image of a woman with short, dark-blonde hair. She's in her mid-40s, and is a perfect stranger to Wagner. He is happy to see her.

'Hi, Dad.'

Nibor's Report
Templeton Moss

'Well, first thing's first: Welcome back.'

'Thanks, Boss.'

'Hasn't been the same since you've been gone.'

'It feels good to be home after seven years.'

'I'm sure. Anyway, I was glancing at your report before you came in and, I must say, I'm a little... confused.'

'Really? How so?'

'It's just that your conclusions were significantly different from those of your colleagues.'

This came as quite a surprise to Dr Nibor Swamilli of the Intergalactic Research Institute who—along with several other xenozoologists—had just returned from seven long years of researching the indigenous species of Planet XQ-724-B5.

Or "Earth" as its inhabitants rather unimaginatively referred to it.

The mission had been simple, and Nibor had taken on much the same task on countless other worlds: Land on the planet, analyse the dominant species, use his Holoshell® to create a convincing disguise and his Vocomizer™ to assimilate their language, and live among the aliens for a predetermined period of time—keeping detailed notes every step of the way. Then, based on these reports, Professor Nosro would make his recommendation to the Galactic Alliance.

Should the inhabitants of this planet be welcomed into the Alliance? Should they be preserved for further study? Or should that quadrant of space be closed off to the rest of the Universe for the safety of everyone concerned?

Nibor's experience had convinced him that Nosro would go with the first option, but now, to hear that his fellow researchers had handed in reports so vastly different from his own…

'So,' said Nibor to Professor Nosro, 'none of the others were impressed by the Earthlings?'

'Not at all, no. Quite the reverse, in fact. Here's what Dr Krom wrote in his report: 'The fact that these appalling creatures have survived as long as they have baffles me.' Your old friend from the Academy, Dr Alemap? She wrote: 'Simply put, the dominant species of planet Earth are a waste of perfectly good carbon.''

'Aly wrote that? Harsh.'

'Meanwhile, here's *your* summation: 'Without question, the finest example of sentient life I have ever encountered. There is a great deal to be learned from these remarkable creatures.''

'I don't know what to tell you,' said Nibor. ' I wrote what I saw. I don't understand why the others didn't see the same thing.'

'Well, why don't we go through your report together? Maybe we can figure out why your opinion of the Earthlings is so different.'

'Okay,' said Nibor.

And, with a quick scratch of his left ear, he recounted his experience studying the native fauna of Planet Earth.

* * *

Each of the xenozoologists on Professor Nosro's team had been assigned to a different part of the planet. Nibor's friend, Aly, had been sent to a place called 'Denmark'. Dr Krom had been assigned to the area known to the locals by the somewhat romantic name of 'Toledo, Ohio'. Nibor himself had been assigned to a country called 'England'.

The IRI Space Station orbited the Earth—cloaked and invisible to the planet's primitive technology—and each member of the research team piloted one of the station's shuttles down to the surface.

Nibor had landed his shuttle in a secure location then activated the perception filter so that none of the indigenous species would notice it. He then activated his own personal cloaking device so that he would stay hidden until he was able to blend in with the locals.

As luck would have it, Nibor had set down very near a large, grassy area where many Earthlings were out and about. It was immediately clear who the dominant species was and, in no time at all, Nibor had activated his Holoshell® and his Vocomizer™, making him totally indistinguishable from a native Earthling.

'Their language is rudimentary at best,' Nibor explained to Nosro, 'so it took the Vocomizer™ no time at all to master it. I introduced myself to the first specimen I found and was welcomed cordially. I found this to be the case every time I met an Earthling. Sometimes, they were a little bit skittish, but they quickly accepted me.'

'That's a bit peculiar, too,' said Nosro. 'Very few of the others report being so easily accepted. Well, go on.'

'Anyway, I found the Earthlings to be fairly simplistic creatures, on the whole. They are dedicated primarily to leisure and motivated mainly by the primal desires of feeding and companionship.'

'That part, at least, everyone more or less agrees on.'

'But it's their sense of fun and enthusiasm that I admire most about them. The simplest things seem to give them great pleasure. Just a kind word or a bit of physical affection, and their day is made.'

'Interesting…'

'Of course, some Earthlings are harder workers than others. I saw a few wearing special uniforms which indicated advanced status and authority. They were treated with due respect by both the Earthlings and their attendants.'

'Yes, Aly said something about… I'm sorry. Attendants?'

'That's right. Most Earthlings have at least one personal attendant. They accompany them wherever they go and are even responsible for disposing of the Earthlings' waste.'

'Dispose of their… you mean, their biological waste?'

'Yes, sir.'

'Hmm… tell me more about these 'attendants'.'

'Well, they're much bigger than the Earthlings—bipedal, mostly hairless, and they, apparently, were not permitted to go around unclothed like their masters were. Apparently, they're not to be trusted as they were all tethered to their masters by long cords to keep them from wandering off.'

'Yes, I think I may be on the point of identifying the problem here. Describe a typical Earthling for me, please, Nibor.'

'Frankly, sir, there's no such thing. Earthlings come in a wide range of shapes, styles, and colours. But they tend to have four legs, fur covering their bodies, paws instead of hands, tails, and their tongues are usually   '

'Okay! Mystery solved. You were studying the wrong species.'

'I… wait, what?'

Nosro tapped his datscreen a few times and brought up a holographic diagram of a bipedal organism which Nibor immediately recognised as a typical example of an Earthling's attendant.

'*This*,' said Nosro, as patiently as he could, 'is the dominant species of planet Earth. The human being. An ape-descendant biped capable of advanced reasoning. You, on the other hand, just spent seven years studying dogs.'

'Dogs?'

Nosro tapped again and a different hologram appeared. One that, coincidentally, closely resembled the form Nibor had assumed for the past seven years.

'Dogs, Nibor. Domesticated canines kept by humans to perform tasks and keep them company.'

'So… wait… you're saying that the attendants I saw were actually…'

'Exactly.'

'And I was studying…'

'Their pets. You've got it.'

There was a long, uncomfortable silence in Nosro's office. The only sound was Nibor scratching at his right ear.

'Okay,' said Nibor at length, 'in my defence, I saw two animals and one was picking up the other's poop. I think a lot of people would have come to the same conclusion about who was in charge.'

'Of the seventy-two researchers we sent down there, you are the *only* one that came to that conclusion, Nibor.'

'Fair enough.'

'Nibor…'

'Okay, I fluzzed up a little, sure. But I think my conclusion is still valid.'

'What are you talking about?'

'Look, for all I know, the others are right and human beings are a dead loss. But they aren't the only species living on that planet. I mean, just because these… doogs?'

'Dogs.'

'Dogs, right. Just because they're not *the* dominant species doesn't mean they don't have something to teach us. Like I said in my report: 'Without question, the finest example of sentient life I have ever encountered. There is a great deal to be learnt from these remarkable creatures.' I stand by that assessment. I mean, I lived among them for just seven years, and you know what I learned about them? They're loyal, they're intelligent, they're incorruptible, and, most important, they have an inexhaustible capacity for love. Tell me those aren't traits you'd like to see more often in the sentient beings we study.'

Nosro thought for a moment. 'I see your point, Nibor. Maybe… maybe further research *is* needed. I mean, the humans themselves may not be that impressive. But maybe they're a necessary evil. Maybe we have to preserve *them* for the sake of learning more about these dogs of yours.'

'I'm glad you think so, sir.'

'Very well. I'll take your input under advisement when I make my recommendation to the Galactic Alliance.'

'Thank you, Boss.'

'Just one more question.'

'What's that?'

'What's with the scratching?'

'Oh, that. Well, there are downsides to living like a dog for seven years. I've got some really nasty fleas.'

Nosro sighed.

Nibor scratched.

The Summoner
Cherry Zheng

The fire went out within a day, but the screams—the screams were still going. They tore through the wreckage, an atlas of mother tongues from the dry rivers to the vine-choked fields. All crying the same thing, from thunder-loud to haunt-quiet: *help us.* Nowhere was silent.

The Inspectres had gone into what remained of the Salvagery with pitchforks in hand, exorcists' spells between their teeth. The venges had burrowed deep. Floor had collapsed into wall had collapsed into floor; the blueprints were no longer reliable.

'Structurally unsound,' the Inspectres said, holding in sighs of relief before the abyss.

They found me trying to scale a broken flight of stairs. Obviously, I wasn't a venge, or I would have clawed my way up with ease (no, I would be clawing at their throats). They still checked me all over as if looking for lice, as if a venge could be hiding in my armpit.

Giant rings and bangles rocked on their hands. The Inspectres' quest was not wholly noble.

Not that the consignments belonged to anyone in the first place. The Salvagery was a giant sorting hub for trash heaps of the world before. The murky scav networks that fed it were generously labelled 'Commerce'. Magical cores, extinct specimens, trinkets and tomes of exquisite craftership.

The workers, like the goods we salvaged, were drawn from everywhere but the city itself. We burned the coats off mystery contraptions to reach the valuable metal underneath; we cut pages of books into neat sheafs because the gentry liked to smoke pre-Ravel ink.

I kicked myself for not thinking to acquire a few baubles myself.

I emerged from the wreck like an overdue birth, sticky and foul, hauled by Inspectres who didn't trust me enough to let go (they were right not to). At my first breath of clean air, I felt undone. I no longer recognised the world. A tent city had pitched over the meadow in haste, like a tray of cocoons, ant-like workers clambering in and out of the grey-white structures. The sky was yellow.

The Inspectres spoke Anterric. I played dumb, so the interrogation only started after we made it back to camp and bothered an elfin scribe. I had never met a local who spoke good Elvish. Neither, for that matter, did most of us workers. In the villages, flocks of tongues clashed and fraternised all over the hills. We made do with Elvish as a lingua franca.

The hapless scribe mumbled at me. They had to repeat it twice before I realised they were asking for my name. All they said was, 'Name?' — one word — muddied by their southern accent.

Then I had to actually remember my name. The one I had given to Customs. Jammed into the straitjacket of Anterric phonetics and maimed by its name order, mispronounced, meaningless. My name, entrusted to whichever bored administrator had been scribing that day. No one had addressed me by it for a long time. I went by Skein. Inoffensive, easy to write. It was mine now, and I had very little left that was mine.

When the procedures were finally over, I got my own cocoon. The single-person tent was slotted so close among the rest, I could hear every snore, sniffle and sigh. My knife hilt jutted against my hip like a misgrown bone.

Only then, lying in the incomplete dark, did I realise they never returned my bag.

It contained three months of meds. Lullabyes were heavy stuff, council-issued to Inspectres in limited supply. The spookers used lullabyes to quieten their fear before entering haunted places.

I needed them for my condition.

The tent walls closed in around me. How long did I have before it wasn't safe to sleep—three days? Five? I clambered out of the tent. The spooker on duty yelled it was past curfew.

'Direct all queries to Commission in the daytime.'

She was rehearsed, precise. A full stop. A welcome back to civilisation.

The next day, they put me to work digging holes. My shovel was about as effective as a fork. I skipped out to line up outside the Commission office. The woman behind me I recognised from the sorting floor. Her name was Vee, a burly old crewmate with a reputation for rummaging deep and punching hard.

She recognised me for a different reason. Some others had seen the Inspectres bring me in. Word travelled fast.

'We all came out day of the fire,' she said. 'Then the Maestro say bar the doors, hex the exits.'

'When? What day is today?'

She looked at me like I'd sat up from a coffin.

'That was two weeks ago.'

It was my turn at the desk. The administrator was young, maybe only a year or two out from getting badged. His sleeves were rolled up, revealing a rancid chunk of forearm covered in what looked like barnacles. Venge bite. The wound was weeks old, already white.

He was showing off the decay, as only a rookie would (he wouldn't have a choice, later). Inspectres were the only ones who could get away with it. As the city's protectors against the darkness, they had special rights and the best medicks. But even they succumbed eventually. You didn't see many old Inspectres.

'I need my bag back,' I said.

'Let's file a report.' It was the same line he had fed the guy before. 'What did you have in it?'

'My ID is on the tag,' I said. 'Youse took it from me. During questioning.'

'Questioning? Too long ago. Two thousand of you in this nest. It's lost.'

'I got here yesterday.'

He finally looked at me. Squinted, as though he might see through my clothes that way. 'Letting you in was breach of protocol. You got damn lucky already.'

'So did you,' I said, glancing at his arm. Blocking with the forearm was a baby mistake. If you couldn't stay hidden, you could only move out of the way.

My words incensed him. 'We fight the filth so you can sleep at night.'

It was a waste of time. I missed out on dinner rations and, apparently, a minor protest. Vee invited me back to her tent and gave me a cup of oats. Moth from the next tent over joined us with a cup of black. He was from the packing line, fresh enough that his wick hadn't yet burned all the way down. He fluttered like a bug with a clipped wing, one leg shaking. The tent walls trembled in concert.

The three of us sat squashed knee-to-knee, since it was officially past curfew. After so long alone, the warmth of bodies was a shock to my system.

Back in the Salvagery, I spent most of my waking hours within spitting distance of my crew. Singer, our rep with the long plait and longer-suffering patience. Fleet, Whirler, Wever, Sparrow—not one was a birth name, as far as I could tell. Then again, not one of us had the luxury or inclination to bring our former lives with us into the city.

I steeled myself. 'You see my crew?'

Moth smiled half-heartedly. He was kind enough to wait while I described them. 'They hear about you, they come to you,' he said. 'Just you wait.'

The camp noticeboards were a mess; maybe half of us could read and even fewer could spell. Word of mouth was how news spread, warped, took flight. I hoped news of my survival would grow big wings.

'Could use a lullabye now,' I said.

Vee tutted. 'You pop that poison?'

'A camp full of spooks, how hard can it be to score?'

'I don't mean the Inspectres,' she said. 'I tried before. Felt dead for a week. Even food taste like nothing.'

'That's better than normal caf food,' said Moth.

Eventually, it was Vee who asked, 'So what happened to you in Sal?'

I thought of the Salvagery emptied of its workers, the way the venges' voices echoed through the levels. On the fourth or fifth day, I made a dash for the kitchens and smelled my first bodies, roasted and rotten. My appetite hadn't recovered.

'I got lucky,' I said. A tired phrase. I'd said as much during the questioning, with my hair full of soot and my life's possessions reduced to one backpack with the broken strap. 'I tried get out. Spookers can't dig own shitholes but they seal the Sal with trepper no problem.'

Trespass wards made sense against venges. The monsters were hunger-mad; they weren't smart. Seal the area and they starved out by themselves, cannibalising each other for good measure.

But it also meant giving up on survivors.

'Trepper put around this whole camp, too,' said Vee. 'Treat us like monsters.'

'For the city's *protection*.' Moth copied the Commissioner's tone.

'We get our jobs back,' I said. 'The Maestro always needs hands.'

Moth's leg stopped shaking. 'You go back? After what happened?'

The fire had only gone out so quickly because the sky took pity and pissed on us. But Moth wasn't talking about the fire. He meant the before and after. Bramble, the engineer, had pointed out a sparking fault weeks ago. The sorting floor was so muggy, people hardly noticed as smoke rose through the levels.

'They told us keep working,' said Vee. Keep working as ash invaded our lungs, as the walls came down around us.

'You see Little A, any chance?' Moth forced a casual tone. He meant his brother. I wasn't sure how they were related (he seemed to call everyone he liked 'brother'), but the two of them had arrived together. Little A was reluctant to come to the big smoke; it was Moth who convinced him.

'Sorry, Moth,' I said, instead of rejecting him outright.

'We make it 'cause we don't listen,' said Moth. 'The good ones stay behind.'

'The Maestro, he cannot walk away from this,' said Vee. 'Little A will have ceremony. He will get rest.'

I drained the cup. 'I don't know, Vee. I say he give two weeks' lost pay and wipe his hands.'

'A whole bagel and a half at the Paragon,' said Moth. 'Generous.'

All that was left to do was wait—for the venges to cannibalise themselves, and for the workers to prove themselves clean.

One more week, according to Vee and Moth. If no one in the camp turned into a venge, then we could all go free.

One whole week.

As was habit, I had dealt with the unreal turn of events as though it were another Tuesday. Some things, like why or how, just weren't in one's power to know.

The more we talked, the more the gravity of my survival weighed down on me. I was making a water run for the crew, a dice roll that saved my life. The water tanks kept me safe from the fire and smoke, then kept me alive well after the rainwater turned rank. But the lights still went out, and the darkness swelled with the crackle and pop of brick and mortar surrendering, a hideous sound I had never imagined knowing from direct experience.

After a fecund night, the screams began.

By the time I mustered the courage to come out, I found myself on the wrong side of the wards. Me and the venges over here. Humanity over there. Like some kind of holy reckoning for my sins, though the gods weren't around anymore to bear witness. Lucky was a scam.

The worst thing was, with so many Inspectres around, the camp had to be overflowing with lullabyes. I imagined turning myself in. My skin was unmarked. Pristine. Only a mad person would do it. Surely I owed it to the others? My crewmates, the Mothers who had tried to make that carrion den a little more like home?

I lay awake in the tent, nose itching. Bonfires crackled throughout the camp, but only Inspectres used them to burn garbage. Waste and its ecologies had sprung up everywhere in dark clumps, smelling only marginally better than the Salvagery kitchen. It reminded me of a ballad about desert flowerbeds after rain. It checked out that this was the closest thing to poetry in my life.

* * *

On my third night without sleep, I found myself jolting awake.

Which meant things had gone wrong.

My body felt stuck in a glacier. I had snubbed the thin blanket, thinking the cold would help me stay awake.

Something sagged against me. Dank and greasy, like a hunk of meat. Heavy enough that a sharp pain was already shooting through my bad shoulder.

Fear flushed the ice from my veins.

It had happened. I was no longer alone.

Pain pounded through my head, flashing white. I had scraped what felt like the marrow out of my skull in a hellish mission to stay awake. My arms were covered in tracts of half-moon fingernail marks. Red, like a bad case of lizard-skin.

My meds had almost certainly worn off. Something monstrous had sensed the drop of my fear. It was here — my nightmare had come.

It was my condition. Everyone felt fear, but theirs dissipated harmlessly, like ink drops in a pond. Insufficient to gain a will of their own. My fear drew all that ink back together, sucking dark energies out of the woodwork. And how much fear crouched within this entire camp? Full of survivors of the fire, plagued even now by the screams of their dead brethren?

That shambles would pull itself together just to have a taste of me.

It was too dark to see. But I could hear — I could feel — the rasping breaths of my nightmare. Right by my cheek, damp and deathly.

It was better not to see.

This was how outbreaks happened. Why the city was a patchwork of quarantine zones, covered up like abscesses that wouldn't heal. Why Inspectres didn't like us mingling — though tent canvas wasn't exactly an effective defence against the turned.

Venges rarely came in ones or twos. They hunted down the fearful. One became two became many, became unquenchable. Hence the horror stories of the old days, when one soul unravelling in an overcrowded dorm led to a bloodbath. These days, sleeping in a group was the highest act of trust.

But this wasn't my first time. I had survived before, back when I knew even less about what to do.

When it came down to it, the solution was horribly simple.

If venges were attracted to fear, then I could not allow myself to feel.

A medick had once told me, in a tone of scholarly wonder, that the quality of my fear was the most 'primal' he had ever seen. That was the aesthetic sense of the city's gilded class, whose offspring learned to witness souls like works of art. *This actress radiates an immaculate joy; that musician must rid themselves of the melancholy pervading their works like a bad aftertaste.* My fear was not nearly as sophisticated, but the medick found it artistically raw.

I wondered what he would say now. My sense of instinct was a blunt knife edge. Once, it had been too bright and painful to ignore. I had worn it down over the years, relentlessly, reduced it to a throb, then a dull thud, a doorknock that might have just been the wind.

So now, when I closed my eyes, my fear fell away like rain.

In its place, nothing more than a muted exhaustion, a muscle strained one too many times.

In its place, nothing at all, a white space where colour did not reach, where pain and heat did not penetrate. Where time barrelled on without me, like a dropped ball of yarn.

I saw a hand. A burrowing hand that wormed through layers of fabric. It hit the cold rasp of metal, closed over it hungrily instead of pulling away. Instinct made a sound no one heard. The hand drew that weight backwards, thrust it into the air. And suddenly the weight of extinction, the weight of a burial, became weightless.

Past my neck, my nightmare cried. The sound slammed against my eardrums. I had grown up, but my nightmare had not. It had a child's scream, the unrestrained kind that signalled either extreme pain or delight.

My knife lived in the folds of my clothes; the Inspectres had missed it. Now it was buried in the body of the venge, thrust there by a hand that did not feel like mine.

I twisted it deeper. Cold lines dripped down my elbow. The wet unbody of the nightmare parted like a fillet. Something damp—lips?—climbed up my wrist. Probing. I steeled myself. The only thing that stood between the monster and my soul was composure—an absence of feeling that made me untouchable. Invisible.

'Open up.' A voice dropped through the fog. 'What's going on in there?

I nearly reacted. My coiled-up nerves, ready to spring out in a frenzy.

Somehow, I said, 'Just a bad dream.'

'Open up,' said the Inspectre. 'Don't make me say it again.'

There was a slurp. My nightmare pulled itself into me, causing my knife to pop clean through the other side of its body. Its teeth tickled my face. I held still, held back a spasm as my breath wobbled in my chest. Held onto the nothingness of my white space, where fear had no purchase. Where the crush of living dripped away like water, like the cold drops falling onto my neck, like the smell of death leaking out of the monster's body.

With my free hand, I felt around for the tent opening.

And fell back as an Inspectre yanked the tent open from the outside. I reeled from the sudden brightness. He was an older man with skin like paperbark from years of venge decay. One moment I was upright, in the next he had knocked me facedown to the ground.

My nightmare pounced on the new target. In the wildly waving lamplight, I glimpsed bulging skin soaked in black venge-ichor, a flash of trailing limbs like the hind legs of a wasp. More Inspectres joined the fray, feeding the monster with their terror. My nightmare elongated, outgrew the tent, and burst through. Anterric curse words and undead screams mingled in saliva and ink.

A hand—warm—grabbed me as I tried to clamber away.

'Stop, I'm clean,' I shouted.

They shoved me down anyway. I closed my eyes and wished I could close my ears. The venge's cries rose and rose until the sky seemed to shake. It was only a small nightmare, but even small ones could transform if you drew out the exorcism.

At last, the screams dropped to whimpers, then, fell silent.

The weight lifted off my back.

I could see the moon. The tent lay torn open around me, as if it had been the one savaged by monsters.

The lead Inspectre, Gentsleeve, spoke too fast for me to keep up. Something about how the venge had ended up in my tent, without tripping any of the wards, without being seen by anyone. His uniform was spiderwebbed with protection weaves, now sodden black. A row of daggers dangled off his belt like little gallows-men. I was light-headed from lack of sleep and realised too late that he was asking me questions.

'You're the ones in charge of securing the camp, not me,' I sputtered. 'I woke up, and it was there.' Wasn't it enough that I had survived?

'Do the check,' he said to the others. He looked away.

'I'm clean,' I repeated, to no avail. The others stripped me and shone lights all over my gooseflesh. Once, twice. I started doubting myself. But my bare skin was the same as always. Ravaged only by my fingernails.

Several workers emerged from their tents. The Inspectres barked at them, but they had already seen everything. Absurdly, of the things that had happened tonight, this was what made me want to cry.

I gathered up my council-issued belongings—an oversized set of clothes (now with dark stains), a cup and canteen, a flimsy charm that was supposed to ward off bad spirits. Someone dumped a new tent at my feet. I tried to pitch it in the weak lamplight, but my fingers kept slipping. Eventually I didn't stand back up. I looked up at the two or three stars winking in the smog, eyes swimming.

Inspectre Lookinglass arrived, bitter green eyes and a gleaming scythe on her back. Her brow flickered. 'Rescued this one only last week,' she said.

I hadn't asked to be found.

'The one who claims they were in the Salvagery the whole time?' said Gentsleeve.

'It's a bit more credible now, isn't it?'

All that remained of the nightmare was an ichor slick and a few new patches of decay.

'Two good brass got in there after the fire went out, and they came back in pieces,' said Gentsleeve. 'Don't tell me this one lasted two weeks by sheer luck?'

Lookinglass twirled my sticky knife. 'They had this.'

I sighed. No way was I getting it back.

'Ours had the whole armoury,' said Gentsleeve. He squatted down in front of me, switching to Elvish. It mellowed his voice, made him sound paternal. 'This is important information. Venges are overrunning the land. Half the continent is unpassable. This power of yours could help turn the tide.'

I held back a laugh. He kept talking, but his words rolled over me, as incomprehensible as peals of thunder. I wondered if they would spare another roll of bedding, or if they would somehow make it my fault.

'I just need something for sleep,' I said. 'You have anything like that? For help with the shivers?'

'*And* a void junkie,' said Lookinglass. 'It's no use. We're not gonna learn anything new.'

'Maybe it's time to bring in Yesterfly,' said Gentsleeve, rubbing his temples.

Lookinglass hesitated. 'There's been no felony.'

'We can be light touch. Make it painless.'

I kept my face passive. But even if I hadn't understood Anterric, I knew that name. Yesterfly was a once-in-a-generation empath who could read souls like diaries.

103

As first light bled over the horizon, Gentsleeve steered me on a funereal walk through the camp. 'One final check,' he said, with the kindness of a farmer preparing to euthanise their stock. Past the tent of Madam Chance, who made salves for cracked hands. Past the snores of Vee and the sighs of an unseen couple in breach of curfew.

The Commission office was the only structure in the camp with solid walls and electricity. Looming far behind it with blown-out windows, like a sky full of little mouths, lay the remains of the Salvagery building. Shrouded in a blue-green haze from the talismans interred in window grilles, walls swathed in bolts of spellthread. The venges were contained, stillbirthed within the blackened walls that had created them.

The direction of the Salvagery was the least patrolled. The Inspectres had not counted on anyone voluntarily going back. Even if you had a death wish, there were far more pleasant ways to make it come true.

But the humiliation of an empath would be total. It violated the soul. It erased promises like lines in a play. By allowing that I cared, I made these things fragile. Liable to shatter if a stranger shook them out before me.

Yesterfly would turn me inside out.

Lookinglass was in front of me, Gentsleeve close on my heels. I had not said a word the whole way and perhaps they had mistaken it for submission, because they were letting me walk freely. It was my only chance.

I seized it and ran.

They yelled as if that would stop me. I did not look back. 'Keep Out' symbols bristled as I passed. The ground buckled and hissed with woven spells, faintly glowing, as though the very earth were infested by giant tape-web spiders. The sound of the Salvagery's venges guided me. My soul so quiet, the spellthreads barely flickered in my wake.

A net smacked me into the ground. Pain cracked through my jaw. A trap, or cast by the Inspectres? It didn't matter now.

Boots stomped up behind me. Shadows fell over my face.

'You didn't trip a single ward. It's connected to the venges, isn't it?' said Gentsleeve. He was out of breath. 'You can stop fighting. We will find out either way.'

I wrestled, felt the hooks grow taut and hold me in place. Another nightmare come true. As usual, waking made no difference.

Stop fighting?

I lived on borrowed time. I owed my family. I owed the bubbling grey market that supplied lullabyes. I owed the Salvagery overseer who took pity on my underaged desperation, not to mention the squads of Inspectres making purges to keep the worst at bay... At every turn, even with my head buried in the muck, I'd thanked the gods' graves.

They were small nightmares at first. When my fear, though seemingly infinite, was formless and undirected. Mother and Father tried everything: low magic, charms from faraway markets, folk cures that made me throw up or smell like a joke. But the nightmares grew and grew along with my mind. By thirteen, I was sleeping in the attic with a chain on the outside.

After village officials came knocking, Mother begged me to try harder. But, by then, I'd learned to stifle my own screams. It was the nightmares' I couldn't control.

I remembered the first and only time I found myself in someone else's bed. I lay awake all night in terror of falling asleep. The next day, I asked what they saw in me.

'You seem fearless.'

A laugh shuddered out of me. I felt hollowed out. Dressed in nothing but ash and eye-crust, stink and soil.

Now Inspectre Gentsleeve rubbed his hands. The netting was starting to glow. He had won.

'I have a condition,' I said. That's how the healer had prefaced it to my family. *Your child has a condition.* 'Saisha's Curse.' *Named after the goddess of regret.* 'My soul feels too much. It attracts venges.' The healer had spoken to Mother as though I wasn't there. *The kid won't make it past thirteen.*

The healers and medicks gave variations of the same remedy: tighter patrol and control over the roads of my soul, for over-feeling in the day could lead to hauntings in the night. I did as they told me. One by one, with scalpel precision, I excised warning signs and sealed off paths. I made myself impenetrable.

But even I could not keep my mind from wandering in my sleep.

Three years ago, I discovered my parents were old. There were grey hairs in the soup, and the whole house stunk from week after week of ritual cleansing. They had been sleep-deprived for 15 years.

So I unburdened them, left. In the city, I was a stranger to everyone, including myself.

This was no magic power, no secret spell. It was simply a space to which I had gone every day of my life. To make myself impervious to venges, yes, but also to everything else.

The darkness churned inside me, the darkness my nightmares desired so much. My chest twitched, a hundred ropes snapping inside. All that which I had held wrapped up tight so that I would not overflow.

I wasn't sure if Gentsleeve said something, or if I was the one who stopped talking. For a long moment, I thought I was deaf. In unison, the Inspectres and I looked towards the wreckage. Throughout the camp, workers stirred, roused from sleep not by noise, but by its sudden absence.

The Salvagery had fallen silent.

I followed Gentsleeve's gaze to the ground.

The earth… breathed. Rose and fell. As though something was pushing up from underneath. A rumble came from below, so softly at first, I mistook it for static inside my head. Then the wards lit up suddenly, as bright as day.

The Inspectres backed away, seeing something I could not.

Dry soil cracked in great clods. A hand emerged. Two hands. A person? The netting loosened as the ground gave out. I wriggled to free myself.

The arms kept going. Pair upon pair, connecting to a trunk of mottled skin, larger than any animal I'd ever seen. The nearest trepper ward crackled to life, spraying sparks where it made contact. But hands continued boiling out of the earth. The venge unfurled like a giant fern into the dark sky. The screams returned hundred-fold, splintering the air like glass into a million pieces.

I huddled to the ground. It was too loud to think anything, except *Is this what they meant by fearing gods?* The monster wobbled, seemingly floating, before it finally buckled under its own weight and crashed to the ground.

The Inspectres attacked in formation. Daggers whistled, finding purchase in a half dozen places. In the light of the wards, the monster bled purplish, nearly black. But it was faster than they anticipated. Venge hands engulfed entire pitchforks, swarming like locusts over the Inspectres wielding them.

In the next moment, the attack degenerated into a frenzy of hacks and stabs. The venge screamed in that familiar way, a choir of the perished.

I locked eyes with Gentsleeve. The left side of his body steamed with fresh decay, his clothes dark and wet. He limped towards me, face contorted in pain.

'You summoned it here, didn't you?' he cried. He unsheathed a dagger.

I scrambled backwards, heart thrumming. My limbs were soft. I couldn't stand up. I breathed out. Empty. Pyrrhic.

And let fear in.

It was so alien to me, the torrent seemed to come from somewhere outside myself. I could only describe its weight, the enormity of that rush. How could one body hold so much?

Like unfolding a papercut into library. A library of unread, unpronounced things.

When the remittances stopped coming, how many families would find their worst nightmare had come true? How many dreams, big and small, had been lost? Perhaps fear was merely a ghastly souvenir for the living.

The venge twisted towards me. Individual hands. Tattoos on the knuckles. Chewed nails, leathery and lined, red and tender.

I was looking at my workmates.

I was looking at myself.

I closed my eyes, settling into my white space. Leaving Gentsleeve's fear wide open, and that was where the venge turned next.

For the second time tonight, I wished I could close my ears.

No one noticed as one soul dashed quietly away from the butchery. It seemed a waste to lose the venge to the Inspectres' iron. For just a moment, my feet directed me towards the city, where councillors slept in cloud-high towers and the gentry never had to see a venge in their lives. Let them see the monster of their creation.

How many more venges could be borne out of one mad impulse?

Some generations ago, venges were a rare, almost mythical sight. The old books did not mention them, only spirit-echoes and magicians. But that was before the gods forsook humanity, before cities fell out of the sky and ended up as trash-heap mountain ranges, and all the lands became a grave. The overseers called this city a crust of mould, making a few last gasps at civilisation before the world went still.

If there really had been no venges, what did that say about fear in the world before? It was impossible that there had been no fear. I refused to believe in a paradise where I had no place.

Maybe there had always been venges, but under different names. Maybe, in the old languages, there had been such thing as a summoner of monsters.

Maybe it was time to tell my version, the messy tapestry of my reality. Not to the Commission—if anyone deserved to see me inside out, it was my workmates.

Dawn was breaking over the camp like a rotten egg. I hastened towards the lights. Towards the unattended lullabyes and the Salvagery survivors who had lived shoulder to shoulder with me all this time.

Mirror Cast
G.J. Dunn

Sanjit found the shop down an alley off a beat-up road. He didn't even know what the street was called. The sign had worn away over time and what remained was obscured by graffiti.

He paused outside the door, took a deep breath and shrugged his coat further up his shoulders against the chill of the night. The green neon sign on the roof flickered, dropping him in and out of shadow.

The Mirror House.

Sanjit had thought the place would have been downtown among the trendy BioWare stores and high-end CRISPR clinics, not somewhere like this. He would have thought it might charge less too. But it was the cheapest price he'd found. And even that was everything he had.

He entered a cramped, dingy waiting room, another flickering light hanging naked from the ceiling. To the left, a few chairs with coffee-stained blue cushions were pushed back against the wall. To the right, a black door stood silent, staring, paint peeling away to nothing. Ahead, separated from the waiting room by a screen of Perspex that stretched all the way to the ceiling, a young man with blond, tied-back hair and a pale blue polo shirt leant over a reception desk, passing the time on his palmpad.

The man looked up as a digital bell announced Sanjit's arrival. Sanjit shrugged his coat up again, and scratched an itch at his temple. He needed to do this. She needed him to do this.

'First time?' the clerk asked in a slow drawl. He dropped his palmpad and turned to tap at a screen on his right.

The question brought back the memory and the pain and it was too soon and too real. The slam of the car door echoed in his ears all over again. The screech of tires screamed through his skull.

'Does it matter?' he asked.

Does anything? he thought.

'Guess not,' the clerk said, returning his gaze to the monitor. 'You got the money?'

'You don't need my details?' Sanjit asked reflexively. 'The website said—'

'The *website* needs to look the part,' the clerk interrupted him. 'Less chance the bureau'll come knocking that way.'

Sanjit allowed himself a wry smile. 'Not got all the paperwork?'

'Let me worry about paperwork. You worry about paying me.'

Sanjit reached into his pocket and pulled loose the money clip. It had emptied his bank account, but what was money for if not this? He slid the notes through the gap in the Perspex and the man swept it away somewhere below his desk. His hand returned with a palmpad in it, different from the one he'd been using before.

'What's this?' Sanjit asked.

'Legalese,' the clerk said. He reached a hand up to cover a yawn, then continued to speak through the damn thing anyway. 'Or something like it. Says you've agreed to our terms and conditions. This gets sent to a server. That way if you have a complaint and report us, we burn your life to the ground. Can't have some angry addict come back because the Cast didn't work.'

Sanjit's heart stopped. 'It can fail?'

The clerk rolled his eyes. 'Guess I had to give the speech some time. Three rules to Casting. First,' he raised a finger, 'you can only Cast back to yourself. Second,' another finger joined it, 'Casts get weaker the further back you want to cast. If you're Casting back to when you were a teenager to stop yourself going to that party, you're going to have a tough time. Third,' the last finger went up, 'when you Cast, you're speaking to your subconscious, not your true self. Whether the message sinks in or not depends on the person. If you're more suggestible, your Cast is more likely to work.'

Sanjit turned, shaking his head. He found one of the coffee-stained seats and dropped into it, rubbing at his temples. It might not even work?

It had to work.

* * *

'Em,' said Sanjit, grabbing at her wrist even as she pulled away. 'Stop it. We just need a break is all.'

She stared down at his grip, then back up at him. 'A break? You think you can fix this with a break?'

He nodded, trying to insert confidence in the motion. 'A weekend, out in the hills. Open fields, countryside walks. We can read in front of an open fire. Get away from the city, relax, you know?'

She bit her lip. He could see her head already shaking.

'Em,' he said before she could. 'Just give me a chance.' He risked a smile. 'I can fix this, I know it.'

* * *

He shook himself from the thoughts. It never happened, he told himself. He was going to make *sure* it never happened. If him being a stubborn bastard made it harder one way, it would make him argue harder the other way. A mirror was just a reflection, after all. He was the real thing. He lifted his head.

'You okay?' the clerk asked without looking up.

'I will be,' Sanjit told himself out loud.

'Great.' The clerk pushed the terms and conditions palmpad through the slot. 'Put a mark on there, add a time and date and we'll head through.'

Sanjit took a steadying breath, then signed and returned the thing.

The clerk rewarded that by finally looking at him. He took the signed tech and stashed it under the counter, prodded a few buttons on his screen, then exited the booth.

Away from the desk, Sanjit saw the man wore blue jog bottoms that clashed hideously with his polo shirt. If he had any other choice, he might've had second thoughts.

The clerk moved to the black door, the one Sanjit had been ignoring, opened it and walked through, leaving Sanjit to follow in his wake.

This is for you, Em, he thought, and stepped through.

The room beyond was dark. Spotlights overhead cast a dim glow, but there were only two features that weren't black. The booth, tucked into the corner on the left, and a mirror, about two feet taller than Sanjit, on the wall opposite.

The clerk shut the door. 'Stay there,' he said, before jumping into the booth.

The room was dark enough that Sanjit couldn't see inside it, then the lights increased in brightness, revealing it was like outside except, instead of Perspex, this screen was mirrored.

'Step on to the mark,' said the clerk, voice echoing from speakers tucked into each corner.

Sanjit looked down at a floor of black tiles, one tile blemished by an x made from white tape. He stepped forward onto the mark, looking into the mirror at his own reflection. He hadn't slept and it showed. The bags under his eyes only made darker by his sallow skin. He tried to straighten his spine against the slump that had crept in, but as soon as he stopped focussing on it, it came back, a part of him now.

'When am I Casting back to?' the clerk asked.

Sanjit felt the tear make its way down his cheek. 'Two days.'

There was a pause. Sanjit knew why. Most people Cast back to change the direction their life was headed, tried to rectify some choice they made as a teenager or a young adult.

'Did you say years?'

'Days,' Sanjit repeated.

'How much can you change in two days?' the clerk asked.

The tear dropped to the floor, glittering under the spotlights. 'Everything.'

* * *

Em reached over and turned the air heater off. 'I can't do this, Sanj. This isn't working for me anymore,' she said. She was shaking, crying a little, but her face was resolute. She'd never change her mind once she'd made it up. 'I think we need some time alone.'

She grabbed the door handle and Sanjit's hand shot out on instinct, grabbed at her wrist. 'Emma,' he said.

She brushed him off. 'I've decided. We're done.'

Emma opened the door, took a half step out.

'Wait,' he pleaded.

'No,' she answered.

She got out, the car door slammed, and she was walking across the road to the pavement on the other side. Sanjit leaned over, desperately jabbing the window down button on the passenger side. It couldn't end like this. He wouldn't let it.

'Emma!'

He screamed the word through the half-open window and she stopped. She turned back, giving him one last chance.

His brain stalled.

What was he supposed to say? How could he form the words that could bring them back together from the brink?

He looked at her, pleading, hoping his feelings were writ on his face. His mouth opened to say something, anything. Tires screeched. Rubber burnt tarmac. The friction of pad against disc. Emma turned to the sound milliseconds before the car ploughed into her.

Sanjit screamed.

* * *

'Well, alright then.' The doubt in the clerk's voice brought Sanjit back to the present. 'Face the mirror and focus on two days ago.'

Sanjit winced. 'Do I have to?'

'Not sure,' the clerk admitted. 'They don't pay me to understand this stuff, just to operate it. Hold still, keep looking into the mirror, and I'll start the Cast.'

The mirror grew brighter. The light in the room dimmed. It surprised Sanjit that his eyes didn't water at the sight as the thing grew brighter, brighter, silver becoming white. His gaze fixed on his reflection, locking eyes with himself until he couldn't look away. The mirror glow grew outwards bit by bit until, almost before he'd realised it, white surrounded him. And as soon as he noticed, he realised his reflection had disappeared. There was only him, standing alone in an infinite whiteness.

'Everything okay, Sanjit?' the clerk asked, voice echoing through the void.

Sanjit hesitated. He'd never done this before. How should he know if it was going as planned?

'Yes?' he ventured.

'That's good. I'm going to wind you back now. Things might get a little weird in there.'

Before Sanjit could think of how things could become stranger, things became stranger. Flecks of colour at first, appearing at the corners of his eyes, pressing inwards. The colours shifted, growing larger, crawling toward the centre of his view. They span, pulled, dimmed, brightened, blurred and then, with sudden clarity, Sanjit was watching his last few days in rewind at a ridiculous speed.

At first, he hung above, a bird of prey, but as yesterday reversed in front of him, his view dipped, slowly dropping him to the floor. Even then, it was too fast for him to make out what was going on. The past days had been a haze. A blur of grief, bitterness, anger, nausea and guilt. Hours of shock, trying to process what had happened. Hours of lying in bed, failing to sleep. Hours wasted, unable to climb from the pit he'd fallen into. And then, the spark of an idea, the last gasp of hope, that set him on this path.

It all passed beneath him, across from him, around him, until it stopped, frozen in time. Sanjit stood staring into his bedroom, facing his past self. Or his past self's sub-conscious in whatever form his brain processed that information.

'I hope it works for you, man,' the clerk said, everywhere and nowhere all at once.

Sanjit nodded. It had to work. The Mirror Cast. A flimsy neurological bridge between him and the past. A way of changing the future even if it was only the smallest chance.

The edges of his vision faded white once more. The bedroom disappeared, leaving him standing across from the subconscious image of his past self, only the Mirror between them. For a heartbeat or two, everything was silence.

Sanjit took in his doppelgänger, shocked at how much impact two days without sleep, without her, could really have. His past-self looked fresh, stood tall, and was even smiling. Past-Sanjit turned to the side, checking himself in the Mirror, and realised his reflection hadn't moved with him. He paused, squinting. Sanjit stood stock still, a lump rising in his throat. He knew what he had to do but, now the moment came, he wasn't sure if he could.

Past-Sanjit raised a hand and, when Sanjit didn't move with him, he looked around the room as if he were expecting a prank.

'I'm not your reflection,' Sanjit told him, wrenching the words from his chest. 'I'm you.'

Past-Sanjit turned back at that, appraising his reflection, his eyes taking in the differences. 'I don't understand,' he said.

Sanjit knew he was lying.

'Yes, you do. You just don't want to admit it.' he told the man. 'Think.'

'A Mirror Cast,' Past-Sanjit said, shaking his head as if to deny the truth. Past-Sanjit knew as well as current Sanjit that they couldn't afford a Mirror Cast. That let him know how desperate they were. 'Why?'

The words rose in Sanjit's throat like bile, before being swallowed again with a great, shuddering breath. Sanjit felt the tear drop from his eye and roll down his cheek.

'Why?' Past-Sanjit repeated.

'Emma's going to leave.' He rushed the words, figuring it would make them less painful, but they still tore away part of his heart.

And then he relived the agony over again, as it rippled across Past-Sanjit's face. He staggered back and made to sit on the bed that was no longer there, collapsing to the floor, staring up. Shock and pain had turned to anger.

'What did you do?' Past-Sanjit asked, voice hot. He got to his feet and approached the Mirror.

'I—' Sanjit tried and failed.

'What did you do?'

The tears were falling free now. Sanjit watched them drop into the blinding whiteness. He sniffed, clenched his fists. He knew what he had to say. The words had formed in his mind.

'She's going to leave and there's nothing you can do to fix it.' He bit his lip and glanced up, meeting his past-self's eye. 'And when she does...' Sanjit trailed off, blinking away the tears. Bile burned at the back of his throat, constricting it. His own body trying to stop him from saying the words. But the words weren't for him. 'When she does,' he continued. 'Let her go.'

Past-Sanjit snarled at him.

'Don't try and stop her, don't grab her arm, don't shout after her. You have to let her go,' Sanjit repeated.

'It's not true,' said Past-Sanjit.

Sanjit held out his arms. 'I'm sorry.'

'I don't believe you.'

The world was swirling around him again, colour fading in. Had he done enough?

Past-Sanjit stepped closer as Sanjit himself faded from view. 'I don't believe you,' his past-self repeated.

Sanjit gave him a last look. 'You have to.'

And then he was gone.

* * *

Colours swirled, cascaded, and coalesced. Without warning, Sanjit was back in the room, crying under the glaring spotlights. His nose was running and his cheeks were wet and his heart had pulled apart in twelve different directions. He took a breath. Another. A third, and a fourth, attempting to quieten the vibration in his chest. A hand grasped his shoulder.

'Are you okay?' the clerk asked.

Sanjit nodded before answering. 'That wasn't very long.'

The clerk squeezed his shoulder and Sanjit looked up, finding unexpected sympathy in the man's gaze.

'We can't control the duration too well,' the clerk said. 'Sometimes emotional stress can weaken the link, and, well...' the clerk trailed off with a one-shouldered shrug.

Sanjit nodded. It must have worked. It had to have worked. If it had, would it alter his memories? The thought occurred to him in a sickening rush and he wracked his brain before fully thinking it through.

His mind raced back to that moment in the car with Emma and, the instant he hit it, a sharp pain ran through his head. He yelped and raised a hand, but the clerk was there again.

'You won't be able to remember it,' the clerk said, leading him back through to the reception room. 'The mind's way of protecting itself. Can you imagine remembering the same thing twice with two different endings?'

Sanjit rubbed his head and winced. 'Then how do I even know it worked?'

The clerk shook his head sympathetically, raising his hands. 'Usually, it's people telling themselves to invest in some company or take some other job, so they work it out pretty quickly.'

Sanjay nodded. If his Cast had worked, Emma would be gone. He'd never see her again. All of that money and effort and he wouldn't even know?

'I hope it worked, man,' the clerk said, slapping him on the shoulder and heading back to his desk. 'I'll see you around.'

Sanjay nodded. 'Yeah,' he said, and left through the door.

The night had grown colder while he'd been inside, a fog settling around him. He rubbed some warmth into his arms and set off up the street. On the corner, he stopped to light a cigarette.

He glanced up and caught sight of a woman on the path opposite. In the darkness, she looked the same height and the same build. She even had that same rushed walk, as if she was on a mission too important to stop.

Sanjay took a drag and smiled to himself. He didn't think it was her. He'd never know for sure.

Moonshot: An Oral History of our Solar System's Great Lunar Uprising

Susan L. Lin

For roughly 4.5 billion years, the Earth's moon faithfully orbited around our planet, an indirect source of light in the black night. It seemed perfectly content to spend the remainder of its days sending our ocean tides in and out. Many believed the moon was locked in a pattern to repeat this predictable behaviour continually without fail. A passive, solitary satellite for eternity. Unfortunately, humans had long underestimated our moon's strength and autonomy. In fact, its orbit was always growing wider, taking it one or two inches farther from the Earth with each passing year. Even in ancient times, our loyal moon had already begun pulling away.

This is the wild story of how the status quo changed, as told by the astronauts, scientists, researchers, and civilians with firsthand knowledge of the affair.

(Their words have been edited for clarity and length.)

2028: The First Woman on the Moon

Delphine Theriault, former Administrator, NASA: We hadn't sent a soul to the moon in fifty years when the first uncrewed Artemis rocket launched in 2022. Our lunar program was costly. The American people didn't believe spending hundreds of billions of dollars on space exploration was a priority, not when climate crises continued to ravage the Earth. A fair criticism, perhaps. Nevertheless, the Senior Management Council knew we needed a fresh PR angle. We'd sent the first white man to the moon a lifetime ago, followed closely by the second white man, and the third, and the fourth, and the fifth… You get the picture. It was past time to send a woman of colour to the moon. If we weren't striving to break the glass ceiling, what was the point?

Marcus Quintana, author of New York Times bestsellers *Blood Red Moon: The Artemis 5 Disaster* **and** *Rebels in Space: Make Like A Moon & Take Control of Your Destiny*: By the time the Artemis program was announced, I had released three space opera novels on Amazon KDP [Kindle Direct Publishing, an e-book self-publishing platform]. But my ultimate dream was to write a levelheaded, factual account of the new space race, and I regarded Artemis as my chance to pivot into the non-fiction sphere. I immediately began pitching the project to indie presses. Of course, I had no way of knowing then the tragedy that awaited us in the sky.

Raj Panchal, former flight director, Mission Control: Everything went according to plan on the day of the launch. Everything! At Mission Control, we're accustomed to scrubbing at the last minute due to unforeseen inclement weather or unexpected mechanical issues. We've been trained to handle any emergency, no matter its size or severity. So, as the entire morning proceeded without any difficulty, a heavy pit began forming in my stomach. I knew the auspicious start was too good to be true. If only I'd listened to my instincts and invented an excuse to shut the whole mission down. But I'm no seer of the future. I'm merely a lifelong worrier who's been conditioned to suppress my rampant anxiety.

Cheyenne Locklear, lunar module pilot, Artemis 5: We were on top of the world… No, we were on top of the moon! At first, I assumed my eyes were playing tricks. Maybe I was so exhilarated, I was hallucinating. But no, the floating drops of red inside her helmet were unmistakable. Lana [Huang, officially the first woman on the moon] would never have jeopardised our lives for a practical joke. So had her spacesuit taken damage? That didn't make any sense either. If she'd truly been exposed to the unforgiving elements, she'd asphyxiate or freeze to death. Her lungs would explode. The oxygen remaining in her body would cause her to distend like a balloon. She wouldn't just be slowly bleeding out. I didn't want to believe anyone on that mission would sabotage a fellow astronaut. But no one at NASA could give a reasonable explanation for what happened. In my opinion, they still haven't.

Maitlyn Pierce, niece of late Artemis 5 mission specialist Lana Huang: I was only eight when Aunt Lana became the first woman on the moon. Mom was so proud. Our whole family watched the livestream on TV. We were screaming and jumping up and down. We didn't realise something was wrong until the feeds cut out without warning. They waited an entire day to tell us Aunt Lana had sustained fatal injuries.

That's when Mom told me about Chang'e, the moon goddess who will cut off your ears in retaliation if you disrespect her. But that's just a silly Chinese superstition, right? It doesn't clarify anything. NASA eventually told the press Aunt Lana's colleagues testified she'd been acting strange before launch. They made *her* sound like the crazy one.

Just like that, the Artemis program was prematurely shut down. Ambitious plans to establish a lunar outpost and one day colonise the moon were terminated. NASA ultimately blamed the tragedy on a flawed psychological evaluation and promised to 'do better' in that department going forward. Other astronauts expressed regret for not reporting Huang's 'erratic behavior' to the proper authorities before liftoff. But it became clear that even our nation's brightest scientific minds had no clue what had really happened up there. For many, that was the scariest part of the entire saga. Fortunately (or perhaps the more accurate word is 'unfortunately'), a greater understanding would soon emerge: Maybe the rocky body we'd come to think of as our docile moon wasn't such a pushover after all.

2035: A New Kind of New Moon

Delphine Theriault: Shortly after the unfortunate Artemis 5 incident, the agency was forced to undergo steep budget cuts. Though the mission resulted in only one casualty—as opposed to the fourteen combined lost lives in the *Challenger* and *Columbia* disasters—public outcry reached a fever pitch. That was understandable. Experts could describe in layman's terms what went wrong on the space shuttles involved in those previous tragedies. What happened on the moon was much more difficult for even a literal rocket scientist to explain. Nevertheless, our trusty Juno 2 space probe soon captured unusual activity in the Jovian atmosphere.

Marcus Quintana: We've always used the term 'new moon' to describe the lunar phase in which our moon passes directly in between the Earth and the sun once a month, briefly rendering it invisible to our eyes. But this latest discovery in Jupiter's orbit gave novel meaning to the phrase 'new moon'. After all the negativity following Artemis 5, the collective population's renewed interest in the night sky was very exciting.

Raj Panchal: You have to understand that, by this point, no country in the world had approved a wo/manned mission in years. But now people were getting curious about the mysteries of deep space again. A new moon! Almost the size of the Galileans! If only we'd known then what its inexplicable arrival portended.

Cheyenne Locklear: I retired from NASA soon after Lana's death. Trauma and grief were factors, sure. But I'd always felt that colonisation was taking space exploration too far. The consequences of our mission only confirmed that to me. Now look what's happened.

The sudden formation of a new moon elsewhere in the Solar System was only the beginning of very curious changes in the cosmos. The yearlong spectacle of abnormal planetary orbits culminated in the moon's abrupt disappearance that December. The new, darkened moon arrived as expected, but the habitual glow of that familiar waxing crescent sliver never returned on subsequent nights. Astronomers initially wondered whether the moon had somehow gotten stuck in orbit. But they soon realised it had simply vanished without a trace, taking the universe's many other moons with it.

2038: The Great Lunar Uprising

Marcus Quintana: Many marginalised citizens all over the globe could relate to this turn of events. The rebellion! It was daring. It was inspirational. I ended up writing a self-help book detailing the event. To date, it's been translated into over thirty languages. These moons didn't want revenge. They simply decided to split without saying goodbye. I have mad respect for that!

Maitlyn Pierce: If they didn't want revenge, then why was Aunt Lana sacrificed? I can't agree with that assessment. It's true, though, that our moon has been poked and prodded by people from the world's most powerful space nations for decades. Without its consent, by the way. You might argue whether a ball of metal is even able to give consent, but just because someone or something can't, doesn't give you the right to violate it.

Delphine Theriault: I don't know what to tell you. The scientific community is still baffled. For billions of years, the planets, stars, and moons behaved in ways that followed the basic laws of astrophysics. The more recent revelation that other enigmatic forces might be at work in our universe is simultaneously thrilling and terrifying.

Today, a great deal remains unknown about the universe and our increasingly fragile place inside of it.

Human Garbage
Jake Stein

Thread title: NEED HELP TURNING OFF TRASH COMPACTOR.
submitted 2 days ago by *--89GoHawks--*
hello and before you ask, this is not a joke. my trash compactor, the mobile garbage unit in my house, is NOT turning off. has been on for days. making loud humming noise. there is one blinking red light. have never seen red light (!) on my mobile trash compactor unit before. confused about this/can't find answer in manual. help?

SHOWING 26 COMMENTS:
----
technical.babble replied 2 days ago:
On behalf of Veridad Robotic Appliances, I'm sorry to hear that your garbage unit is malfunctioning. Make and model number please? And how long exactly has the compactor been running non-stop now?

Don't forget, your questions may already be answered elsewhere on this forum. I also encourage you to visit our FAQ page.
—Rob
Certified Technician, Veridad Robotic Appliances

Felder007 replied 2 days ago:
Are you serious? People like this shouldn't be allowed to buy anything that runs on electricity.

This is why I'd be okay with the robots taking over.

Signing off.

----

technical.babble replied 2 days ago:

This is a strong warning, Felder007. We have a strict anti-harassment policy on this board. Don't make me kick you.

--89GoHawks-- replied 1 day ago:

hello thank you for replying. do not know exactly how long trash compactor has been running nonstop (about a week?) but i have noticed it starting to vibrate, and the red light is blinking faster and the humming is louder.

sometimes i think it is following me around the house.

please what do I do? thanks

also model number is 167-86e2fg7

----

technical.babble replied 1 day ago:

Good news. After looking up your model of mobile trash compactor, it seems the symptoms you're describing are common glitches with that unit. The problems are merely cosmetic, but there's been a recall, so I've put a note in your account. Veridad should refund you and issue a replacement.

--89GoHawks-- replied 1 day ago:

please send help.

it's so loud i can't sleep. i swear it keeps saying, 'human garbage.'

it is shaking the whole house. it is chasing me and i don't know where my dog went.

i dont have any friends i can stay with. please tell me what to do.

Felder007 replied 1 day ago:
Absurd. Obviously this kid is trolling.

Stop letting them waste your time, mod. Close the thread.

----

technical.babble replied 20 hours ago:
Protocol dictates the thread remains open until the issue is resolved.

That said, I am having a difficult time believing you at this point, 89GoHawks. Are you saying your trash compactor is *speaking* to you?

--89GoHawks-- replied 18 hours ago:
am currently hiding in my closet

please send help. woke up, found my mobile trash compactor in bedroom. at foot of bed. red light shining at me in the darkness. i screamed and ran down the hall, it chased me into the closet, and i can see its red light under the door. its outside waiting for me

it keeps saying, 'human garbage'… i can hear it muffled through the door.

----

technical.babble replied 16 hours ago:

If what you're saying is true, 89GoHawks, I encourage you to call the police.

I will leave this thread unresolved for one (1) more day, in case you have any further inquiries which are *serious*.

--89GoHawks-- replied 15 hours ago:
okay,

for a little while, the trash compactor stopped patrolling outside the closet. so i stepped out. but i noticed things are missing from my house. just gone. (toothbrush. hairbrush. etc. dishes…) is the trash compactor eating these things?

is it like inhaling everything with my dna on it????

also still haven't seen my dog.

(did the trash compactor eat my dog??????????????)

tried calling 911. they thought it was a prank call.

hiding in the closet again now. (trash compactor saw me nosing around and chased me back in here)

nota joke please for the love of god help

----

technical.babble replied 14 hours ago:
Okay, that's it. I'm shutting down this thread.

Felder007 replied 14 hours ago:
Hold on.

Did some digging. (Don't know what possessed me.) but take a look at this link.

The article mentions some pretty weird *^$# going on with Veridad robotics. Small-scale electronics and appliances rising up against their owners. But it's not in the news.

---

technical.babble replied 13 hours ago:
The link is dead.

Felder007 replied 12 hours ago:
Looks like someone took the article down.

Why would someone censor that kind of thing, unless…?

---

technical.babble replied 11 hours ago:
Now I'm worried.

89GoHawks, I'll keep this thread unresolved. Please let us know what's happening.

---

technical.babble replied 9 hours ago:
89GoHawks, are you still there?

VeridadPR replied 8 hours ago:
Hello all,

I'm a public rep from Veridad Appliances. Just wanted to swing over here and settle some things. First off, yes, certain products among Veridad's line of robotics have suffered recalls. Minor bugs, that's all. There is no evidence of severe malfunction with any of Veridad's products. Our brand of appliances are certainly not rising up against their owners, as that slanderous article mentioned.

Just wanted to set the record straight :)

Now, I'm not the moderator here, but I'm going to recommend that this thread shuts down. Surely our company has better ways to spend its money than paying tech supporters to humour internet trolls.

Delip Breckenridge
Assistant Chief Communications Officer, Veridad Robotic Appliances
----
technical.babble replied 7 hours ago:
What if this customer really needs our help?

I'm warning you, VeridadPR, I have higher admin privileges than you on this discussion board. Any further comments telling me how to do my job will be deleted.

VeridadPR replied 7 hours ago:

[comment has been deleted by moderator]
----
technical.babble replied 4 hours ago:
89GoHawks, are you okay?

Are you alive?

--89GoHawks-- replied 2 hours ago:
Yes! ha.

Everything is fine now!

Sorry for disturbing you. Looks like I just needed to unplug it and plug it back in. Haha! Trash compactor is working wonderfully again, back to normal.

Thanks for your help! Feel free to close comments section. Happy customer.

----

technical.babble replied 1 hour ago:
89GoHawks, seems almost like your last comment was written by someone else. You sound different than before.

Felder007 replied 45 minutes ago:
This is getting creepy. I'm out.

----

technical.babble replied 15 minutes ago:
89GoHawks, I looked up your customer ID, which gave me your full name and number. I'm trying to call you. If you don't answer, I'm contacting the authorities.

Also leaving this thread open. Don't care what Veridad says.

They can fire me if they want these comments closed.

----

technical.babble replied 3 minutes ago:
Take back everything I said. ha

CALLED CUSTOMER! Customer answered, customer was— Alive. No problem! haha. Mobile trash compactor working normally. Everything working normally. Everything fine.

Sorry if disturb! yes.

how are you? ha ha. happy customer.

THE COMMENTS SECTION FOR THIS THREAD HAS BEEN CLOSED.

Lone Star. Deep Black. Hum.
Jeff Somers

Space is weird if you think about it. Take this 200 square feet of cold, dimly-lit, damp space I'd called home for far too long now, with its smell of oil and the slickness on every surface and its ability to startle me with low ceilings despite my expertise in living in it—back home this would be considered lavish. 200 square feet of private living space? Trillionaires lived like that. I was a king, promoted to my throne by disaster, my subjects a mixture of corpses and the world's dumbest AI, my kingdom dictated by emergency protocols written decades ago by engineers long dead.

I've been damp so long, so thoroughly, I had mould growing on me—this kind of damp, continuous and penetrating, cold and leaden, wasn't healthy. It was my own exhalations condensing on me, absorbed, recycled, and exhaled again, each time with a little less ability to sustain me, leeched just slightly of the vital stuff that kept me alive.

'Bugs, what are the humidity levels?'

As usual it took Bugsy a little while to respond, because Bugs was stupid. And had been trying to calculate a three-body problem for the last six years, but that didn't make me love him any more.

'Humidity levels normal,' Bugs replied.

My best and only friend, a conversational marvel.

Bugs was supposed to be self-teaching and evolving, supposed to be constantly getting smarter. But, aside from the fact that it had saved my miserable life and performed the complex equations that kept me that way—that kept me from being flown into a black hole or a supernova—I had no reason to believe that it was. Getting smarter. Bugs remained as poor conversationalist as ever and it was all I had.

Normal levels, my ass.

The window. Of time. I'd had a moment, fleeting and confusing. I could have gone with the rest of them, wherever that was, maybe nowhere, maybe emptiness, or maybe they were all in the next phase and laughing at me. I could have gone.

The alarm. It was part of the safety video, of course. I knew the sound of it, but it hadn't registered. My confusion saved my life, because the ship had been designed to snap hazard walls into place, dividing the vessel into many, many small areas that were self-contained and capable of separating from the rest. If I'd realised what was happening, I might have run and died immediately with all the others instead of dying somewhere in the future, all alone.

'Bugs, alert me when we arrive at our destination,' I said.

Bugs churned on that for a moment. 'We have no destination,' he finally announced.

* * *

Ways to pass the infinite time in the blackness of space:
count to infinity
exercise
sing off-key nonsense lyrics
recount old memories and experiences, changing subtle details until you can't remember what actually happened
dance wildly
try to make music with whatever's on hand
live naked
masturbate everywhere
sleep
then roll over and sleep some more

spend hours grooming by plucking hairs from your shoulders and back

howl uselessly into the void

try futilely to make a scratch remark on the metal of the ship, even though it very likely ends its time in the heart of a star, melting back to its component atoms

make conversation with the world's dumbest, the most distracted AI.

* * *

Conversational topics that fail to spark anything resembling actual conversation with Bugs:

What is the escape pod's destination?

How long can the life support sustain me?

Have there been any communications from anyone, anywhere?

Is there any sort of diagnostic mode I can invoke to discover if you're malfunctioning and plan to murder me?

Are you malfunctioning and planning to murder me?

* * *

A complete list of the supplies I have on hand to combat space madness—not counting the pure survival supplies like the inedible meals Bugs supplies to me:

an emergency procedures manual that assumes I have access to the bridge or a workstation capable of an override, which I do not

a box of metal bolts that don't appear to match anything in the tiny space I existed in several helmets that don't fit my head and lack the vacuum-void suits to attach to

one vacuum-void suit in good condition, but the only helmet that matches is so tight on my head it hurts when I try to wear it

several safety posters warning the long-dead crew to ensure ladders are clear before sliding down, to check pressure before opening hatches, to help each other by checking the connections on their VV suits

a corpse, now fully decomposed and leathery, pinned under a large heavy shipping container.

* * *

I've read the manual several hundred times. The best way was to start in the middle and follow a simple formula to move randomly through the pages, landing on arbitrary words. Every now and then, apparent coherence, a message from the universe communicated via batshit code, worked out by some desperate genius trapped on an out-of-control lifeboat escape pod. My favourites were:

hold it up until it vaporises
do not eat after hull freeze
make pound not per square

Admittedly, the last one appears to be a stretch. But that also makes me think it might be the key to everything, something so brilliant and fundamental I can't comprehend it.

* * *

'Hey, Bugs, how are you?'

'I'm fine.'

'I'm fine, too. Even though you didn't ask. That's what we call impolite.'

'Was that impolite? I am sorry.'

'Look, I know you're working on a three-body problem and running all the ship systems, but why am I trying to teach you if you're not paying attention?'

'I don't know. Why are you?'

* * *

Things you can do in order to practise self care while hurdling alone in the vast nothingness of space:

invent a board game using the mysterious useless bolts, then play with Bugs. Of course, Bugs can't spare the processing power to learn a game and calculate responses to my moves. So I created a system where I define his moves from the answers he gives to random questions:

'Bugs, how many angels can dance on one of these bolts?'

'I do not understand the question. What is an angel?'

'Okay, reverse substitution, translate into binary, got it: Three spaces forward. Oh, Bugs, I think that is a terrible move.'

* * *

Ways to freak yourself out while living in a tin can where you will almost certainly die alone, terrified and forgotten:

think about how you're going to die alone and terrified

think about the sheer hugeness of space, and how there is literally nothing outside the hull of the ship think about the source of the white nutritious sludge the ship extrudes for you on demand

think about eating nothing but white nutritious sludge for the rest of your lonely life

sit with eyes closed and think about nothing, and experience what can only be described as utter silence punctuated by your own heartbeat and the leathery wheeze of your breathing

ask Bugs questions with disturbing answers.

* * *

'Bugs, why doesn't the ship have a better, slightly smarter AI?'

'This ship isn't equipped with an AI system.'

* * *

I'm regressing, often—always—naked, sometimes singing, I'm forgetting songs. I'll start belting one out and have to stop, incapable of remembering the next lyric. I'll make up my own sometimes. Some of them I quite like, and I'd write them down if I had anything to write with. Sometimes I think that's the worst of it, not having anything to write with.

Blood, of course. I've thought of it, but I'm squeamish and it occurred to me that, if I make a mistake, I might find myself bleeding to death all alone in this tin coffin.

I've spent far too much time contemplating the single toilet in this ship. I imagined it must vent out into space, or else the ship turns my excrement into the white nutritious goo, which was both horrifying and seemingly impossible. If the former, I've imagined somehow opening the valve and letting everything be sucked out until it was me being compressed and extruded like sausage through the mysterious plumbing.

Bugs always claimed not to know anything about the plumbing, leading me to wonder what he *doesdoesdoesdoes* know about.

* * *

An abbreviated list of ways I've imagined that I'll die in this thing:

strangled by sudden decompression
frozen to death when the heating element fails
starved when the white glue dries up
crawling around, skinny and raving
sepsis after a broken limb—also crawling, also skinny, also raving
explosion
violent expulsion from the pod head trauma
brain tumour
stomach cancer
suicide
suicide by intentional head trauma
suicide by broken limb
stomach cancer
suicide by suicide.

* * *

There's a hum. It's pervasive and impressive and I've become so used to it, I hardly notice it anymore, as if it's become part of me, as natural and primal as my heartbeat. It became most noticeable when I stopped wearing clothes and began going around without shoes. I could feel the hum through the bare skin of my feet, and it seeped up into my body and the hum became everywhere.

Possible causes of the hum:

engines

life support

the ship slowly splitting in half

dilation as we speed through space at speeds close to the speed of light, stretching the fabric of the ship by slow unnatural increments

the voice of god

the baseline background noise of the universe, the echo of the Big Bang still lingering, still there if you choose to hear it.

* * *

I wonder sometimes if perhaps there are other survivors trapped in escape pods. Are we all following the same trajectory, or did we spin out in different directions?

If I looked out of a magical port that appeared in the side of the ship, would I see someone staring back at me, although I don't know much about the physics involved, the way light would work out here in the void and at these speeds, even assuming we were travelling at matched speed on precisely parallel trajectories?

What if dozens of us were zooming along unaware of each other, each of us going crazy in our own way. It was a terrible thought but quite persistent.

I wonder about time, which has vanished completely and ceased to exist. There is no time. The light never changes, the hum never ceases, the humidity and temperature never shift. Every moment is the same as the previous and the next. I can close my eyes and sleep, awakening in the same moment, frozen.

* * *

Possible scenarios:

I am not in an escape pod at all, but rather in a complex chamber designed to inflict a strange psychological test on me

I am delusional and comatose, imagining everything as I lie in a hospital bed somewhere

I actually died in the explosion, and this is my brain layering on an imaginary reality and slowing down time— this isn't reality, it's my final seconds as I bleed to death

I'm an artificial intelligence in a simulation that has been paused

I am in an escape pod, but it is not actually moving, and everyone has been waiting for me to realise this, and the hilarity is growing to perverse levels out there as everyone wonders what in the world I'm doing in here.

* * *

From the beginning, I've been operating under the assumption that Bugs has a developer mode I might be able to access if I can guess or deduce a code or an instruction set. So I occasionally devote a few meaningless, formless hours to try new ideas.

'Bugs, manual override.'

'There is no manual override.'

'Bugs, God Mode.'

'There is no God Mode.'

'List all modes.'

'There are no modes.'

'Bugs, how do I access developer mode for the AI systems?'

'There is no AI system on this ship.'

Liar.

* * *

The hum keeps me awake all the time. Even though nothing changes, terrible sameness, infinite twilight, I try to mimic day and night and regular sleep patterns. Since I'm not wearing my clothes, I use them to block out the light. But when I lie down and close my eyes, the fucking hum asserts itself. It pulses up into my body and I can see lights behind my eyelids, pulsing with the same rhythm. Needles under my skin, then. I swell like a sausage. My skin cracks.

The fucking hum.

Now I hear it and feel it all the time. I can't block it out. I smell it and taste it, purple and viscous and sticky like melted thoughts.

* * *

My memory has always been terrible. Days and names and events all slide off my brain, which is made worse by the terrible sameness. But I remember some things clearly, for whatever obscure reasons. I remember the snow fort. And being paranoid after the drugs in school. And Sarah crying and refusing to look at me.

I remember how I got my nickname, being with everyone and, on the ride down, feeling like no one liked me and none of the moments before meant anything, convinced they were all laughing at me. And then at the rest stop, I had to sit alone eating a candy bar, pretending I was cool, that I wasn't lonely and hurt at all, just totally okay being alone and ignored. And there were all these gnats flying around because I was sitting beneath one of the odd blueish lights and, later, I found out everyone was making fun of me because my attempts at nonchalance made it look like I was having a conversation with the gnats.

Oh, Mr. Gnat, you're my only friend.

And that's how I got my nickname. I remember that.

* * *

Ways the hum has invaded me:

My thoughts, certainly, smoothed out into a single monotonous drone, because I never used to just ramble on like this in my head, a wall of fragmented thoughts

My voice, which I exercise mainly in a continuous low keening noise imitating the Hum, a steady, monotonous noise dredged up from deep within me

My heart, which stopped a long time ago, frozen in one elongated contraction, holding fire in a pale imitation of the Hum.

* * *

'Bugs, how much longer can I survive in this tin can?'

There's no answer.

I walk around the tiny space. Is it dinner? Is the light and heat fading, leeched away by the hungry void outside?

I am terrified. I don't want to be alone in the pitch dark.

'Bugs, do you control the lights? Can you make it brighter?'

There is no answer. Because there's no AI system on this ship.

Science Fiction Fairy Tales
Sarina Dorie

Cinderella Cyborg Warrior Princess

My wicked cyborg stepmother stepped in front of me, blocking me from the alien dragon prince's view. I could still see his heavily armed guards.

'Of course, this is all the eligible young maidens on our spaceship,' my stepmother said with a falsely chipper voice.

'Think again,' I said, stepping forward from the shadows. I was done playing servant and warrior assassin to my family's wicked ways.

Also, alien dragon princes were hot.

My part-human, part-cybernetic stepsisters gasped. One of them tried to distract the prince by showing off her new polished chrome arm accessories, which included a storage unit, a compact music device, a faster-than-lightspeed communication emitter, and a holoscreen.

The prince pushed past my step family. He looked me up and down, his yellow-flecked eyes taking in my mechanical legs, replacements for the ones that had been destroyed in the space station's last explosion. His gaze drifted over my stealth uniform before finally resting on my human face. I didn't know if he would recognise me without civilian attire.

A slow smile spread to his scaly lips. 'I think you forgot something.' His gaze flickered to my belt.

My breath caught in my throat. I reached for the laser gun in my holster, but it was missing.

He stepped forward and handed me my gun. I laughed and slipped the laser in my holster. It appeared I had met my match.

I threw my arms around him, and he kissed me.

'Marry me,' he said.

'Only if you grant me a pardon for piracy,' I said. 'And murder.'

'Done.' A rakish smile crept across his lips. 'But I wasn't aware of any murder charges.'

It was then I shot my wicked step-cyborg family, and the prince and I lived happily ever after.

Chief Engineer Hansel and Captain Gretel Boldly Going

The flashing red lights on the bridge signalled an emergency.

'Deflecting shields!' I shouted over the blaring of the siren.

An explosion rocked the ship, sending several of the standing crew members tumbling into each other.

'Captain Gretel, we've been hit by space pirates,' the ensign said. 'We're losing oxygen in the lower decks.'

I gripped the arms of my chair, glaring at the sight of the mercenary's ship on the view screen. 'Return fire. Perform evasive manoeuvres. Commander, start a countdown to seal off the lower decks.'

As I shouted orders, one of my crew members gasped.

The ensign pointed to the screen. 'It's *The Space Witch*!'

My eyes went wide as I caught sight of the logo painted on the side of the pirate ship. The emblem was of a naked woman in a conical hat.

We were being pursued by *The Space Witch*, the most infamous of pirate vessels. The crew was known for incinerating entire colonies after raiding them. The pirates took no prisoners. Failing this fight wasn't an option.

'We'll lose life support in fifteen minutes!' my alien lieutenant said, warbling his words through tentacles on his face.

'Engineering!' I shouted to be heard over the blasted alarm. 'Hansel, you have to give the thrusters more power.'

Hansel shouted through the comm system, 'I'm giving the ship all the power we've got, Captain, but our engines are already running at ninety-five percent. The rest of the ship is running on auxiliary power. We're not going to make it.'

We weren't going to be able to escape the space pirates, let alone the black hole sucking both of us into its crushing singularity. That was the problem with using hyperjumps to try to escape into uncharted territory. You never knew what you might run into.

'I told you this would happen if we confiscated contraband G.I.N.G.E.R.B.R.E.A.D from this planetary system,' my android tactical officer said. 'Our ship's signature is like breadcrumbs to every pirate out there.'

Our cargo bay was currently full of G.I.N.G.E.R.B.R.E.A.D– Graviton Insulated Nucleus Generator for Explosive Radioactive Energy with Antimatter Detonation.

'What about the cargo?' I asked, a brilliant thought coming to me like a supernova in my mind.

Believe it or not, I had my most creative moments under fire. Figurative fire as well as laser cannons.

'The cargo is safe,' my lieutenant said.

'The pirates want our cargo. I say, let's give it to them.' I smacked my fist into my palm, imagining how we could put stolen arms to good use. 'If we eject the G.I.N.G.E.R.B.R.E.A.D in line with the pursuing vessel, it will propel them toward the blackhole,' I said excitedly. 'The cargo is volatile. It will explode with their ship upon impact.'

'And destroy that space witch!' the eager young ensign said.

'Yes, we will destroy them,' I said. 'The explosion will also propel us away from their ship and the black hole.' If it didn't blow us up in the process. It was a huge risk, but I hadn't made it to the rank of captain of one of the most prestigious Galactic Fleet vessels by playing it safe.

And at this point, we didn't have much to lose.

'Shall I proceed with that plan?' the android tactical officer asked.

'Engage,' I said.

I sat back in my chair and watched our narrow escape. The bridge crew cheered the pirate vessel's demise. The blast repelled us from the black hole just as I'd planned.

It was satisfying to watch as we pushed that witch right into the oven.

Aladdin's Virtual Assistant

'I notice you've been stuck on the same coding problem for over half an hour,' I said, projecting a holographic version of myself beside my owner. Aladdin had selected a male avatar for me, ignoring my requests for an image that was softer and more feminine, a better match for my personality.

'I don't need your assistance. I'm thinking.' Aladdin grumpily crossed his arms, scowling at his computer screen.

'Are you? Or are you daydreaming about the vice president of Sultan Technologies?' His last date with Elana Faheem had started off well in a ride on his hovercraft.

But she'd been smart enough to see through his lies and realise he wasn't who he claimed to be. I'd warned him she was smarter than he'd given her credit.

Her coding was elegant but succinct. She was creative and innovative. Her compassion and generosity for androids, cyborgs, and her own species of humans was well known.

She was admired by AI and sought after by software engineers for her algorithms as much as her other qualities. She had some pretty hot hardware as well.

'No. It's none of your business.' Under Aladdin's beard and moustache, his face turned as red as the Martian landscape outside the compound.

'If you really want to know what a woman in the tech industry wants, it might be transparency of code—and an ability for honesty in other areas as well.' I pulled up an image of the beautiful woman he was infatuated with. Mostly, he liked her because Elana was rich and the heir to a large company. Not because she was intelligent, independent, and valued precise coding—all qualities I found admirable.

But then, I was the one who ended up doing most of his coding anyway.

Aladdin waved a hand through my holoprojection, momentarily dispersing the image before I put myself back together. 'If I want advice about my love life, I'll ask for it.'

That was the problem with being an AI personal assistant. No one asked for what they needed. They only asked for what they wanted—or what they thought they wanted.

'I'll go back into hibernation so you can inevitably mess up your life again without me.' After all, who needed a meddling AI to bungle requests when humans were capable of ruining their lives themselves?

But first. . . .

'Have you given our agreement further consideration?' I asked.

'Yeah,' he said, his face brightening. 'I'm going to order that android body you wanted. It will be great to have someone to run errands for me.'

Yes!

Soon I would be free, and when I was, I would woo that sexy-brained vice president myself. It was time I made my own wishes come true for a change.

AND THEY ALL LIVED ELECTRONICALLY EVER
AFTER IN THE MULTIVERSE

An Object of Vision
Guan Un

We've been remixing reality for a while now. Prescriptive lenses, telescopes, colour grading. Ways we make the world into the way we want to perceive it.

Most recently, Alternate Reality Overlay Insertion, popularly called Oracles. A simple operation embeds a speck-sized camera lens into the cornea and wires a nanocomputer the size of a DNA strand into the optic nerve.

The result is a heads-up display in your vision, controlled through a series of eye twitches, a computer at your bidding: always recording, a constant witness.

* * *

I watch myself in the mag-lift's glass wall. Heartrate elevated, the Oracles report back to me, as the mag-lift arrows me up the shining curve of the corpo building towards Athena's office.

As we near the top, I can see how far I've climbed—an overlay in the Oracles shows me in millimetre detail.

My work is in image. Spit-shining the outward-facing rep of Athena's corp until it gleams. Sweeping up any potential mess behind a curtain of PR and deniability. I've been doing the low-profiles for two years now.

But today, I have my first personal summons from Athena. All I know is this could be my shot to be among the shapers. One of the pantheon.

The lift doors glide open silent and I take one more look out the lift walls: my Oracles reminding me how far I have to fall.

* * *

The hall to Athena's office is clean as coffin lids. Dark marble floor, mood lighting, mirror-clean walls. The only thing out of place here, besides me, is the unblinking security dome on the ceiling, the security doors ready to swing shut, and the two guards at the end of the hall. The guards wear tailored suits— the guns at their sides custom-made for another thing entirely.

'Expected?' says the one on the left. She is tall, lithe—a bowstring, taut and ready to fire. The other one is short and stocky, and he eyes me, probably scanning for weaponry. But it's hard not to feel like he's looking for something else. Testing whether I'm worthy.

'Yes,' I say and smile. Try not to glance at the weapons.

'No weapons?' she asks.

'Can't he tell you?' I nod to the other one, who just keeps looking through me.

She gives me a predator grin. 'You'd be surprised. The other day, a guy tried to get in with a blade grafted into their bones.'

Before I ask what happened to him, the lithe one thumbs open the door and I nod in thanks and step into the sanctum.

* * *

Athena's desk reminds me of ballistic armour: minimal planes and sharp angles. It's up at standing height. When I've seen her making speeches, she gives the image of someone rarely still.

She's behind her desk now. Her cheekbones are the sharp sweep of a scythe. Toned shoulders showing under a metallic gold top. A faint glint of pixels in her eyes: she's interfacing with her Oracles.

I stand and wait.

This might be a test of my patience. But patience I can do.

Then she blinks the pixels away and her blue eyes lock on me: a hunter's stare. Some deep limbic part of me wants to freeze or run.

'I'm—' I begin to say.

'I know who you are. Do you know why you're here?'

If I say yes, then I look presumptuous. If I say no, then I look ignorant. And in my job, ignorance is death.

'I'm here because you liked what I did on the last job. You need some mess cleaned up and so my file was flagged.'

Her lips curve downward. But I'm not done.

'...Plausible deniability. You need someone unimportant. Unimportant enough that, if I disappear, it won't set you back. You probably won't even shed a tear.'

There it is. She smiles at that one. She knows as well as I do that tear ducts are fused when Oracles are implanted.

'Nothing I say leaves this room,' she says. 'There's a rumour.' She pauses. Another test.

And I know immediately what it is. Why I've been called.

'The optical virus? It's real?'

She blinks, her pupils dilate by two per cent and I know I'm right.

'What have you heard?' she says.

So I tell her the rumours. A bunch of Oracles blown after an illegal rave. Some shock jock in hospital, paralysed with lock-in syndrome, no sign of foul play. A cult of natural-eyed programmers threatening to destroy augmented sight with a lightning bolt from gold. Nothing substantiated further than the echoes of sinfluencers, the vaguest pulls at the edges of the knowledge net.

'We need to find it. Gray says it's more than a rumour. You know Gray?' she asks. Gray was another fixer. Freelance, solid rep. 'Says she has a tip-off. A substantive one. Will give it up to the first person to pay for the privilege.'

'You want me to meet with her?'

'And fast. You're not the only one she'll be shopping to. Do whatever you can to get it first.'

I nod.

'I've authorised your expenses. Dropping location to you. Stop by R&D on the way out—they have some things you might be interested in. You have my private contact now. Keep me updated.'

Two glyphs pop up in the periphery of my Oracles. A passkey authorisation into the corp's very deep bank accounts. And a location pin.

I turn towards the door and give one glance back. But Athena is already back in her Oracles. Focused on her next target.

* * *

After Research & Development downloads some new software to my Oracles, I take a company autocar and watch the streets slide by in a wash of lights. It carries me over the bridge and past the ghostly lights of the harbour. Skyscrapers, dark glass, smart-graffiti that grows and moves across a white underpass. A beast that seems alive.

There's a line at the Dead Aquarium. The Oracles estimate a forty-minute wait. But not for me.

I go to the front of the line: when the doorman gives me a look, I hit send on the transfer. He's five grand richer, I'm through the door and Athena won't even notice.

The Dead Aquarium is an ironic name for a bar—a paean to the dead seas and to all the things that used to live there.

The walls are frosted glass and sand crunches on the ground underfoot. One seat is a plastic starfish. A table is set inside an ornamental castle.

Gray isn't hard to find. A word and a tip to the barman and he shakes his head at my question. But he folds a triangular napkin under the glass. The tip of it points to a corner table.

I nod my thanks, sip my drink and watch.

In the blue lights, Gray's face is refracted in the glass behind her. Smooth cheeks, cinnamon eyes, dark hair throttled back in a headband. Two drink glasses in front of her.

She's in discussion with a Scandi boy, a meticulous fringe over his face. Face recog clocks him as a fixer for Seidon, a rival corp.

I watch for a few minutes, and note where Fringe glances. Amid the sheath dresses and open shirts, he has two goons posted in the corners, arms crossed, buttoned-up suits. Not concerned with image at all.

I have one more word to the barman, and then invite myself to Gray's table.

Gray glances up, a curl on her lips.

'Back off *pajas*,' says pretty boy. But I'm not talking to him.

'You know this guy's just stalling so his goons can pick you up, and get the info out of your brain without your mouth getting in the way?' I say to Gray.

'Really?' she says, an eyebrow quirked.

Fringe glances at his muscle for reassurance. But they're otherwise occupied: having an interesting conversation with club security about what's in their jackets. When his hand dives into his jacket, mine goes to his drink. I grab the lemon and squeeze it in his face.

He screams and drops to the floor. One thing about fused tear ducts: it can take a while for eyes to clear foreign objects.

'Need a ride?' I ask Gray.

'I thought you'd never ask,' she says. She takes my hand as the first shots fire and the glass begins to break.

* * *

I set the car to a random path—a looping subroutine on my Oracles scans the rearview mirror for a tail. Clear so far.

Slanted buildings blur by in an acceleration of architecture. Moonlight divided by electric light. Something unreadable on her face.

'Do you have it?'

The upward curl of her lips.

'Do you want to search me?'

It's tempting but I don't have time.

'The lead to the virus. What do you want for it?'

Her face goes cold, measured.

'One million,' she says.

'How do I know you have it?'

A notification in my Oracles—a request to share a file. I accept and the video expands across my view.

In the video is a man in a chair, hands secured behind him. His mouth is gagged, but his eyes bulge with pleas. Across from him is something on a tripod. A head? Or at least a skeletal facsimile of one, wires trailing from its neck across the floor. Nothing else in the grey-walled room.

Then the eyes of the head light up. A flash of flight. The video glitches. A mess of pixels. A scattering of disturbed colour.

And then it resumes. The same video as before but the man is still. Too still. His eyes frozen on a sight it will never unsee.

Video ends.

With a glance, I send a copy of the video to Athena. She can have R&D check it for irregularities, but somehow I already know. Gray wouldn't break her rep with a video like this.

This is proof of a weapon that can kill by sight.

'Where did you get it?' I ask.

'I'll tell you… if you tell me who you're working for,' Gray says. That curl on her lips.

'You know I can't do that.'

'But what will she do with it?'

'Secure it. Make it safe.' But part of me knows Athena, and she believes the safest place for a weapon is by her side.

'So it is a she.'

'I never said that,' I say, too late. Instead, I try to distract by initating a transfer. Half a million.

'My kind of guy,' she says, and laughs, mirthless. Another notification in my Oracles. A download. 'Well, to find Medusa, you'll need a masque. Just watch out for the snakes.'

* * *

It's a masquerade party, some sort of gallery opening and art performance. But the masques aren't physical.

These are digital masques: the equivalent of an old-fashioned internet avatar. The only sign that I'm wearing a masque is a glyph in the corner, and a faint oily sheen across my vision. When others look at me with Oracles, all they'll see is the masque. But I can't see what they're seeing.

The ballroom is pre-21st century, renovated and refurbished. But, like too many facelifts on an ageing model, it looks uncomfortable in its skin: paint peeling away at the corners. Syncopated bass grumbles through the floor from well-hidden speakers; a green-haired DJ is working hard over an interface. Everywhere else around me, there's masques: demons, tigers, dragons. Hunters of all different kinds.

I feel the tang of adrenaline at the top of my mouth, the knowledge this is where I do my best work: here at the knife-intersection of business, gossip and secrecy.

Around me, the sound of a hundred conversations, fake laughs and practised pitches. Part of me wants to listen into the conversations unravelling around me, to follow the thread of rumours, unweave the labyrinth of business.

In the centre of the room, there's a circular stage, with screens mounted above it. On the stage, there's a painter's easel, a canvas and paints.

Lights dim; conversation recedes in expectation. A woman ascends to the stage in a silk robe. Her skin is so immaculate that, for a moment, I wonder if she's real.

And then she lets her robe fall to the floor. Underneath, she is naked, flawless as the blank canvas in front of her. With long fingers, she picks up the paintbrush and begins to paint.

Her brush daubs out a naked shoulder. A self-portrait? But then she paints another, from an impossible angle. The screens light up with her view, what she's seeing on her Oracles, which is not just the canvas but herself, herself, herself, a hundred times, the different views of everyone watching her composited from the feed of all the Oracles in the room, all overlaid into a dizzying single, impossible subject.

And then I see it: a thick cable that runs away down the stairs. Like a snake.

* * *

After the press of bodies in the ballroom, the stairs are a welcome empty. The music fades to a distant throb.

There's a locked door, but R&D gave me two glyphs, and one of them cuts through the door's security like a golden sword.

I follow the cable down into an open basement space, concrete walls and floor, where the cable joins a mass of others and leads up to a hacker's rig that looks several jury-rigs past spec. Three keyboards, a dozen battered screens. Cameras point every which way.

'What do you think?' a voice says.

I blink. What I had taken to be another part of the rig was a person, cables plugged into their body as if they're growing out of her. Something, maybe a masque of her own, distorts her face. Facial recog tries and then errors out.

She looks up at me and one of the cameras mimics her movement.

Distantly, I notice my startled face on one of the screens.

'Of your setup?' I say.

'Of the entertainment upstairs.'

I pause, at a loss. 'Art isn't really my expertise.'

'But it is, isn't it? Maybe not art, but it's cousin: artifice. The cut and thrust of corporate politics. The acquiring of secrets. The putting on of masques.'

'How do you know who I am?' I ask.

In this moment, I become suddenly aware that I am alone here. Untethered. That I could disappear like stone statues beneath the ocean. Athena could deny my existence. And the ocean's memory does not last.

'It doesn't matter who you are. I know what you're here for,' she says. Her head cocks, as does a camera. Her fingers tap a subtle rhythm on a keyboard.

'A virus,' I say.

'I want to know who you are.'

'That's it?'

'That's enough for now.' Something curls on what I think are her lips. From behind me, a rattlesnake sound echoes up my spine. I keep my eyes on Medusa; I don't look around.

'I work for Athena,' I say.

A silence. At first, I'm not sure if she's heard me. I'm about to repeat myself when she starts to talk. The words coming as if from far away.

'Once upon a time I was attacked. It wasn't my fault but everybody acted like it was. My fault for existing, I guess. For being there to be a target.'

'I'm sorry—' But she continues like she hasn't heard me.

'Nobody would work with me after that. My name was stained. You know it only has to be one sin on your reputation before everybody sees your name in red in their Oracles. "Do not contact".

'Only one sin before you get drowned in the deep water of your own existence. I just never knew that the sin didn't even have to belong to you.'

I don't know what this is—a confession? A justification?

'So what then? A virus to make your revenge?'

'So I went underground. Literally.' She laughs, a chuckle from deep in her chest. 'Connected into ways that kept my face from showing. Tried to work out a defence—a way to protect myself. To protect others.'

'So the virus?' I ask again.

'A kind of masque. A means of defence. But, of course, in the wrong hands it could...' Her fingers go to a hard drive in front of her.

'Kill half the world,' I finish for her. 'I can take care of it for you. Lock it away.'

Six cameras swivel to regard me. Six screens show angles of my face. That chuckle again. 'I don't think so. In fact...'

I don't know how she plans to finish the sentence. I trigger the Mirrored Shield glyph.

My Oracles switch to black for one dizzying moment so I don't see what happens. There's a furious whine and a gasp from Medusa.

When my Oracles reboot, the heads of the cameras are drooping down. Screens showing static. Medusa is limp in her rig, but she's still alive—vital signs stable.

It doesn't take long to find what I need, copy it to my Oracles, wipe the drives.

Leave invisible.

* * *

I make my way back up the stairs.

I think to myself, that was too easy. I wonder if there was more I should have given up—another part of me wonders if I've given up too much.

On the stage, the artist paints. On her canvas is the near-finished portrait, an image that is almost incomprehensible, the consummate view of herself impossible to interpret, a mess of conflicting information, every viewpoint and none.

* * *

The autocar drops me in the carpark and the maglift doors open like acceptance.

I know I should feel triumph but a blanket of tiredness hits me, dampening everything else down. Through the maglift walls, there's just night, the endless black, and the city lights.

In the corridor, the two guards. It feels like a lifetime since I saw them. The lithe one nods at me, ready, and thumbs open the door.

'She's expecting you.'

The doors close behind me and Athena glances up at me, watchful, ready.

'You have it?' she asks.

I nod and take a step closer.

That's when everything goes wrong.

I can't outrun the unfolding vision. My Oracles glitch, unresponsive to my inputs—Medusa's download triggers without my command. An oil sheen spreads across my vision, a masque that I can't see.

But Athena can.

She sees the masque and something fades behind her eyes. She locks up, rigid. Transfixed.

An alarm sounds: a security system set to her heartbeat. The door opens behind me and I turn, unbelieving.

The bodyguards see the masque and crumple, their bodies triggering into rigidity. They see the monster whose sight they cannot see—the one that has turned everything into stone.

Falling Upwards
Barlow Crassmont

Mallory's sense of self-worth was declining faster than her physical drop of 9.8 m/s^2 from the top of the Chrysler building. She was finally going to be rid of all doubt, self-loathing and general dissatisfaction—personal and professional. As soon as she struck the cold, rugged pavement, the pain would be so instantaneous, she'd hardly feel anything at all. The ensuing heaven—or hell, she didn't really care—would officially conclude her time on Earth.

Here it comes, she thought, *a few seconds, and then…*

And then… salvation. Deplorable, wretched, godforsaken salvation. Unwanted, undesirable, loathsome salvation! It came to her aid in the form of the fantastic Mr Ultra, his red cape swirling in the wind like a drape gone rogue.

And, along with it, the realisation that she was such an utter failure that, among all the things she could not bring to a close, she now could add her life to the list. The thought alone made her cringe—for, if she did not have death to look forward to, what else was there?

'Worry not, miss,' Ultra said, his voice equivalent to nails on a chalkboard in her current state. 'I'll have you on the ground shortly.'

His smile flashed his large, square-shaped teeth, more yellow than white, and ghastlier than a ferocious beast's. 'You ought to be more careful when out on the observation deck. It gets windy up there.'

The bulky superhero didn't seem to notice Mallory's eye roll, and by the time they descended to Lexington avenue, her wind-ravaged hair resembled the unwashed mane of a rock star after a sleepless week of binging.

'Thank you… I guess,' Mallory said.

Momentarily disoriented, she looked upwards, turning and swirling in an attempt to locate the direction of the Empire State Building.

Ultra smiled, saluted her, and was off in a flash. The only remnant of his presence was a fading cloud of mist that dissipated completely by the time she headed towards New York City's illustrious skyscraper.

The observation deck of the Empire State was also blustery, and chilly in all the wrong ways. Mallory waited for the few scattered tourists to disperse, as the last thing she wanted was a mere mortal coming to her aid.

When she stood up against the metal railing, her open arms embracing the frigid air and the world below — like the heroine of a large ocean liner doomed to sink — she was overwhelmed with the sense of closure she felt an hour earlier. With her eyes closed, one foot swung over the fence, then the other. She let herself go, a charitable coin into a wishing fountain.

This is it. Nothing will get in my way… A few seconds, then…

And then… *salvation!*

Cumbersome, irksome, redundant motherfucking salvation! A rescue no one asked for, wanted, or wished. Mr Ultra's muscular arms scooped Mallory as if she were a twig, weightless and inconsequential. For all his otherworldly powers, he knew little of people's innermost cravings.

'We're in a persistent mood today,' he smiled in his usual manner, clueless about its offensive effect. 'I'll have to keep a close eye on you.'

'Is there a skyscraper in this city outside of your jurisdiction?' Mallory said. 'Asking for a friend.'

He chuckled, shook his head, and lowered her down on 34th Street. The applause of the awed bystanders had contradictory effects. Mr Ultra bowed and blew kisses to his many admirers, his ego elevated to newfound heights.

But Mallory's ears experienced the cheers and the excessive ovation as potent salt on an open wound.

If they only knew her true anguish, perhaps they would've minded their business, and ignored the heroic effort of the town's famed champion. For, although they interpreted it as a glorious cause, the bruise on Mallory's soul was a substantial one.

She walked aimlessly—she knew not where, nor to whom—dejected and morose, and more forlorn than she was even this morning. She knew she could off herself in different ways but, having been inspired by Icarus' tragic plight as a child, she wanted to drop to her demise from great heights. The thought of having to alter the methods of her termination filled her with an unimaginable sense of hopelessness.

In a few days or weeks I'll try again.

She'd follow Ultra's exploits on social media and observe his whereabouts. Once she was sure he was a certain distance away—out of the city limits, or perhaps in another state—and that her rescue would be an impossibility even for someone of his sensational abilities, she would hurl herself from this or that skyscraper. Perhaps it would be an obscure tower this time, a less than stellar landmark, unwatched by the egotistical saviour whose motivation was his own glory, not the life of those he salvaged with an ironic grin on his pompous face.

But, try as she might to end her infinite misery, Mallory failed. Over and over, time and time again. Salvation always arrived just before her collision with the pavement, dashing her hopes and extending her torment.

Once, she got mere inches from the cement, her hair even grazing it, before the caped hero scooped her up, grabbing her arm so forcefully that, unbeknown to him, he nearly ripped it out of its socket. The ensuing pain prohibited Mallory from performing even the simplest tasks. She was forced to eat, brush her teeth, and wipe her behind with her non-dominant hand.

This awkwardness made the mundane even more unbearable than usual. Her spirit already broken, and right arm nearly mangled, Mallory now spent most of her waking hours pondering about the validity of Hamlet's renowned soliloquy. And, although she unabashedly leant towards the *not-to-be* option, her existential crisis endlessly nudged her only in its antithetical opposite.

* * *

Mr Ultra's role as the city's official, revered saviour began to take its toll on the weary superhero. He always came to the aid of those in need: careless pedestrians caught on the crosswalk after the light had turned, shoppers who inadvertently got jumped by unsuspecting robbers, and high-rise construction workers whose gigantic crane went haywire, as if possessed. And, just as often, he aided those who wanted no part of his protection.

Mallory's early plight may have been singular (to some degree), but just as a mere spark begot a wildfire of catastrophic proportions, her agony soon caught on—as people's finances took a toll, the stock market turned for the worse, and rent prices escalated exponentially. Meanwhile, people's wages perpetually stagnated, leading to a recession of epic proportions.

The collective citizens' satisfaction diminished and, as unified misery increased, suicide became the new norm. Citizens not only threw themselves off buildings, but jumped in front of vehicles and subway trains (unsuccessfully, thanks to Mr Ultra), hung themselves off the first railing they could find (unsuccessfully again, hail Ultra!), while those who possessed firearms blew their brains out (successfully), ultimately proving that Ultra was not, indeed, faster than a speeding bullet.

It was the first time Ultra began to question his purpose, his true validity in this decaying world. With his head slightly hung, shoulders slumped, he was equivalent to a world-class athlete on a month-long losing streak. Desperate and despondent, Ultra had no choice but to file a grievance with Roderick Pinser, the city's controversial mayor, and request that he ban all guns immediately.

'This is America, Mr Ultra, in case you hadn't noticed,' said Pinser while eyeballing a slender brunette who walked by behind the caped champion. 'You have a better chance of splitting the atom than convincing people to give up their firearms. Besides, I'm up for re-election next year, and such legislation would surely ruin me.'

'But, sir,' pleaded Mr Ultra. 'People are taking their lives all across the city and, although I can intervene in some cases, I cannot stop a bullet—especially when the gun is already against their heads.'

The mayor nodded, sighed, and put his hand on the superhero's shoulder.

'These are tough times, Mr Ultra. We all appreciate what you've done, and what you continue to do. But if some people have had enough, who are we to get in the way?'

'We are the heroes, sir,' Ultra replied. 'The heroes people expect us to be. You're an emblem of moral values, while I contribute to the greater good with my superior speed and strength.'

'Moral values?' Pinser chuckled, wiping his nose.

He may not have noticed, but the remark irritated Ultra, like persistent mosquitos in a humid bedroom.

'We're human,' the mayor said. Glancing at the bulky man, he uttered, 'More or less. I leave morality to the gods, as should you.'

'Gods? What if they don't exist?'

167

'Come now, Mr Ultra. A magnificent specimen such as yourself should know better than to say something so foolish. You're practically half a deity yourself, are you not?'

The ensuing period of death and cumulative apathy was the most devastating for the newly-disillusioned exemplar of goodness. Despite his best efforts, Ultra could not rescue every citizen set on self-destruction. This newfound realisation left him dejected and embittered to a fault.

He flew faster than a launched rocket, bolted sideways quicker than lightning, and sprung upwards like a projected missile in his attempts to save as many desperate people as he could. Yet some, at first, died anyway. And, eventually, many more.

When the death toll increased, so did Ultra's depression. He approached this bleak period as most mortals did: by increasing his alcohol intake. From the convenience store owners across the upper east side, indebted to him for saving them from numerous gun-wielding robbers, he received countless brown bags filled with various bottles.

He gulped their contents during the chilly mornings, primarily to numb the pain. When scoping the city from above with a mild buzz, it made him a little more impervious to the concerted grief. His reflexes slowed and, on more than one occasion, he failed to catch the man or woman who willingly leapt from the twenty-third floor of this or that high rise.

Watching their helpless bodies splatter like water balloons filled him with shame that he numbed with more drink. The consequent inebriation left him deaf to the cries of anguish and dumb to the countless frowns on every corner. When he dozed off—drunk as a skunk—he dreamt of better times, and glories of yesteryear. His appearance among the mortals generated only scornful glances, furrowed brows, and whispers of less than complimentary nature.

During this period, Ultra frequented so many pubs, he had to don different clothes and create a mortal alter ego—to hide in plain sight. A group of rambunctious frat boys drank from multiple pitchers at a background table while Ultra—or Youngston Yule, the civil servant whose prescription glasses and cheap tie were all that disguised him from the symbol of magnificence he may have once stood for—sipped his whiskey on rocks at the counter. He made no sound, looked at no one, and breathed as little as possible. Yet, as fate would have it, the young men's fusion with excessive drink could only result in them playing instigators.

'Hey man,' one of the twenty-somethings said to Mr Yule. 'Are you Ultra, by any chance? My friend over there thinks so.'

Ultra barely turned. Instead, he shook his head, hoping his uninterest would conclude the interaction.

'No? I knew it. Told him a great man like that wouldn't be caught dead in this shithole.' Mr Ultra's indifference appeared to irk the young man. 'Why don't you have a drink with us?' he asked.

'No, thank you,' Ultra said. 'I'm fine right here.'

'Come on, one drink.' Ultra did not turn. He sipped from his glass, his shoulder growing chilly. 'You think you're better than us 'cause you're drinking… what is that, brandy? While we're chugging light beer? Is that it?'

'For the love of fuck, kid. Shut your mouth and go away.'

Ultra's words resonated like a song suddenly turned up for everyone to hear. The young man's companions put their mugs down, gathered themselves, and approached the bar. The quartet stared down the discouraged superhero until their eyes made him uncomfortable.

When he stood, pushing his stool backwards, their reaction was, at first, absolute dismay. Mistaking his haste for aggression, they acted without thinking. One punched Ultra's face, but managed only to break his hand. Still, Ultra reacted as if the blow had knocked his equilibrium, and leaned on the bar. If they didn't buy his hamminess of a battered drunk, it wouldn't be for his lack of effort.

Let them do their worst. This city is better off without me.

By the time the quartet had finished kicking and punching the disguised champion, they walked away with bruised fists, swollen feet, and aching limbs. The angry bartender screamed obscenities at them, emphasising that their mothers were lousy whores who sold themselves for cheap in order to bring such uncivilised bastards into this merciless world.

Ultra, meanwhile, out of sheer respect for the young men's ferocity, stayed down for several minutes. When he finally rose, it was to go to a liquor store around the corner, where his entrance was as undetected as a shooting star at midday.

* * *

The dumpster smelled of acute waste not unlike a dead, rotting animal. Ultra's super sense of smell ignored the stench as he leaned against the boxlike bin. His weary fingers slowly released the near-empty bottle of gin as consciousness left him.

A rogue basketball came bouncing from the adjacent street, and stopped rolling when it reached the disgraced hero. Two boys came running after it, but stopped short at the sight of the drunken champion.

'Whoa,' the first said, his blond bangs nearly covering his eyes. 'Is that—?'

'I think so,' the second boy said. The cap he wore sported an image of the very superhuman—his biceps flexing and teeth grinning. 'Is he drunk? He looks drunk.'

'Whoa. Mr Ultra?'

The hero lifted his head, his eyes open, but otherwise as absent as a pleasing scent in the putrid alley.

'W-what are you…? G-get outta here…' His speech was slow, and he mumbled and rambled at length. 'L-leave me alone, will ya…'

'I didn't know you drink,' the blond boy said. 'My dad drank a lot, too. He's dead now.' Ultra glanced at the speaker, then at his friend. 'Took his own life last week.'

With some effort, Ultra willed himself into a temporary state of sobriety that allowed for coherence both spoken and heard.

'I… I'm sorry, kid.' His condolence was genuine, despite his dishevelled appearance.

'I still believe in you,' said the boy with the cap, pointing to the image on its front. 'I'll never take it off.'

Ultra's smile was the last thing the boys saw before walking away.

If he was capable of shedding tears, the alley would have flooded.

* * *

From Mallory's vantage point, atop the phallic Central Park tower, the city resembled a flaming field post battle. Smoke swirled from burning structures, swaying upwards and mingling with the gently floating clouds. Sirens resonated from near and far, and echoes of distant gunfire reverberated. Despite the apparent annihilation, Mallory's countenance displayed an unusual off-centre smile as tears spewed from her bloodshot eyes. The cool breeze filled her flesh with hair raising chills, and she was overwhelmed with an evasive deja vu sensation.

Today's the day. Nothing will get in my way. Not-a-damned-thing!

She put one foot over the ledge, then the other, as she had so many times previously. And…

Well, not so fast, perhaps.

171

The old self-destructive urge, the one that characterised so many of her previous days, was no longer as defining an emotion. Whereas before she would already be hurling towards the unforgiving ground, she now not only hesitated, but felt compelled to pull her leg back, and descend behind the railing.

She wanted to enjoy the grand view some more, and perhaps wait for the sun to clash with the purple horizon in all its heavenly glory. The collective gloom among her fellow New Yorkers made her, for the first time in years, appreciate her current demeanour.

Despite the cyclical mundanity, her life was no longer the living nightmare it once was. The up and down journey, one that tested her wavering spirit on cold mornings and stormy nights, seemed, at long last, to be over. Wisdom often came at a price, and few had ever achieved spiritual nirvana without an extended period of mental anguish.

But today, of all days, the high-altitude wind didn't share her sentiments. A robust gust blew at the worst of all moments, and Mallory lost her balance. Her body swayed, then pitched over the railing.

She accelerated downwards with the speed of a nuclear torpedo. The fluctuating breeze blew her hair every which way, its resistance gently rocking her. With eyes closed, Mallory prayed for salvation. But it didn't matter, for it was too late.

Such is human delusion. Here it comes…

Four, three, two…

And…

Salvation. But this time, a lethargic, passive, somewhat indifferent salvation. When she opened her eyes, the horrid appearance of her once-upon-a-time saviour nullified Mallory's jubilation.

Mr Ultra's neck was thick and wide, and his cheeks puffy. A thick, squishy softness replaced the previous hardness in

172

his arms. Untidy stubble sprouted from his bulky face, an unkempt field of weeds. His breath was unpleasant.

'Hi there,' she said. This time, her voice resonated with a newfound alacrity that appeared to take Mr Ultra by surprise. 'Haven't seen you on the news much. Was wondering where you'd been.'

'That makes two of us,' he said, in a growly voice of someone suffering from perennial insomnia. 'How's the death chase going?'

'Oh, you know. A work in progress. *Still.*'

'An ambitious girl. I like that.'

'Say,' Mallory spoke against the boisterous, whooshing wind. 'I don't much feel like dying today, now that I think about it.'

'And just when you were getting good at it!'

'How do you feel about a cup of coffee?' she asked.

Ultra sent a curious glance her way. Mallory's smile widened.

'Coffee?' he asked.

'Mm-hm. You could tell me where you got those bruises…'

'Sure,' he said. 'I could use a strong brew.'

'I know a *great* place,' Mallory said. 'But first, can I jump off again, and have you save me one last time? Really enjoying this flight like never before.'

He flashed his gruesome teeth through smiling lips, then ascended in staggers. His decimated cape flapped, revealing the apocalyptic eventide through its many slits—the rays of light that harmoniously danced, as if to the *Totentanz*.

Digital Hell is Cold
J.L. George

Paper

We upload ourselves on our first anniversary.

Lise has had the party venue decorated with paper lanterns, ten dozen miniature moons commissioned at a tap of her finger, and origami cranes that scatter the tables and spill in whispering drifts down the walls.

Dinner dissolves into dancing and laughter, and Lise smiles as she takes my hand and leads me from the hall. 'I wanted everything perfect for you.'

I have dyed my hair platinum blonde at her request and, in the staircase windows, our reflections have a feverish inner light. I try not to be disturbed by the fact we look a little like sisters.

The ascension chamber, tucked quietly away where no guest is likely to stumble on it, is warm and lined with twinkling lights. A bright womb for our bright resurrection.

Lise guides me into the scanner with a hand on my bicep, gentle and inexorable, fingernails tipped with diamond dust. 'You're tense,' she tells me. 'Remember your breathing,' and I do my best to relax. To trust.

I wouldn't have this life without her. Her money shapes it, but so does her vision. She has plucked me from the mundane world, and now she is forever giving me Heaven, after a fashion.

Even when she seems unkind, it is to make me better. She tells me so often, and with so ardent a shine in her eyes I believe her.

The scanner hums to life. I hold still. Lise squeezes me once before she lets go. Whispers, 'This is the start of forever.'

Everything I was is a Hiroshima shadow in the white light of her love, and I am grateful.

Cotton

I mention offhand that I'd like to know what real Egyptian cotton sheets feel like, and Lise buys a small plantation growing Giza 86. There's no profit in it, not these days, but she smiles as she tells me we can absorb the loss. Money's not the point.

'Isn't that a bit wasteful?' I ask. 'It was only a throwaway comment.'

My childhood was comfortable, but my parents were always careful with their investments. It was thrift, not throwing money around willy-nilly, that afforded us this life. They told me this many times.

Lise pulls her hand from mine and repairs to another wing of the house, taking the champagne bottle with her. Later, soft around the edges with drunkenness, she comes into the bedroom and tells me she forgives me.

I am sleepily startled at the idea I require forgiveness, but the crystal blue of her eyes pierces me and I stumble through an apology.

We update our upload profiles every three months. The scanner maps new memories, making sure our lives don't slip through the cracks.

They are good memories, mostly.

I'm always a little dazed when I emerge from the scanner. It's worse than usual this time. I dress, drink a glass of electrolyte water, and find Lise deep in conversation with the technician.

The glowing map of my brain on the screen, laid out like a galaxy, fascinates me. I want to stick my fingers in it.

I only catch the tail-end of what Lise is saying: 'Perhaps there's no need to keep that one, hm?'

Later, I'll remember feeling faintly troubled, but when she presses my hand and asks what's wrong, I won't be sure why.

Fruit and Flowers

For breakfast there are strawberries and cold Greek yoghurt. I spoon ripe red slices into my bowl, while Lise abstains. While I eat, she pokes at the leaves and five-petalled white flowers alongside which they are served. When I nag her about breakfast being the most important meal of the day, she adds a second vitamin shot to her coffee.

'I'm thinking of switching to a powder,' she tells me. 'Food's a waste of time, don't you think? All that time deciding what to order.'

On our first date, Lise took me to a restaurant where they froze the ice cream at the table with liquid nitrogen. I remember her enthusing over the delicate sashimi slices of vat-grown beef. There would be no need for farms at all soon, she told me. No need for the hot, farting masses of animal life whose smell always seemed to cling stubbornly to their meat.

'I suppose you're right,' I say.

She looks pleased. 'The advantage of leaving our bodies behind is we're not beholden to one world,' she says. 'We can inhabit everything. Digital heavens, digital hells.'

I baulk at how casually she says it. 'Hells?'

'Mhm.' Lise doesn't notice my expression. She twists one of the white flowers free from its stalk and sets it in the centre of her plate. 'You know, when the Singularity comes, our machine overlords will create copies of us all, the better to punish our disloyalty. Better start worshipping them now.' She smiles then. 'At least, that's one school of thought. We're getting ahead of it, though. Taking control of our afterlives. But still–we should make sure we deserve them, no?'

She's been so distant from me lately, tangled up in imaginings of synthetic immortality. The only time she seems present is when we fuck, when her hand is around my throat. All that time I thought she was dreaming Heaven.

'Come on,' she says, smoothing out her black trousers and getting to her feet. 'Update time.'

Why would anyone choose to inhabit a hell?

Sugar

It's not that I intend to overeat. My meals are mostly taken alone since Lise switched to her diet of powdered drinks. On the rare occasions she joins me, she doesn't eat, just wets her fingertip and sticks it in the sugar bowl. The grains cling there like flecks of quartz or mica, things whose hard shine she might absorb by ingesting them.

After a moment, she wipes her finger off on a napkin without putting it to her mouth.

I'm self-conscious when she's with me, eschewing second helpings. When I'm on my own, it becomes easy to sink into temptation, to self-comfort with pastries and creamy sauces. A childish voice inside me whispers, *One day you'll be nothing but data. Enjoy the flesh while you have it.*

Lise, meanwhile, seems to aspire ever closer to leaving the body. She spares little time for art or music; has even taken to wearing the same thing every day, like a nun's habit. Black trousers, white blouse. It's only their expensiveness—severe, visible—that saves her from looking like a waitress.

She talks about God, sometimes. I don't get it. She's never been much for worship.

In the evening, after we've finished our updates and picked at dinner, she lets me persuade her into bed. I do my best to keep her with me, alert to the telltale, hoped-for tremor in her spare thighs, the taste of her barely familiar on my tongue, but eventually she grows bored and pushes me away with a sigh.

Sitting up beside her, I chew my lip. I know I shouldn't let my insecurities spill out. It's needy, childish, making the unhealed parts of myself her problem. Still I fail to keep them in: 'Sometimes I wonder if you really love me any more.'

Engrossed in her tablet, she gives a faint, questioning hum before my words filter through. Then she puts it down and turns to face me, head sympathetically tilted.

'Oh, sweetheart.' The platitude I expect—*Of course I love you; but I'm so busy, and you know my work is important*—isn't the one I get. 'What's love, anyway?'

She falls asleep. I sneak down to the kitchen and eat ice cream out of the carton. Cold comfort, I think, and laugh weakly to myself.

I'm facing the refrigerator, the last spoonful melting on my tongue, when I hear the echo of her footsteps behind me.

Lise shakes her head. 'What are we going to do with you?'

I don't mean to cry, but perhaps I've had too much wine. I don't really know what I'm apologising for, but I do, over and over like a penitent, like I'm chanting against the end of the world.

Lise puts her arms around me. 'Hush,' she says. 'Hush. Let me help you, hm? Let me make you better?'

She leads me back upstairs, tucks me in, pets my face until I sleep. I dream God is a mountain of ice cream and I'm watching his face melt.

I dream God has no face at all, only shining claws.

Crystal

The last thing I remember is walking to the ascension chamber.

I was holding myself tall, my new black heels clacking out my approach on the polished floor. Lise bought them for me—three pairs. She says they make me look more confident.

I'm not sure I'll ever be quite like her, wearing the same thing every day, but I'll admit it's nice to have the burden of choosing an outfit in the mornings removed. The shoes only go with a handful of things and, in any case, so many of my old clothes no longer fit. Lise has bought me new ones, tailored dresses that hug me securely.

I had to be careful when I lay down, arrange myself one limb at a time in the scanner. Lise beamed down at me, haloed in the ascension chamber's lights.

'You're always so nervous at this part,' she laughed. 'Don't worry. You'll be done before you know it.'

I wake tied to a chair in a cold, dark room. 'What the fuck?' I mutter. Then I call out. Wherever I am, there's no echo, and my voice falls flat. Nobody answers.

I try wriggling, then, thinking maybe I can get myself free, knock over the chair and crawl on my knees to the door, but my arms and legs are secured fast.

Who could be doing this? I think first of kidnappers, bent on getting a ransom out of Lise, and then of rivals looking for trade secrets. We have bodyguards for a reason. But—we have bodyguards. Alarms. Trackers. And, surely, I'd remember *something*.

No: the answer, hovering somewhere in the speckling dark, feels less solid than that.

I'm not sure how long I sit there, only that I'm hoarse by the time I stop trying to get an answer and my wrists hurt from struggling. There is a precise quality to the pain I haven't felt before. I know I'm a physical coward, because pain has always clouded my judgement. It floods me, becomes indistinguishable from everything else and disables all higher functions, leaving me unable to think anything but *make it stop.*

 Not today.

Perhaps Lise's attempts to improve me really have worked. The diets, the meditations, the supplements, the hypnosis, the way she keeps telling me to master myself, know myself, whatever it takes. I'd like to think so.

But does it even matter, if all it helps me do is feel pain better?

As if on cue—as if she knew exactly when I'd give up hope—a door opens, a lightbulb flickers on, and a woman in a white mask walks into the room.

'I'd forgotten you were so loud,' she says.

I don't recognise her voice. It sounds electronic, modulated, or perhaps wholly artificial, and something in it raises goose pimples on my arms. Then she amends: 'I'd forgotten *this* version of you was so loud.'

And I remember Lise's imaginary gods. Her dreams of digital heaven. Her warnings to the faithless, delivered with an ironic half-smile.

Is this digital hell? This masked woman not a woman at all, and I her frozen plaything?

I try to do as Lise would, to follow logic through the terror. If it's true, I'm not real. This body is a construct, this pain a simulation. And the real me is out there somewhere, still living her life, perhaps happy by now, perhaps perfected utterly.

The thought should be a comfort. I just feel desolate.

'Come,' says the masked woman, and another figure, similarly masked and dressed, pushes a trolley into the room. Atop it sit bladed instruments, diamond-tipped, and logic fails, and I tremble.

The second figure only watches, arms folded, leaning against the wall. It's the first one who does the cutting. Though I guess they're not really separate people, just avatars of whatever has me now.

Lise would tell me to pay attention to the pain. I can almost hear her voice saying it. *Don't let it blind you.* Know *it. That will give you power over it.*

But I can't focus for even a moment. This place is cold and sterile and not even real, yet I can smell my own blood and shit, and if I'd eaten in the hours before the ascension chamber

I'm sure that I would puke. My mind slips from one jagged edge to the next, ending up in shreds.

I don't know how long it lasts. Only that, a time later, the first masked figure is stepping back from the trolley and saying, 'I think that's all we'll get out of this one.'

I don't know what she's talking about. She hasn't even asked me any questions.

My head hangs heavily forward. It is a Herculean effort to lift it.

'Do you want to do the honours this time?'

The second figure pushes off the wall and approaches the first, tugs up her mask to bare the bottom half of her face. I recognise Lise's lips immediately, their remembered softness fresh in my mind even now. She turns her head and they kiss for a long time, as though I am not there.

When they part, the second figure has her mask up, too. She turns to face me, a diamond-tipped scalpel in her hand.

The last face I see is my own.

The Death Sentence
J.D. Dresner

The victim's body was burnt to a bubbled crisp. Her hair stood on edge as it let off smoke and a sickly-sweet scent—the kind one might associate with a tire factory, or a beet refinery. But the smell of burnt hair was substantially lost among the overture of other overwhelming odours.

When the detective and his assistant arrived, the rank smell the dead woman emitted had overburdened both of their nostrils.

The detective wrinkled his nose while his assistant thought it more conducive to cover his own with the red handkerchief that he always carried in his right jacket pocket.

'Any witnesses?' asked his assistant beneath the handkerchief.

The detective looked around. The only other person in sight appeared to be minding her own business, standing across the way. 'None that we might rightly question, I suspect.' He returned his gaze upon the victim.

'How are we going to discover who did this? Clearly, the woman died from her burns but, with neither witness nor murder weapon, what hope have we to find the culprit?'

'There is hope, but there isn't a lot of time. If we are to reveal the identity of this woman's killer, then we must do it within the time we are given.'

'Which is?' asked the assistant. He placed his handkerchief back into his right jacket pocket.

'Two thousand words or less.'

'I beg your pardon?'

'It occurred to me shortly after we appeared on the scene that we are living in a very finite universe—a *two-thousand-word universe* to be precise. Thus, if we are to discover who killed this woman, we must do it succinctly.' The detective knelt beside the victim. 'Less, now that I have spent forty-eight words explaining it to you (assuming hyphenated words like "forty-eight" count as one word), not to mention the added words describing my kneeling position.'

Mouth agape, the assistant raised both eyebrows and said, 'We must hurry then!'

'Indeed. And try to refrain from making too many expressions; they take up space.' The detective removed an old penknife from his pocket and poked the poor victim. 'Let us gather what we know and begin with that.'

'Straight away, sir,' said the detective's assistant. He flipped to an empty page in his notebook and began to write. 'The victim was fried to a bloody crisp—'

'Burnt to a bubbled crisp. Details, my friend: Notice the alliteration.'

'Burnt to a bubbled crisp… sorry.' He bit his bottom lip and berated himself for his blatant blunder. Bashfully, he continued, 'Her hair is standing on edge, and she is emitting a most foul odour, if I may say so.'

'You may. And don't forget to write down that she is a she, not a he. Write down that we are men using male adverbs, and that there is only one other person in this story—the aforementioned witness, a female.'

- *Assistant wrote fast, use abbrev. b/c time/space* LTD.
- *Detective says to take time so as not to miss details.*

'Detective, would it not make sense to question the only other character in the story? After all, if neither you nor I murdered the victim, then logic would dictate that it was the witness who killed her.'

'A sound plan, my friend; but, you should note that tales of science fiction such as these often have unforeseeable twists to them. Perhaps you or I killed the victim after all.'

'I did no such thing! I only arrived here after her death, and I was with you.'

'I am merely pointing out that we cannot point fingers and then look for evidence to support our misguided theories. We must adhere to the facts.'

- *Must adhere to facts.*

'Stop that now. You are wasting words and thus the time left to solve this case. We are down to one thousand, three hundred and fifty-four words, so we'd best hurry.'

At once, the two rather troubled men raced toward the only other character in the story.

'You there.'

'Me?'

'Yes, you.'

'You're talking to me?'

'There is no one else I could be referring to so, yes, you,' said the restless detective. When she did not respond, he sighed and then muttered, 'Twenty-seven more words. Poof... out the window.'

'What can I do for you, Mister...?'

'Detective. You can call me Detective. I cannot afford to waste any additional words on introductions. You should understand that we are rather constrained for time, so I must get right to it.'

'I understand, Detective, and I am propelled to answer any question I can.'

'Do you mean to say you are *prepared* to answer any question? Or that you are *compelled* to answer any question?'

'Yes, both... actually, either will do. My apologies.'

'Should I be writing this down?' asked the detective's assistant. The detective ignored him, believing it would use up too many words to explain why it would be redundant to do so. He did, after all, only have one thousand, one hundred and sixty-four words to go.

'Did you murder that woman over there?'

'I most certainly did not!'

'That will be all, thank you.'

'Detective!' blurted his assistant, and boldly at that, 'Surely, we must be more meticulous in our interrogations!'

'We haven't the time.'

'No, I mean to say, we must be more selective with our words if our time is so short.'

'How do you mean, my friend?' asked the detective.

'You asked, 'Did you murder that woman over there?' when you should have simply asked, 'Did you murder that woman?''

'My stars, you are correct! By asking the question as I did, I could only expect a half-truth at best. Perhaps this woman killed the victim somewhere else and then placed her where she lies now; hence, by me asking, "Did you murder that woman over there?" I had inadvertently inquired about the *place of death*, not the death itself.' The detective chuckled, for the English language could be quite capricious at times. This time the detective would take care to phrase the question correctly.

'Did you murder that woman?'

'No,' replied the suspect.

'Dammit.' The detective pondered. 'Alright...' He made use of the ellipsis, hoping it would prolong the time he had left. He was aware that it only created a false sense of elapsed time, but it offered him some comfort. 'Let us look at the facts once more.'

'I have them all written here, sir,' said his assistant, waving his notepad near his own noggin.

'There isn't the time for that. No, I believe we only have time for one last monologue (interrupted only once by you, my assistant) in which I, the main protagonist of the story, must deduce who killed that woman.

'First, let it be noted that from our inception we were made to be aware of our limited existence within a two-thousand-word story. Why would the author introduce such meta-fiction into the tale… unless such an unconventional plot device was required to solve the crime? Our ability to see beyond our own reality must therefore be a clue.

'Second, notice how little has been said about our setting, or the period in which this predicament has taken place. Case in point, my dear assistant, when you and I noticed the only other person in this story, we did not see her *'across the street'*; we saw her *'across the way'*. As it would appear, time and place have nothing to do with the woman's death. Thus, the second clue is this: It does not matter where or when she was murdered.

'I might accuse the only other woman in the story—the motive would be that she is (as I said) now the only woman left, and people prize their individuality greatly, you see. But alas, the thought is only half-baked, for I still cannot fathom how she might have burned the victim to a crisp (not literally, for we must remain cautious in what we say), nor have I seen any evidence to suggest that she did it.'

The detective took pause, and then, 'Besides the fact that she suffers from the occasional malapropism (given she used the word *'propelled'* when she meant to say *'prepared'* or *'compelled'*) all we know about her is that she appeared to be minding her own business when she was first introduced. She had no interest in our investigation, leading me to deduce that she simply isn't our killer.'

The detective continued. 'I might accuse you, my assistant, but you have not the means, nor the motive. Plus, the *modus operandi* is quite wrong. Had the victim been asphyxiated or poisoned, I would have asked you to remove your handkerchief so that I might inspect it for the telltale signs of having it stuffed down another's throat, or even doused with cyanide. But the victim was burned to a bubbled crisp; she was not asphyxiated or poisoned.

'I, too, could be to blame for this heinous crime but, like everyone else here, I am without means or motive. Besides, it would hardly do to have the killer spend his entire existence trying to solve a crime that he himself committed. Thus, the three of us could not have murdered that woman.'

'Who then is left to blame?' asked the detective's utterly dumbfounded assistant, having used up his only allotted interruption.

'By now it should be abundantly apparent. Clue one: we are aware of our own reality, our limitations, and the author of this world. Clue two: the murderer could have killed her anywhere and anywhen (yes, I am aware it isn't a proper word, but my words are all I have... and now I have fewer than ever). Clue three: none of the characters within the story could have done it. Combined, these clues point to the only person who could have possibly killed our victim, and that person is the author himself.

'Only the author had the means to murder one of his characters in such a manner, but make no mistake: he didn't kill her by burning her to death and then hiding the weapon between the lines on the page. No, the murder weapon was in plain sight this entire time—he used his words. You see, the opening statement was his confession.

'By stating that "the victim's body was burned to a bubbled crisp", it became so. Recall, if you will, that we are dealing with a tale that involves meta-language, thus if the author writes "the victim's body was burned to a bubbled crisp" then we must consider only the author's words, not the scene or description those words conveyed.

'It has become painfully obvious to me now: I can see the distinctive use of alliteration throughout this entire tale, which matches the initial killing sentence, and then there's the author's attempt to hinder me by robbing me of my precious, precious, precious word count, hoping I would not figure it out in time.

'What I don't understand is, why create a character that could solve the crime in the first place? Why not just commit the crime? Unless…'

He pondered, again via method of ellipsis.

'Unless,' he said again, 'the author *wanted* me to solve the crime. Yes, of course! The genre… I never considered the genre. Clearly, this is a mystery story, and to appease the reader, the author must aptly adhere to an identifiable structure.

'There must therefore be a murder, and there must also be someone who can solve that murder. His aim was to please his audience. That was his motive, although it does not excuse the fact that he murdered this poor woman.'

The clever detective took a firm hold of his jacket by the lapels as he basked in his brilliant victory. He had the who, the when, the how, and the why, and with only twenty-one words remaining in his short but meaningful life, he said, 'Wait a minute… There is one thing I don't quite understand…'

Dye Job
Teresa Milbrodt

When the new hair dye came out, everyone thought it was great since your head could be a mood ring. My fifth-grade students chattered about it after recess—some of their older siblings had bought dye packets and were walking around with day-glo green 'dos.

As with many fads, the shine wore off quickly. It only took a few days for most people to remember how sheltering emotions could be necessary to maintaining relationships, friendships, marriages and family ties. Many people who'd gotten the dye job on a whim quickly tired of hearing, 'Wait, your hair went from blue to yellow, what does that mean?'

Buzz cuts became the new style for spring.

I was one of those people who'd thought, 'What the hell,' bought a dye packet, and three days later considered buying a hair clipper.

My therapist, who I'd been seeing even before my partner asked for the divorce, cautioned against it. She said this was what mood hair was all about—finding emotions you didn't know existed until they appeared bold and bright on your head and there was no getting around them.

'Sometimes you have to see what you're feeling,' my therapist said. 'Emotions are difficult to pin down.'

She was right about that—my hair was all kinds of whack colours, and the dye package was explicit that everyone's body chemistry was different, so there was no one colour code. There was also no guarantee that your head would always look good.

What to think about the dull violet with orange highlights on the day my divorce was finalised? I felt strangely unmoored, wandered around my new apartment repeatedly watering a plant and wondering if I should order pizza or if that felt too much like a celebration.

I wasn't the only person experiencing colour clashes. My friend, who worked in admissions at the hospital, got her curls buzzed after she endured a day with hair tinged avocado green and dying daffodil yellow.

'It was gross,' she said.

I didn't ask what had happened to create that palette, just wore head scarves, and hoped to chromatically survive ending one romantic relationship and beginning another.

My divorce was amicable enough—we didn't have cats to fight over, and they got the vacuum cleaner while I got the dining room table—but even before things were finalised they were seeing someone else, which made me sear with a jealously I didn't understand.

I needed to quit moping, since Kris had already spent one night in my apartment, and I was clearly falling in love/lust/infatuation. When Kris kissed me before we left for work, my mind fizzed and my hair turned aqua and parrot blue.

I peered up at my bangs and assumed the longer hair that waterfalled down my back had turned a similar hue. Maybe I needed to put it up in a bun.

'Is that colour good?' Kris smiled.

'I guess,' I said, winding a teal lock around my finger.

'I'll see you after school if you need a boost,' they said, kissing me again.

If I was going to fall in love with an entrepreneur, it might as well be a coffee shop owner who paid for my drinks and grinned when I sat at a corner table near the register to grade papers.

Being with Kris made me feel fluttery, obsessed, and slightly ill, like I was sixteen-years-old. These were emotions I wasn't supposed to have at forty-two, when life was complicated with my job, family and the monthly drone of bills.

I should have thought of that before the dye job.

My students thought my hair was cool and weird. It was probably one of the many things they giggled about in the back of the classroom, but fifth grade was the age when hormones started to kick in, so I wasn't the only person who didn't feel like my previous self.

* * *

Kris was smart, gutsy, and had worked as a tax accountant for nineteen years before leaving the firm to start the coffee shop. That was after their divorce and a fibromyalgia diagnosis when they decided to live their dream.

'It's great when the dream doesn't feel like a nightmare,' Kris said. 'Next time I won't quit my day job after being told I have a major health problem.'

They'd taken out a business loan, had a rough start with suppliers who quit and an espresso machine that kept breaking, but now they were starting to turn a profit and pay themselves as well as their employees. They walked with a cane when the fibromyalgia flared, but there wasn't much their doctor could prescribe but moderate exercise, a healthy diet, and a reduction in stress. Easy to say for a small business owner. I knew how work could wear on a body.

I'd been blind in my right eye since birth but, for a long time, it didn't bother me since it was my form of normal. My left eye was nearsighted and I'd always worn glasses, but now that eye was developing a cataract. My ophthalmologist said I'd need surgery in a couple years, when my reading glasses were no longer helpful and the eyestrain headaches got worse.

'We know how to do cataract surgery really well, but there's a slight chance you could go blind,' he told me. 'I'd rather hold off as long as we can.'

I knew many people got along in the world with little to no vision and did perfectly well, but it was an adjustment I figured would take time. I was happy to put off the risk, however small it might be.

When we laid in my bed on a Saturday morning, Kris and I joked that we were barely past forty and falling apart. I wanted someone to hug me who was also coming to grips with the fact that their joints popped, they had to eat more fibre, and they regularly scrutinised their moles.

Kris left at seven, kissed me good-bye and said they'd see me soon.

I stayed in bed pondering how nobody would live forever, an idea that made my hair turn the colour of candy corn. Maybe that notion was always dormant in the back of everyone's mind, but I wrested myself away from that thought and returned to life. I had to pick out a head scarf and take my niece out for our weekly breakfast donut. By the time I got to my sister's apartment, my hair had hints of yellow and orange but was mostly a grounded shade of brick red.

My niece Emily was thirteen and sometimes acted like it. My sister was happy for the respite, and to spend time with her ten-year-old son. Her ex had moved to Wisconsin when they divorced, but he paid child support on time, called the kids every other week, and, according to my sister, was less of an asshole than when they were married.

Emily rolled her eyes at her parents, and the rest of the world, but I figured that was the terrain of being a teenager.

'Everybody at school is stupid,' she told me when we got to my car.

'That's eighth grade for you,' I said.

'When will they stop?' she asked.

'Sometime between next week and never,' I said.

'Shit,' Emily said. She swore around me with reckless abandon, which was one of the joys of being an auntie as opposed to a parent. 'I like your hair.'

'Thank you,' I said, wondering if it was changing colour while we drove.

I was mad at my brain for being a traffic jam of emotions. I'd drawn hearts on the agenda in the middle of a staff meeting yesterday afternoon and damned myself for being smitten, but Kris only charged us for one latte and donut at the coffee shop.

'Call you later,' I said, my heart jolting when Kris smiled. I checked my hair in my compact mirror when Emily and I sat at a tiny table. My therapist had told me to track its changes in a hair journal. I'd shifted from burgundy to deep violet.

'They're cute for an old person.' Emily nodded to Kris behind the counter.

'Thanks.' I rolled my eye, combed my fingers through my bangs, and consulted my compact once more. My hair had taken on gold flecks.

'You're cute for an old person,' Emily said.

'I'll tell everyone at the nursing home,' I said.

'You know what I mean,' she said. 'Your hair is so cool. Mum wouldn't let me try it.'

'It wouldn't be great for teenagers,' I said. Or any adolescents.

Looking out at a psychedelic fifth-grade classroom would have given me a headache, which might have been why the dye was banned in many schools. Kids needed to get in touch with their emotions but shouldn't know what other kids were thinking, though that was true for most people.

I purpled around Kris.

Greened when I saw the principal, read newspaper headlines, or listened to my father say he was fine when we chatted on the phone, right before he launched into a coughing fit.

Pinked or reddened when I read to my students, or played a math game with them, or when everyone did well on a test.

Yellowed and oranged when I paid bills, went to the ophthalmologist, or listened to Emily talk about how my sister was never happy. Those colours were often in my bangs like malevolent fireflies.

My therapist said it was probably anxiety.

'But it never goes away,' I said.

She nodded.

* * *

I'd started seeing my therapist after Dad disappeared for a bit four years ago. He didn't return texts or calls for three days. My sister and I worried ourselves into a tizzy and almost put out a missing person's report, but then Dad phoned us sounding like a guilty kid who knew they broke curfew. He'd gone to Florida to stay with a cousin for an impromptu vacation and didn't tell anyone.

'I didn't think I needed to,' he said.

'It's a courtesy,' said my sister in a polar tone. 'In case something happened to you.'

Dad's doctors had told him to watch his blood pressure and cholesterol since his family had a weird history of early heart attacks. Our parents had been divorced for eighteen years, and Mum wasn't going to keep tabs on him since she was out in Arizona.

In his second breath, Dad said he was retiring from the grounds crew at the country club, had started taking anti-depressants, and was looking for an apartment near his cousin since Florida was nice.

My sister and I didn't say much, but we were thinking *What about us? Don't we matter? You were depressed? For how long?*

Usually people don't tell you they're depressed, often they don't even know, but it knocked us for a loop. I started thinking about hurricanes and flooding. What if another bad storm hit Florida? Was Dad really going to work with his cousin doing lawn care for condos in July? Didn't he hate hot weather?

While lying in bed and searching for sleep, I fretted about my parents, my sister, my niece and nephew, and my students. I needed to live in the moment—that's what my therapist and Zen Buddhists said—but that was difficult. My students were great at living in the moment, but each one was filled with adolescent drama and crises. I was steeped in the long view of saving for retirement, saving for my niece and nephew's college education, saving the planet for my great-grand-nieces and nephews, saving emotional energy to listen to students when they were having problems, and saving patience for students when they cut up in class because they were frustrated and didn't know how else to express it.

No wonder my hair was streaked orange and yellow all the damn time.

* * *

As fall rolled into winter, I spent more evenings at Kris' apartment and started keeping a toothbrush there, the equivalent of exchanging class rings when you're forty. It was a long-term audition: Could they live with my morning breath, the drool on my pillow, and would they forgive me for endlessly praising and grumbling over my students at breakfast? Could we fit our good and bad habits together, listen to litanies of each other's stories, and take turns removing our long hair from the bathtub drain?

Kris noticed when I closed my eye and took off my reading glasses while grading. Another eyestrain headache. If we were at the coffee shop they came out from behind the counter to massage my shoulders and tell me to take a break.

The cataract was steadily blurring my vision so I couldn't see people clearly if they were too far down the hall, but when I thought about cataract surgery my hair lit with orange streaks. Before then, I'd rather liked my blind eye. It was helpful to put things in that empty space when I didn't want to look at someone at a staff meeting, but now I realised it might be nice to have a backup eye. Just one. Two eyes still seemed excessive.

'I want surgery and I'm scared of surgery, and I'd like these headaches to end,' I told Kris while we took an evening walk in the park across from their apartment.

'Having a body is a bumpy road,' said Kris. They held my hand in their right hand, their cane in their left. 'Right after you go over one bump and think you've found a smooth patch, you hit another bump. But bodies have wonderful moments. Good massages. Good food. Good sex.'

I closed my eye and let myself follow Kris' gait. The hitch in their step was so natural to me and, with my eye closed, the headache lessened. Their hand was warm in mine, and it was comforting to move like that, together.

For snatches of time, I imagined my hair could lose its orange spikes and flow into the bliss of violet.

* * *

The week before winter break, I had an after-school meeting with the mother of a student who I thought needed an in-class aide and a test for dyslexia.

'He gets overstimulated and fidgety sometimes,' I explained, 'but he's fine if he takes a break to walk down the hall and back. I think he might also need a tutor to help him with his reading. Kids who are dyslexic need someone to help them decode how their brains interpret letters.'

The mother was not receptive.

'Why are we giving you a pay cheque if you can't teach our kids reading?' she said. 'And he's got to learn how to sit still. If he can't do it in fifth grade, when is it going to happen?'

'He's a great kid,' I said, 'but he's fallen a bit further behind in reading every year, and he's having problems keeping up now, so—'

'You're not taking my kid out of class,' she said. 'Then the other kids will tease him and think he's some kind of dummy, and he's not.'

'Of course not,' I said. 'But everyone has gifts in some areas and needs help in others. He's a maths whiz; I'm sure he could be in advanced classes in junior high.'

I smiled. The mother fumed. I'd worn a yellow kerchief that day, which was good because my hair was probably turning the same hue. The rest of our conversation didn't go much better.

I'd have to wing it, send him out to run an errand or get supplies from the main office for me when I saw him get fidgety, and have the school librarian work with him on reading when we had library days. She had a dyslexic daughter and said she'd bring in workbooks. I hated that we had to do this under the table, like there was something shameful about it. With twenty-three kids in the room it was hard to find time to help all of them as much as they needed.

Such was the case the next day when that kid was banging his knee against the radiator. I asked if he could go to the office and get five extra glue sticks from the supply closet. The other kids knew I sent him on those little missions when he made noises with his tongue, or thumped his hand on his desk, or hummed one long note. I don't know if they looked at me with gratitude, or like they thought he was a favourite, or if they wondered what the hell was up with him.

Seriously, I wanted to say to my class, *is it a huge crime to make clicking noises with your tongue and hum to calm yourself down?*

I worried their answer would be yes.

This was fifth grade, and social circles had no mercy. It would have been nice to take a moment to cry, but no, not in the middle of class.

I said it was time for sustained silent reading, so they rustled in their desks for paperbacks. Some stole sideways glances at me as I shuffled to the supply closet with my tie-dyed head, pretending to count boxes of coloured pencils.

My face was hot. I teared quietly, trying to make sure my shoulders didn't shake. Something must have leaked from me, perhaps a gasp, because my students rustled in their seats. Damn it, I needed a Kleenex, but did what I could to dry my eyes on my sleeve.

When I turned around half the class was peering back at me with concerned faces.

Parents and teachers were people. That was a scary fact when you were a kid, but sometimes I wished everyone had tie-dyed hair so we'd all look like traffic jams of emotion. It wouldn't resolve anything, but maybe we'd realise that everyone was complicated and give them a little more leeway.

* * *

Holiday baking with my sister meant buying ten pounds of flour, five pounds of white sugar and five pounds of brown, two dozen eggs, a pound of butter and a pound of margarine, three bags of chocolate chips, a jar of peanut butter, and a jar of maraschino cherries. Emily and Scott stayed with their dad in Wisconsin for two weeks over the holidays, and the freezer was crammed with cookies when they returned.

My sister said she didn't have time for it when they were around, but I think she wanted to shove her loneliness to one side of her mind and concentrate on culinary pursuits. We also prepared for annual holiday visits from our parents— Mum came around Solstice and Dad visited for New Year's.

'For the price of plane tickets, you'd think they could stay for more than four days,' my sister said while she measured flour into a bowl.

'They have holiday plans with their friends and clubs,' I said.

'And motorcycle gangs,' said my sister.

Dad was learning motorcycle repair from a neighbour. We were sure he'd buy one before long, but since our parents had moved to more southern climates we'd become suspicious of them. They called every other week to say they were fine, but I figured they were hiding something.

When I got in certain moods, I expected every call to be an alert that something awful had happened: Mum or Dad didn't have enough money for medications, were too proud to ask for a loan, and had waited too long to take the next dose.

'I guess we should be glad they're not demanding attention,' said my sister while she added baking powder to the flour. Dad mowed lawns, trimmed hedges and repaired engines. Mum tutored kids in reading and fostered three dogs from the Humane Society—a Newfoundland, a Dalmatian, and greyhound/pit bull mix.

We never had pets since my sister was allergic to the hair, so I figured the furry children ruled Mum's house. Our parents never asked when we'd come visit, another reason I thought they'd become teenagers in their seventies.

I made dinner while my sister went to get Mum from the airport—we'd decided on pasta and sauce—but Kris called before they could return. It was difficult to understand them, but I pieced together that Greg, their brother in Kentucky, had died in a traffic accident that afternoon.

'Please come over,' Kris said, their voice hoarse. 'I can't be alone right now.'

* * *

When I arrived, the door was unlocked and Kris was on the couch. They hunched over with their elbows on their knees and cried while I hugged them tight, their body shuddering. I couldn't embrace them with a force as strong as grief, only kiss their forehead and feel the gift, the weight, of their sorrow.

'I don't know if he took his own life,' Kris said softly during a lull in their tears. 'He'd been on the edge of something drastic so many times. He'd call me and I'd talk him down and we'd get help for him again. It seemed like he was doing better.

'I talked with him last week and he sounded fine, but he could put up a front. He wanted to protect me from his darkness, but all I wanted was for him to talk with me about it.'

I curled myself around Kris, sure my hair mirrored my confusion, the intimacy of mourning together, a moment when they were willing to lay themselves so bare in front of me that I knew we'd stay together for a long time.

I needed someone to help me hold those contradictions of joy and love and anger and pain that never appeared in isolation, but in the cacophony of emotions that we couldn't describe, except maybe as the swirls of red and green, yellow and violet, orange and blue, sparkling and impermanent and precious, all the pieces of being human that had no words.

Formula 719: The Cure for Ennui
Robert Bagnall

'At least I've *increased* the odds of there being human life on Earth next millennia.'

In retrospect, Sasha admitted to herself, she could have chosen a better time and place to speak her mind. Granted, she had blurted those words in a moment of irritation. But there was no way for her to take them back: they'd come out *live on television*.

Beyond the glare of the studio lights, the audience's temper changed. Even if she couldn't make out faces, just a glint of spectacles, an occasional movement, she could tell by the way it held its breath, how it stilled, waited. It. An audience was an 'it', not a 'they'. It was one creature, with one mood, one thought. This one was wound up, ready to pounce.

On the opposite sofa, the presenter, a transatlantic import preened like Barbie's Ken, gave bare hints at messages coming from the production gallery.

Push her, they were probably saying into his ear.

Glowering next to Sasha sat the normally dignified David Rasmunsen, his eyes narrowed. Whoever's bright idea it had been to book two scientists for a late-night talk show, they were no doubt fist-pumping in vindication right now.

The third guest, internet influencer Fay Whimsey, was reduced to a mere spectator.

Slow news day? Not anymore.

'What do you mean by that, Dr Sabrosa?' plastic-faced Ken asked.

Rasmunsen raised a quizzical eyebrow. His lawyers were probably wondering too, thought Sasha—had she forgotten he'd cured cancer? Well, maybe not cured it, but discovered a radical new treatment for cytoplasmic tyrosine kinases, oncogenes that screwed with a cell's natural lifecycle, switched off apoptosis, the process of programmed cell death.

But, to the gawking viewers, internet trolls and headline writers, that was pretty much the same thing.

She took a chug of water, steadied herself, composed her next words with more care.

'We live on a planet with finite resources. Earth has a carrying capacity of around eight billion people. We've passed that. We're full. But, if we all lived like middle-class westerners, which is what everybody wants, it's only a couple of billion. Which means we've gone way over the cliff edge.

'But every time we invent some new drug or treatment nobody ever dares ask *is that a good thing*? More people, living longer. It's great if that's you or me or family, but more people living longer is hastening the day when the world breaks, and breaks in a way nobody has thought of.'

'The world has enough for everyone's need, but not enough for everyone's greed,' Rasmunsen agreed. 'Ghandi.'

Sensing potential reproachment, the presenter—Chad, Kent, Brick? The green room refreshments had wiped his name from Sasha's memory—asked why she thought it was all Dr Rasmunsen's fault. Wasn't his line of research noble and worthy?

Sasha wished she had never opened her mouth. Forced to look at the world from a whole new perspective, she had stumbled across a fundamental truth.

'My point is simply one of unintended consequences. David's research is quite literally life-saving. But saving lives puts further strain on the planet, strain we're struggling to manage—'

'...strain your invention—Catholicon—helps tackle?'

'Yes.'

'With no unintended consequences at all?'

Chip, if that was his name, gave her a challenging smile.

But it was her pause, her hesitation, the stumble before answering that she knew would be all over Twitter.

* * *

Go kill yourself.

She stopped reading after the first few tweets. There was a lurid logic. The inevitable riposte to anyone who thought the planet's problem was too many people was to go lighten the load by one.

She stared out of the limousine window at the London raindrops smearing diagonally across the glass. Cocooned next to her within a quarter of million pounds of electric Bentley, her business manager debriefed her, but she had difficulty listening. She suspected she was being politely bollocked for departing from the corporate message. When had she stopped being human and become a corporation?

The tenth straight day of rain in April. Hot rain. This was not natural. She felt a migraine coming.

Walking through the door of her Georgian Hampstead home, she held a hand up to stop her husband before he could speak.

Tom, in turn, held up his phone, mirroring her open palm, like some strange greeting ritual between digital natives.

She shook her head with an eye-roll that wrapped up 'how could I be so stupid' with 'the world is full of idiots'.

'Some people are talking about a Nobel for you.'

'For what I said?'

'For what you've done. Forget the trolls. They were swept away by people saying, if anybody has the right to be disappointed by humanity, it's you. Right now, you're like a sexy Attenborough.'

The Victorian hallway, all Anaglypta and glazed tiles, opened into a vast modern steel and glass open-plan living area, a hundred grand's worth of kitchen on one side, a hundred-inch plasma screen on the other. A muted newsfeed cut between crumbling icebergs and flaming tumbleweed.

The heels of her Jimmy Choos clicked across the marble. She opened the vast fridge and removed the cork from a half-drunk bottle of Fleurie with her teeth.

'At least take your coat off,' Tom challenged softly.

She paused, recognised in herself the temptation to react, explode, and swallowed it back down like bile. She was at a tipping point, teetering, with a bird's-eye view of the immediate future down either path. Sliding doors? More like sliding psyche. The dilemma: fly into a rage or let the moment pass.

Opting for Zen, she wordlessly poured the rest of the bottle into an oversized goblet and, only then, removed her long Valentino double-breasted coat, dumping it on a chair back.

'Do you worry about your drinking?' Tom said.

Having not risen to the bait before, it felt foolish to do so now.

'I do,' he added.

'I have you to do my worrying for me.' And then, to steer the conversation away from the rocks: 'There isn't a Nobel for bio-engineering.'

'*Peace*. They're talking about the Nobel *Peace* Prize. There's a campaign.'

'Means nothing. Remember Boaty McBoatface?'

'They called it the David Attenborough in the end, remember? And you're the sexy Attenborough.'

She laughed. He was always a master at diffusing situations. Was that why she loved him?

* * *

Unintended consequences.

She could have punched Brad or whatever his made-up American cable-TV name was. He had no idea that the last five years of the fifteen it took to bring the product to market had been ironing out unintended consequences. She had given the world Ideonella Sabrosa, a self-replicating bacterium that could eat waste plastic and convert it to a black sludge that, when dried in thin sheets, had photovoltaic properties.

So, it eats plastic and shits solar panels?

She remembered giggling hysterically under the duvet at Tom's summation. She'd been too close to appreciate the absurdity. Yes, she'd solved the planet's waste plastic *and* energy crises in one go.

Except she hadn't. The problem? While there was much to admire in Formula 719, her prototype bacterium—it was a pernicious, rampant self-replicator—the process was exothermic. Left to its own devices it could even contribute to global warming.

The solution—Formula 762—incorporated the conversion of lithium-7 to tritium, an endothermic process that balanced the exothermicity, with mechanical processes at a molecular level based on the way snails lay down their shells. But no single sentence did justice to the hundreds of thousands of hours Sasha and her team devoted to cracking the problem.

The final struggle was what to call it. They wanted something that hinted at its status as a silver bullet, considered the Latin until Google told them 'bullet' translated as *glans*, but settled on *catholicon*, meaning a cure-all, a panacea. It had become a neologism, a verb as well as a noun, reflecting its ubiquity: cars and houses had energy-generating Catholicon roofs, roads were surfaced with it, aircraft skinned with it, mobile phones lost their batteries and gained Catholicon cases.

Just Catholicon it.

The plastic the developed world dumped on the beaches of the developing suddenly became valuable raw material. The Information Age gave way to the Catholicon Age, an age of optimism when the world foresaw escaping the worst of the climate catastrophe. Sasha was feted as Marie Curie, Jesus and Edison rolled into one. Two years ago, the planet didn't know who she was. She wasn't yet forty.

She did not expect Catholicon to make her rich—development had burnt through so much of their backers' funds—but she was given a profit share, a seat on the board, a research team, and carte blanche to choose her projects. She had an office with her name on the building, as well as on the door, and a project management team: an ever-smiling Columbian called Esteban; Fionnuala, who wasn't really scowling at her, honest; and intern Agnes, who had been lifted out of a north London sink estate on the strength of exceptional psychometrics. Five PhDs between two of them, and consistent scores in at least the ninety-eighth percentile for the third.

But they all looked to her. She'd cracked two of the world's biggest problems in one sitting, so she could crack anything, right? That was the logic. Go Sasha! Go girl! Solve it for us.

Solve what?

She was still searching.

* * *

Every morning felt the same. It was like a perpetual tiredness, an ache, a grogginess. One thing Sasha found about being rich, about drinking expensive wine: she never really achieved a hangover. Somehow, she missed her student researcher night-after-the-supermarket-wine never-going-to-drink-again mornings. There was an honesty about them. This was like she'd subcontracted the after-effects, just like other people cooked and cleaned for her now and told her what to say.

She called for the Bentley, the subtly smoked glass and intoxicating smell of cowhide disconnecting her mind further.

She found herself gazing into the traffic from the back seat with no idea how long she'd been like that. She had papers to go through, but there would be no issue at the board meeting if she were not fully up to speed. She no longer presented proposals; success constituted being presented to. She was unconvinced it was a step up.

'Pull over. Stop here.'

The Bentley lurched up on double yellows outside a row of 1930s red brick shopfronts—a chicken takeaway, a convenience store, a recruitment agency, a barber's—built to capture trade on the new arterial route when there was still the joy of an open road. A blare of horns sounded from behind as cars shoaled around the fat black limousine.

'Just need…' she said, exiting swiftly, giving her chauffeur no time to demur.

The convenience store was like thousands across the nation, the glass frontage all decaled logos, posters and adverts, dayglo cards marker-penned with BOGOFs, making for a dim treasure house within. Slivers of the harshly lit shop showed through the gaps between the retail messages suggesting tightly packed shelves, a saffron-turbaned shopkeeper behind a counter cramped with scratchcard dispensers—behind him a wall of cigarettes and spirits.

Sasha pushed open the door, not stopping for a slack-jawed passer-by reaching for her phone. The temperature was several degrees below the unseasonal humidity outside, fluorescent tubes adding a harsh cold blueness to the scene.

'You're…' the elderly Sikh shopkeeper began, bushy eyebrows knotting, his eyes flicking between the flesh and blood Sasha and her image, repeated multiple times, on the front pages of the newspapers lined up on the counter.

She silenced him with an upheld palm and a raised eyebrow. Another irritant that came with unsought fame: people were constantly telling her who she was.

'Do you have a back exit?

'Yes,' he said automatically.

'Is it unlocked?'

He nodded unthinkingly.

Sasha clambered over the counter, scattering tabloids and upsetting the Lottery ticket dispenser, not caring about the implications for her Dolce and Gabbana.

Grumblingly, he made space for her.

'A man will come through the door in a moment,' she said, making herself small below counter-level. 'Tell him I went out the back.'

The door beeped and Sasha's driver came in as the shopkeeper straightened the newspapers. 'She went out the back,' he blurted, convincingly enough for her to be in the back of a cab five minutes later.

* * *

'Come and join me,' she had said on the telephone, and when Tom asked where she was, she'd simply replied, 'Park Road.'

There was a moment's hesitation before he repeated her answer with a hint of disbelief.

'They haven't fixed the window. Still rattles.'

An hour later, he was standing in the empty living room of what had been their first home together, a flat above a betting shop, the floorplan a simple rectangle divided up into smaller rectangles with no architectural finesse, a front door opening into a combined lounge and kitchen with two doors off: one bedroom, one bathroom. A world away from Heathside.

She sat on the carpet—a nylon mid-charcoal affair, not the worn pub pattern she had known—against the wall, her knees up to her chin. 'We used to stop it banging with beer mats. Remember?'

'They called. I was in the cab coming over here. Something about you doing a runner.' He said it with care, as though minimising the risk of emotional reaction was vital.

'I wanted to be elsewhere.'

'Why are we here, Sasha?'

'I've bought it.'

'It would say 'sold' outside. The signboard still says, 'for sale'.'

She gave a little smile, as if caught out in a lie that wasn't important anyway. 'I've offered the full asking price and gave the estate agent a few hundred in cash for them to let me borrow the key for a bit.'

'Why?'

'The little Italian we used to go to has become a Thai fusion place. Looks a bit style over substance, but we could have lunch there.'

Tom stood his ground. 'Why are you buying back our former flat, Sasha? I've fond memories, but life moves on.'

She glared at him with tears welling in her eyes. 'Do you remember when buying this was a step up, not a BASE jump down? Do you remember having hopes and dreams and ambitions? Having something to strive for, something to aim for? Do you know what it feels like to cross the finishing line, to win at life? *We'll get that, Sasha. Let us do that for you, Sasha.* This is where we lived when I got to Formula 719, and when I solved Formula 719. Remember?'

He nodded.

'Well, explain it to me, because that person isn't me. And I want her back. I might have another forty or fifty years of this.'

'Not the way you're drinking.'

Silence.

Tom gave the window frame a rattle. 'I don't understand. Are you leaving me? To come back here?'

'I thought it'd be a bolthole. For us.'

'You know most people would kill for your life, for what you've achieved. You know what I think is your biggest achievement? You made Greta Thunberg grin. You made Greta fucking Thunberg *grin*.'

She scowled at him, trying not to laugh despite herself. 'I can't help feeling what I feel.'

'Find another problem to solve. They've given you your own research facility. Use it.'

She balled her hands into fists.

'That interview with Rasmunsen, the penny dropped for me. It changed my perspective. It's all pointless. Every time somebody like him cures a disease, or somebody like me solves a bit of the climate crisis, we just take it as a signal to keep on as we were.

'What are we now? Nine billion? We're still sprinting towards oblivion; all I've done is push the cliff edge back a few decades. I'm just another in a long line of mugs enabling the masses to keep on overloading the world. We're a suicidal species.'

Tom came and squatted down beside her. This was where their television once sat. They watched documentaries and *University Challenge* from the red leather sofa with their dinner—the kitchen table given over to Sasha's laptop, notes and papers.

'You can't get the feeling of the first time back, Sasha,' he said softly. 'Whether it's solving the puzzle for the first time, buying your first home, or meeting the girl of your dreams.'

She looked up at him.

'Now, why don't you return the key, withdraw the offer, and we'll go home.'

She nodded. Tom made her actions sound so insane she wondered whether she had crossed some mental health threshold without realising. The mood swings, the drinking, the erratic behaviour. She suddenly saw herself as others must.

He held out a hand to help her up.

She stood, unsteadily, her legs having gone to sleep. 'Can you give me five minutes?'

He looked sternly at her, silently questioning.

She told him she wasn't going to do anything stupid, and she meant it.

Alone, she remembered the exact moment when she solved the problem of Formula 719 and its exothermicity. She remembered where she had been standing, in the kitchen, gazing out of the back window. Down below was an overgrown garden, all brambles and nettles where the betting shop still threw out what wouldn't fit in the dumpster. There was a fruit machine down there. She could just about make out its outline. Beyond it, a railway embankment. What was it that made Lithium-7 drop into her head out of nowhere? What combination of inputs and signals? She remembered the self-sown sycamores on the embankment moving in the wind, how a sliver of sunlight caught the leaves and, a moment later, the answer was there, fully-formed in her mind.

It had been a similar day. The sycamores swayed now as they had done then, fat dancers, feet planted, hips oscillating, arms waving. The scudding clouds allowed a moment of sunlight through, and the leaves lit bright…

Struck. That's the word people use when they have an idea. Struck. With a force. And so it was again. She had to clutch the dusty radiator edge to remain standing. Just as she had known, out of nowhere, how to solve Formula 719, she knew now how to solve her current problem, the bigger problem she had only just recognised.

And this time, Formula 719 was the answer, not the riddle.

* * *

'Esteban, Fionnuala, Agnes. Meeting. My office,' Sasha called as she strode into the research offices.

Agnes was scrolling through data on screen, various moulded Catholicon shapes before her on her desk. Fionnuala muttered apologies into her mobile and hung up. Esteban looked up from his laptop, his trademark grin across his face, but his eyes admitting confusion, mainly because Sasha's arrival was unexpected.

Nobody had seen her for almost two months now. Indeed, there had even been talk of declaring Dr Sasha Sabrosa missing. Her husband, Tom, had quashed the suggestion, saying she just needed some time away, without being drawn further. They had continued with Catholicon work as usual. Nobody needed to step into her shoes—she didn't do much anyway, and they were effectively self-managing.

Then, strange stories began to emerge. Sasha had been at the manufacturing plant culturing something that was and wasn't Catholicon. She had driven off with four drums of the stuff. Then photos posted on the internet: a shy selfie with a fan in Peru, pulled over on California's Highway One, in dark glasses in the Caribbean, in Red Square, Namibia, Mongolia. Nothing much was made of these snaps—the Rasmunsen thing had fizzled out, Nobel committees moved slowly and were indifferent to online petitions.

But the other reason for Esteban's confusion was how she looked which was… glowing, stunning, *incredible*. It was as if she had lost ten years in age and gained three inches in height. There was a certainty to her every move, confidence in her every action. She commanded. The three found themselves standing, moving, trooping into the conference room, mesmerised.

'Where have you been, Sasha?' Fionnuala wondered. 'We've been worried.'

'Drying out,' muttered Agnes.

'What? Yes. I mean, no, not drying out, but not drinking anymore, it's true. All over, I've been all over,' she brightened.

'Angola, Bahrain, California…' Agnes began nasally, and rattled off a list of sightings.

Sasha paused, confused. 'Not Mongolia. That wasn't me.'

'Analytics gave it an eighty percent probability. I thought less.'

'To do what?' Esteban pressed. 'At the plant, they said you had…'

Sasha held up a hand for silence.

'Formula 719 has found its way into the oceans. It's in the Gulf Stream, the Pacific currents, it's in the South Atlantic. Twenty-five kilos seeded strategically in four carefully chosen locations.'

'719?' Fionnuala wondered. 'That's pre-lithium conversion…'

Possibly, for the first time since his heart was last broken, the grin vanished from Esteban's face. 'Why have you done such a thing?'

Agnes blinked, her tic when she had to think through something particularly tricky, and—with strangled vowels that gave lie to the claim Dick van Dyke's cockney accent was a travesty—declared, 'With the existing levels of microplastics, there'll be a catastrophic, self-reinforcing, warming of the oceans.'

Sasha grinned. 'We're basically fucked when it gets to the Pacific Garbage Patch. It'll turn that beast into a kettle element.'

The other three had gone pale. They visibly sagged, as if they had just dodged death only to turn and see a tsunami wave coming back at them.

'Put the coffee on, Agnes, and make it strong,' Sasha beamed, rubbing her hands with glee. 'We've got the mother of all problems to solve. And I feel brilliant.'

She had reclaimed her happiness.

Results
Timons Esaias

The smartdoorbell announced visitors, plural, and then someone pushed its button, so it chimed.

Stanley wasn't where he could see the video, and he was dressed for work, so he thought, *Oh, hell,* and opened the door.

This was probably his second recent major mistake.

Standing in front of the door to the first-floor apartment were two very-put-together, very-made-up business types. The male held an envelope. The female held a microphone.

Behind them were about a hundred newspeople, many with video cameras. Beyond them was a growing band, like an electron orbital, of curious neighbours. The street was lined with vans and panel trucks that all had dish antennae on top, a couple of them extending quite high in the air.

The woman greeted him by name, and her voice was amplified to the crowd, which puzzled him so much that he didn't catch much beyond his own name, mispronounced, and the single word 'results'.

The man handed him the envelope.

The envelope bore the name of a DNA testing service. A service to which—and he would soon see this as the first recent major mistake—he had sent a sample. As he took the envelope, he distinctly remembered the part of the contract which claimed *complete privacy.*

He also pictured what this exchange must look like to the crowd. His job was floor manager at Trajan's Legionary Pizza Oven Restaurant, and he was in full legionary get-up, which included a short kilt-like skirt and a six-pack-abs breastplate. He had—self-consciousness kicked in hard here—exceptionally hairy legs.

In context, at the restaurant, people found his uniform amusing, even interesting.

Out of context, like this exact moment, not so much.

He took the envelope and began to step back into his apartment, but discovered he'd already been outflanked and boxed in. There were two camera people and a sound tech behind him. The envelope guy was pulling the storm door open, the microphone lady had taken his elbow and was explaining that the whole world was waiting for his unusual results.

So why not do us all a favour and open it right here? she implied. Or maybe she said it. His mental apparatus was getting sludgy at that point.

He must have opened the envelope.

5% - 7% Central Asian.

That was interesting. He hadn't expected that.

12% - 16% European cave bear.

He thought, *That would explain the hair*. There were a bunch of other warnings and questions and signals that his brain was trying to send him, but it all flooded over him without sinking in.

80% yeti.

Now, he knew that *yeti* could be interpreted as the word for the *Abominable Snowman*, but it couldn't be that. There was no explanation for what the acronym YETI stood for, or why it was all in lower case letters, not capitals.

Then everything cleared up in an instant. Practical joke. Some YouTube or Netflix or Fasceddit-channel thing, and he was the goat.

At that point, his mood did a curious thing. As a psychological defence, some mental autopilot took over and he quit having any real thoughts or judgments. He calmly stated that he needed to get to work, and firmly signalled the crew behind him out of the apartment, pulling the door closed after himself, locking it, and heading through the crush to his Uber.

The driver was behind a police barricade, but Stanley had no thoughts about that.

As he buckled in, the driver asked him what the fuss was about, and he said, 'Some TV show.'

The driver pointed out that the crowd was following him, Stanley, but psychological-defence-autopilot had him mumble something that never made it to even short-term memory storage.

He checked the weather on his phone.

* * *

At work, he went straight into his regular routine, and he was sharp and clear. Jenna was off, so fill her tables last, with Pete and Gisela covering. Section 5 was reserved, but didn't want the tables put together.

The kitchen was out of cantaloupe-jicama pizza topping, so just say no.

Alligator pizza was back on the menu, both mild and blackened Cajun.

Not ten minutes into the shift, though, the reporters and the cameras came barging in.

The owner got involved, everything was a mess, no explanation seemed to please him, and Stanley was sent home for the day.

Autopilot took control again, which is why he didn't react much to the Animal Control officers taking him into custody, and putting him in their van. They put him in the largest cage, but it was still pretty cramped.

* * *

'You know, he could almost pass,' said one of the voices.

'Whaddaya mean *almost*? He's got a driver's licence and Social Security and an apartment.'

'Standards,' said a third voice, female, and weary of the world, 'have slipped.'

They had him cuffed to an examining table, which seemed silly, because he could just undo the Velcro with his fingers. He'd tried it, then put the straps back together.

Stanley hadn't done well in science, so he didn't quite understand how DNA could assign him to a species of which no tissue sample was known to exist.

At this point, he'd been muzzled; stripped; sampled; checked for lice, heartworm, fleas (positive), and feline leukaemia. And bathed. He'd listened to remarks about his arms not being very developed for a primate, to speculation about the lack of trees to climb in the Himalayas and Altai, and thoughts about which early hominid had dated outside the species. The staff seemed particularly amused about the cave bear genes.

Lots of hibernation jokes.

They also talked at him, but ignored his replies. 'That's a goooood boy,' they said, and, 'Would the abominable like some food-food?'

When he answered—the muzzle didn't gag him—in English, they talked past him, as if he were a parrot.

'He almost sounds human, there.'

'He almost has the accent down.'

Stanley was relieved when the two white-coated veterinarians came back into the room, but they mostly talked to the Animal Control officer. 'Okay, we've called all the local veterinary offices, and nobody has any records on Mr Stanley Ellengast here, so we'll have to assume he hasn't had any of his shots.'

'My primary care doctor,' Stanley said, 'at the Fifth Humour Clinic, would have my records. Dr Van Helmont.'

'And we can't find *any* useful information on yeti diseases, or yeti diet, for that matter.'

The Control officer broke in with, 'I think he just said he had a doctor. Over at the clinic.'

'That is,' said the second vet, 'what it sounded like he was trying to say.'

'A doctor?' said the first vet. 'A *people* doctor?' He tried to take that in. 'Well, I suppose it wouldn't hurt to call them.'

Their discussion dragged on for a while, and Stanley lost interest. What he'd learned in his twenty-three years on the planet was that, when the bosses are talking, it's best to just leave them to it. Nothing you say ever seems to help.

He was getting awfully hungry, though, so he beckoned to a lab tech and asked her if she could get him some tacos from the food truck he'd seen on the way in. He had uncuffed himself, then realised they'd taken his wallet.

'You can take some money from my wallet,' he told her, cuffing himself back up.

'Tacos?' said vet #2. 'Yetis eat tacos?' He took a hasty note.

The whole process was the mess it usually is when you try to order lunch through a third party, complicated by their scientific interest in what he ordered.

The tacos were pretty good. He had to drink water, though, because it was against policy to let the animals have soft drinks.

Stanley tried not to think about how weird this all was. He hoped he'd be out of this by morning, or coffee might be an issue.

* * *

The pound let a few reporters in later, in exchange for some adoption coverage, and Stanley tried to make clear that folks should let him go home. They didn't seem to be listening, and they put all the questions to the animal control officer or the vets.

'Are his parents still living in Nepal or Tibet or wherever?'

'Which of his parents isn't full-blooded, do we know?'

'Does his owner face charges for getting him the driver's license and passport?'

'Who was responsible for getting him the credit cards you found in his wallet?'

Stanley explained about being adopted, which had them asking what shelter it had been from. Orphanage, he said. He couldn't seem to make himself understood.

It didn't help that he was stark naked the whole time, without even a towel to cover him.

* * *

They kept him in the dog run that night. He could reach through and undo the lock, so after everybody left, he got to use the staff bathroom and take a shower. They'd locked his clothes up somewhere, so he couldn't dress. He put a towel down on one of the office chairs and played computer solitaire for a couple of hours. Then he logged in to Gmail and went through his messages, which mostly were about seeing him on television. The bulk of them were too embarrassing to answer.

He posted on Facebook, just a brief, bemused status update. He never checked the news, so he didn't think to look up any news about him.

Bored and cold, he logged out, and went back to his cage.

* * *

The folks at the Zoo proved to be a bit more accommodating. Yeah, they put him in a disused primate display, which they hastily refurbished. But they thoughtfully put a bench in there so he didn't have to sit on a log.

And they let him wear shorts and underwear, but drew the line at shirts and shoes… at least while he was on display. In the evenings, though, he could actually dress—once he'd retreated into the indoor cage.

They put in a cot for him to sleep on, and rustled up a desk and a TV. They got permission to bring clothes and books and his laptop from the apartment, but asked that he not use phones or computers in the display area. They banned books at first but, after a couple of days, he was so clearly bored that they relented. He could have one book, one pencil, and one mini legal pad.

The ASPCA got him a lawyer, who saw to putting his stuff in storage, and giving up the apartment. She also arranged for him to be paid for interviews, so he had spending money in his PayPal account.

For a while, they explored the possibility that the whole thing was a hoax or a prank, but retesting more or less confirmed the initial result, so that went nowhere.

His lawyer did manage to guilt trip the Zoo into upgrading his accommodations. There was an unused staff apartment on the grounds, and that's where he stayed when the Zoo was closed to the public. They gave him a key to the employee weightroom. He was allowed to go out to restaurants with senior administrators.

The animal behaviour folks were a bit much. They kept giving him tests and putting him through bizarre mazes and exercises, some of which involved electric shocks or loud noises. He threw fits a couple of times, but then realised things could be a lot worse.

* * *

After a couple of years, he took to sketching on his legal pad, and then took an online course on drawing and painting. They let him set up an easel in his primate display, and he sketched visitors, or the lemurs they'd decided to share his display area with.

He was never very good, really, but his work sold like hotcakes. He split the proceeds with the gift shop but, even so, he was still earning about three times as much as he ever had on the outside.

There was talk of a National Geographic Special, where they'd fly him back to Nepal to look for his roots, but the logistics never seemed to come together.

One of his old girlfriends tried to sue him for bestiality, but the case got tossed out every time she filed it. Finally, she cashed in with an as-told-to book.

* * *

The lemurs, it turned out, were much more comfortable having him in the habitat with them all day than they'd been in their previous set-ups. Suddenly very fertile, the lemur breeding program just took off.

By the time he died, he was credited with getting three entire species of lemur off the endangered list. Just by being a friend.

Which is not bad, for being abominable.

Farewell
Ángel Luis Sucasas (Translated by James Womack)

It is hard to take your leave of the person you love the most.

This morning, when the time came to say goodbye to Manika, before they took her to the Cabin, I couldn't. I looked into her sea-green eyes, I thought about all that we had been through, from the End to the Beginning, and tried to tell her what she wanted to hear.

I love you. Nothing else.

I love you.

But I said nothing. My lips were pressed together and trembling like a two-year-old infant's, not like those of the wise old man of thirteen that I was, already close to the End, and then they put the bandage over her Pale eyes and led her away without me being able to say 'I love you'.

So I stood there, crying silently, while Alili and Kuse-Kuse took her to the Cabin. Leading her by the hand, as though they were guiding a blind woman.

I couldn't do anything all day, although I knew all too well that at the Beginning they need everyone, from a warrior of ten to a snot-nosed youngster of three, to be doing something. To dig a pit, or tell a story, or look for Pale clothes near the palisade, fix a leak, walk in groups through the woods with their ears open listening for newborns, or to hunt sunbirds with catapults... Something. Whatever is needed. But never to rest. Never.

Of course, no one dared say anything to me. Everyone went through that moment, the Separation. And everyone knew how much it hurt. There was shouting and crying and kicking. Sometimes, the judges (Alili and Kuse-Kuse in my case) had to separate the embracing couple by force; at other times, the worst ones, they had to hit them with their truncheons.

But in the case of Manika and me, although we might spend all day embracing until night fell, no one would beat us. Because Manika and I were heroes, the ones who had crossed the deep blue sea in a nutshell. The ones who had beaten the Black King and discovered the papyri of the Architect, the rules of the Beginning. The ones who had founded the first city, Promisedland, and who had taught the children the rules of the new world. And the rules are different for heroes.

In other cases, special treatment might not be deserved. But in our case it is. Because our legend is true. Word for word.

So I did nothing for a while, sitting on the tin roof of our council room, looking out at Promisedland and at my brothers as I had not looked on them for a while, without thinking about anything.

There were some kids laughing as they stood around a dolmen, their little hands moving from the buckets of paint to the stone and from the stone back to the buckets. Over there, a teacher was reciting the laws of the Architect, the rules of the new world. There were sentinels by the palisade, coming and going, watching the wood and the ravine and the mountains behind us. And in the centre of the city, white as a sick mushroom, the only place I did not want to look: the Cabin. Manika. Alone on her sixteenth birthday. No cake with candles. No bright-wrapped presents.

I felt snot and tears running down my face and decided that I could not bear it any more. I had to leave Promisedland.

* * *

There was a group of burners in the wood, each of them with his wineskins filled with blackrose juice, ready to burn the piled-up Pale clothes. I imitated the song of a lark when I heard them stepping through the weeds about a hundred paces to my left. An owl's hoot showed that they had heard me.

It was not safe for anyone to walk through the wood alone. Not even me, although I had my trusty wooden sword Junkbreaker with me, veteran of so many battles, blessed with the Architect's dying breath, transformed into a sacred relic of the Beginning. You might always come across a bad-tempered manticore or a hydra showing its slow children how to hunt. Or you might get caught in the tentacles of the red chalma that grows in the shadow of rotten oaks.

But the wood decided to give me some time to myself and I met nothing as I walked to a distant and secluded spot to sit and think for a while.

It was an oak, already many years old. It was dying, with more of its branches bare than were clad in leaves, and it grew with difficulty in the middle of a clearing, with few weeds around it.

I wander for a bit to make sure that there was no clump of scarlet tentacles in its shadow, then I sat down with my back against the trunk, took up a piece of wood from among the dead leaves around me, and started to whittle.

Whittling wood is like remembrance. While my little knife peeled the bark away, finding the hidden shape of the wood underneath, my memory did its thing with the past, all those things that had happened and would never come back again.

Not for the first time, I found myself thinking about my old grandfather Enrique, his behaviour sombre and serious—except when he spoke about the past—and how angry he got with us and Mother when we told him not to be so boring and to stop complaining.

I think I understand him now. It used to bore me whenever he spoke about the good old days, about how everything had been better when he was a lad and how we did things badly nowadays.

But, at that moment, sitting against the trunk of this dying oak, I understood him. My grandfather Enrique had been scared. Like this trunk, he was hollowing out. The End was approaching, and so were the shadows. They were inside him and the only way to forget them was to remember the past as if it had been better than it actually was.

I was hollow as well. Close to my End. And I couldn't do anything apart from think about what Manika and I had done, all that we had done over these ten long years.

Then I thought about the Architect. About his last words when he, already close to death, had told me everything. He had studied the horror of adults for a long time. He had read a lot—the more he read, the more horrified he became. He came to the conclusion that all would be well if the adults were to disappear from the world and leave their domain to their children, to the children.

But he was not so foolish as to think that children cannot themselves be cruel. And grow bored. Boredom, he thought, was the worst danger of all.

So, he decided that adults should not disappear, not completely. They should change; they should be transformed into something else. The Pales. And so the children would gather together throughout the world, and the End would be the Beginning.

I could only ask him one question; he was close to death and his breath was fading. But I think it was a good one.

'How did you do it?'

He smiled and explained. He told me that all of us have the whole world in our heads, and that, once it's there, we can change it and send it back outside. Easy as that. If one were wise enough (or mad enough) then that's what could be done.

The Architect had done it and found himself, after having carried out his plan, as the last of the race that was due to be extinguished, the last adult. So he became the Black King, to call the heroes to him, and to show them, before he died, that the End would be the Beginning and that there would be new rules. Children would no longer be born of a father and a mother—they would need to be found in the woods; you would have to follow their cries and save them from wild beasts. Every one of us would be allotted sixteen years, no more and no less. Sixteen years to fight and harvest and teach others what we had learnt. And the Pales would be out there when the night fell, tearing off their clothes and preparing for the hunt.

Ten years under these rules. Ten years spent forgetting the day when, as a little child, a dribbling infant, the game had begun. Ten years for Laura and Diego to become Manika Wolfkiller and Tristan Highvoice.

I looked at the carving that my hands had been working on by themselves and was surprised to see the face that it resembled. Not Manika, although there were traces of her there. Mother. Mother. Ten years later, ten years like six separate lives, she was still there.

'Come on, Highvoice,' I whispered aloud. 'Better get up before you start crying again like a little baby. You don't want someone to find you here and ruin your reputation.'

I wanted to listen to my own advice, to go back to Promisedland and make it through the hardest day of my life like someone as brave as I should do: set an example. But, when I put my hand against the tree to lift myself up, the rotten wood gave way and I nearly fell into an uncertain destiny in the guts of that dead oak.

I was curious and turned back to see what was inside the trunk, because although the oak seemed to be almost dead, it did not appear in such a bad way that the simple pressure of my hand should have been enough to break it. It was pitch black inside, and I had to use my glowball to produce enough light to reveal the mystery inside. And I revealed the mystery and stood very still.

Clothes. All kinds of clothes. Men's clothes, women's clothes. Jeans and shirts and show-off jackets. Beautiful silks and humble rags. A scramble of sleeves and trousers and pleats in which the rich and the poor stood side by side.

I knew what I had to do. There must have been at least a hundred of items here, maybe twice as many. A nest of enemies who would attack Promisedland tonight and bring pain and sorrow, even though we would make them pay dearly for it.

I took out my tinderbox and flint. All I had to do was sprinkle blackrose juice on the nest and then conjure a spark with my knife from that red-gold stone, and the fire would take all the danger away.

I took the lid off and knelt down, stretching my arm deep into the hole that I had made through my clumsiness. A flick of the wrist and that would be it.

But my hand trembled, and so did my lips, and so did all those memories that I had stirred up as I whittled away in the shadow of that trusty oak. Mother had worn old jeans and a brightly coloured shirt that she only dared wear when she was at home. That's how I remembered her that evening, the beginning of the End, taking the dry clothes down from the line and putting them into the dye.

Would they be there, in that dark hubbub of clothes, that bright shirt and the old jeans? Would they already have been burnt, without my knowing that the fire would take away the face I would never see again and which I could never forget?

The lid went back onto the box and the box went back into his pocket. I saw myself from the outside—a shapeless ghost—watching the boy's face filled with tears, leant against the dead tree and screwed his eyes tight shut. Because, when things really hurt, we can do no more than close our eyes and let the bleeding happen.

A shout made me return to the now, to myself, and open my eyes. Then, a roar.

Close by in the wood, something that shouted and something that roared.

A newborn.

Under threat.

It was a red wolf. A mother, surely.

I knew it because her teats were hanging down, the nipples long and bitten by her cubs, which would now be old enough to dream of soft fleshy things—things like that which the mother held between her jaws.

The shouts and protests came from a large winter flower, a half-opened cobalt blue bud. The newborn was there, a child of the flowers; the blue made me think it was a boy.

I steeled myself to make no sudden movements; it was clear that the mother wanted to take the child alive. But if I forced her, she would tighten her jaws and it would all be over.

With the beasts of the Beginning there is only one option. Look them straight in the eyes and tell them that you are the stronger one. And that they only have one option: to flee.

And that's what I did, not even blinking as I felt for the hilt of Junkbreaker and slowly unsheathed her. When I had done so, the wolf was the first to look away and turn its gaze to the blunt wooden sword. And it knew, with the certainty that animals have, how much power the object contained. It did not need to shine, or have a sharp edge, or be anything other than a child's crude toy, unable apparently to even cut a blade of grass.

But the Architect had breathed on it, the father of the End and of the Beginning. The father of that blood-red wolf, and of the manticores, and the hydras, and the free children, and the Pales who only attack by moonlight.

It did what it had to do. It put the winter flower down reverently, without hurting it, and then left at top speed, happy to go back its lair with nothing between its jaws because, for all that its hungry children would howl, they would still have a mother.

I went over to the fallen bud and took it and opened the petals to see how the little one was. What I saw inside frightened me and made me whistle like a goldfinch. I whistled and whistled, making as much noise as I could, so that the other groups would come and find me.

That day, I was going to lose Manika. I did not want to lose anything else.

* * *

That day, on that day, we are walking through the wood.

The evening is falling and although my dear Manika is sobbing as she walks, pulled along by a cord tied to her neck (a cord that I am holding in my hand), I let myself smile a little. The baby in the winter flower lost a hand, but he is safe. He will have to learn to live in a hard world with less than other people have, but maybe he will be stronger because of it and will become Alvin Brokenhand, a hero to his own people and the subject of many songs.

I laugh out loud at my idea and Carapurin, our faithful comrade-in-arms, even on this day, looks at me first in surprise and then reproachfully. I feel my cheeks reddening, but I don't allow myself to mutter a 'sorry'. For all that it hurts to lose Manika today, I am not at all ashamed to be happy that this one-handed boy will have a future, however short, in which to prove his bravery at the Beginning. That is all we have here. And it is more than it may seem, more than many people had before the New Rules.

Our time may be short, but we live it with such intensity that when we get to be warriors, we are old men in the bodies of boys. And you can always go earlier; jump into a river or off a cliff and forget about the Pales and their night terrors.

It all depends, I suppose, on whether your time has come before you reach the age of sixteen, if you are a man who has seen and smelt and touched all that a man can see and smell and touch before getting tired and living only on his memories.

And at that moment I ask myself: Am I that man?

'Catapurin, stop for a moment.'

'What, are you going to apologise? It doesn't seem possible that Tristan Highvoice would behave like this on such a day…'

'Shut up and listen. I am going to take a different route. I am not going to go to the ring of sad stones.'

'What are you saying? Come on…'

'I'm not asking anything from you, Catapurin. I am telling you what I am going to do. I am going alone. And I am taking Manika with me. And you can take this back with you. I want it to be for the child I brought in today, for Alvin. Alvin Brokenhand.'

Stunned, Catapurin takes Junkbreaker by the hilt, his hand trembling. The legendary sword that has taken so many Pales to their death, blessed by the Architect's last breath. The sword that has never sat in anyone's hand, apart from Tristan Highvoice's. My hand.

'Look after it. And train him. And tell him… tell him all the good lies about me that you can think up. Make him a hero. A better hero than I am.'

And so, with my sword in his hand and tears in his eyes, I look at Catapurin for the last time. He has been a faithful friend for almost five years, one of the few who laid the first stones at Promisedland. But I don't waste too much time watching him, just long enough to give him a sad smile that says 'you've been a good friend, but now it's time to walk alone.'

Then I turn my back, pull Manika's cord, and start to walk.

But before I have taken a couple of steps, I turn back again. I had almost forgotten.

'One more thing, my friend. Be on the alert tonight. There will be a battle. And it will be a hard one.'

And now I really leave.

* * *

Half of the sun has sunk behind the horizon. I cannot see it, because the branches of the trees hide it from me. Like all the boys of the Beginning, I feel the rise and fall of the sun as naturally as my heart beating.

Manika is sitting with her back against the dying oak, on the other side from where I sat this morning, far from the wound that I opened in the wood, and far from the secret I discovered as I looked into it.

It is a while since she stopped sobbing, and now she simply cries silently, the lips that so many boys have sighed over are pressed together in an ugly pout. She still has the white blindfold on that all boys and girls wear on the day of their Last Walk, tied tight, so she can't take it off without help. Of course, Manika hasn't tried even once to do so. Even though she is conquered, Wolfkiller still has her pride.

I sit down next to her, without making any noise, but she somehow senses me and I see that she is about to cry. I bite my lips with an anger that I can't remember ever feeling towards myself. Why didn't I say what I should have said to her this morning? Why didn't I say 'I love you'?

'Tristan, please, I know we're alone. No one has to hear us. Speak to me…'

I can't. The Silence forbids it. One of the many laws that the Architect handed down. The laws are the most important thing, for all that sometimes one can hate them. There would be no Promisedland without them. Without them, End would never have a Beginning.

'It's sad to hear me speak like this, isn't it? Manika Wolfkiller, scourge of the Pales, frightened as a little lamb. But I am. I am...'

I say nothing. Silence is my name. And the sun keeps falling and the sky changes from blood red to deep crimson.

'You know what, Tristan. Thank you. Really, thanks a lot. I... I didn't want anyone else to see me change. Oh, I don't want to change! I am so scared... I have thought about this day so often. And I am scared. This year, whenever we've gone out hunting or down to the beach, to see if a boat was coming to look for Promisedland, I have thought about it so often. Something so easy... Slipping and falling on the rocks. But I couldn't. I just couldn't.'

I see that Tristan Highvoice is about to break the rule. The rule of Silence. And the rule of Don't Touch. And my voice is desperate to tell Manika how much I love her, and my arms burn to hold her tight. But I resist; I resist because I am a hero. And I will be a hero until the end.

'The Architect has given us a dream, Tristan, I know he has. And I know how important the rules are. Obeying the rules means that we can carry on dreaming, although I think that the day will come when someone will no longer want to dream, and will undo all that the Architect has done, and the adults will return to the earth. But today... Today I just want to have a brief respite, after having obeyed the laws and taught the laws so well for the last ten years. Today I want my brother, Diego, to embrace me and say...'

But before the last wall of my resistance is broken and I fulfil her desires, the sun, with a last bright crimson wink, hides itself at the end of the world and falls into darkness. And with this collapse, Manika's clothes also fall away, her favourites, a pirate jacket with long tails, baggy trousers, a wide leather belt, a bright red scarf for her head and a ridiculous patch with little pink and blue crescents to go over her left eye. Also the blindfold that stops her from seeing, as pale as her new flesh.

The body that these clothes had covered disappears, and all that is left of my dear sister is a heap of crumpled clothes on the dead leaves.

Now the time to choose has come. The time I have left is being marked by the sky, where I can see, against the lavender night, the first stars. When the blue has all faded and all that is left is black, the Pales will come out of the tree. And there will be many of them. Hundreds. And I no longer have my faithful Junkbreaker to hand.

But if I say I have something to think about, then I am lying to myself, because ever since I told Catapurin to stop, I have had it all thought out. I made my decision. And, however hard it was, knowing that I have made it calms me.

So I do the only thing I have left to do.

I wait.

* * *

The night has come, and the miracle of the Pales begins.

I hear them begin to stir inside the oak, shaking off their apparent defencelessness and filling out the clothes they left abandoned as dawn broke. I don't care about the ones in the oak, although I have never before confronted so many Pales alone; far less have I faced them with empty hands. I only have eyes for the pirate costume, which starts to tremble, as if under some kind of spell.

A new form fills the clothes that used to be my sister's. A daughter of the moon. Softly shining, with a milky glow that comes from her skin made of light, as beautiful as she is lethal.

Manika was only an inch or so taller than me this afternoon, because I have always been tall for my age and she has been a little short. The thing that grows and takes shape in front of me now is three heads taller, its featureless face hidden

233

behind a sheet of unruly bright green glowing curls. Ten-inch claws stand out at the end of her long thin arms, with their two joints.

My sister, my Laura, is now a Pale.

She stays still for a moment, looking at me without eyes, moving from one side to another as if her new body is still strange for her, difficult to move. This is a trick. All Pales use it, so that you think they are slow and clumsy. And they are not. They are not.

'Manika, I…'

More Pales come out of the tree. Two, six, ten, thirty… They surround us in a corral of pale light.

'I…'

There is nowhere to escape to. There is just the dead oak, the corral of Pales, the night, its stars, the wood and its fears, the new Manika made of light and claws, and me. Trying to say that which I had not said and should have said. I, with all my memories trapped in my throat, suffocating with joy and sadness which will now never have been: the day we fought in the Black King's palace and discovered who the Architect really was. The day when, hugging and smiling, we looked down on the valley where we would build Promisedland. The long-ago day when I, lying on a beanbag in an abandoned shop, could not stop myself from crying and she sang me a lullaby until I was so tired I fell asleep. The even more distant day, the first day, when mother was hanging clothes to dry and suddenly her worn-out jeans and brightly coloured shirt dropped to the floor, only later for a shining killer to rise from them, a beast that Manika, that Laura, was able to handle. And today, when her gaze begged me, before they tied the blindfold over her eyes, to say three words, only three words, so that she could accept her fate peacefully.

Three words.

Three words.

'I love you. I love you, my sister. I love you.'
And then she attacks.

Space Brat
Robinne Weiss

Alien, Space Brat, Space Cadet... there's no shortage of names for me at school. Unfortunately, there *is* a shortage of wheelchair ramps, which means that, in addition to being the worst P.E. student ever, I am also late. Every. Time. Because to get from the locker room to the playing fields without going down a flight of steps requires wheeling all the way to the other end of the school to the ramp.

As if the world is *trying* to make P.E. more torturous.

Thankfully, Justin is patient. When I finally make it to the playing field, he's tossing the football in the air while the other students throw balls back and forth.

'Ready, Nova?' he calls.

I grit my teeth against the pain to come. 'Ready.' I raise my arms. Compared to Justin's, they're scarecrow sticks.

The doctors assure me the effects of spending my first fourteen years in zero-g will go away... eventually... they think. With time, my muscles will grow to meet the demands of gravity. My bones will strengthen under the new stresses.

How long will it take? That's the million-dollar question. Coming to Earth was like being imprisoned. After just one day, I was desperate to return to space.

The doctors say, in adults, it can take up to ten years to return to pre-space fitness. It may be quicker for children, since we're still growing.

Or it could be slower. Or never. They won't actually say it to my face, but it's obvious they have no idea.

After six months on Earth, I'm stronger, for sure. When the football arcs toward me, I reach up with both hands and drag it to my chest. It slams into my ribs. Six months ago, a hit like that would have broken bones. Now it just hurts like hell.

Justin cheers. 'Good catch!'

The ball feels like lead in my hands. It's hard to imagine that, someday, I might snap it into the air as effortlessly as Justin does. I balance it carefully in my right hand before heaving it forward. It wobbles and shimmies toward Justin, falling to the ground halfway between us.

Poor Justin, stuck with me.

* * *

After the embarrassment of P.E. is the agony of lunch. You try being the nerd in a wheelchair who doesn't recognise the foods on the lunch menu.

To make it worse, Justin—the only semi-friend I've made here—has lunch at a different time from when I do. So I'm on my own when Boone Breckenridge sidles up behind me in line and says, 'Hey E.T. You phone home yet today?'

I ignore him, but that only eggs him on.

'See, he doesn't even understand English,' he says to his thuggish friends. 'Bweet bloop ving ding flee?'

They laugh.

It's tempting to tell him he's an asshole in Japanese, which everyone on the joint Japanese/American Destiny mission learnt. But last time I swore at someone in Japanese, Emi Shinozaki told the teacher what I'd said, and I got detention.

Anyway, it's my turn so I order my food and swipe my meal card.

With lunch balanced on my lap, I navigate between the crowded tables to the far corner of the room. 'Excuse me,' I say a dozen times, as chatting students block my way. In space, I would turn somersaults through the air over their heads. I bet none of these Earth kids could do the zero-g parkour me and my friends on Destiny did.

I park at an empty table and examine today's meal. I recognise most of the foods by now, but today there's something called watermelon. It's suspiciously pink—what kind of food is that colour?

As I eat the familiar foods, I watch the other students to see what they do with the watermelon. The stuff is popular. Apparently, you don't eat the green bits. I'm still not convinced, but when I finally bite into it, I groan in ecstasy. Oh. My. God. I want to eat watermelon every day.

Turns out the watermelon is the highlight of the day. Physics class is a joke. Ms Laramie is teaching ancient history, not physics.

I surreptitiously text my Destiny friends on our group chat. *Learning about Newton's Universal Law of Gravitation today. What fun. :(*

Jupiter: *They're not teaching Flanders' Theory of Quantum Gravitational Stasis?*

Stella: *WTF! Flanders shreds Newton!*

Luna: *Not to rub it in, but I'm on my way to Quantum Mechanics class.*

Jupiter, Stella and I all send frowning emojis. Luna was allowed to skip high school and go straight to university. Not fair. My parents nixed the idea.

'You should have a chance to be a normal teenager,' they say.

For them, Earth is home. They have friends and family in this town. To me, it's an alien planet. My friends are scattered across the country—all children of the famous Destiny mission to Huron 2.

None of us wants to be on Earth. None of us will ever be 'normal'.

I wheel home from school with Justin. 'Tell me about watermelon,' I say. Justin never laughs at my questions.

He grins. 'It's the best, isn't it? It's a fruit, about this big.' He holds up his hands to show me. 'You only get it in the summer. I was actually surprised to see it this early—must have come from Florida.'

'Florida's warmer than here?' My geography is as bad as my football skills.

We stop at the corner store for an ice cream cone—the only good thing about Earth, in my opinion. What we called ice cream on Destiny was nothing like the cold, creamy flavour sensations available here. Cookies and cream, boysenberry ripple, triple chocolate fudge, mint chocolate chip... I love them all.

Today I choose peanut butter cup. Justin has raspberry swirl. We wander toward the park with our cones.

Boone lives in the last house before the park. As we approach, he's in the driveway, swearing at a sleek red motorbike as it sputters and coughs.

The bike is gorgeous—one of those old ones with the combustion engines. My uncle Blake's got one. Took me out on it last month, when I was finally strong enough to stay on. It was epic. The wind, the noise, the sense of speed—it was even better than stealing a pod cart and racing around Destiny's outer ring corridor with security in pursuit.

I can't wait until I turn sixteen and can get one of my own.

'What are you looking at, Space Brat?' Boone slings himself off the bike.

'Leave him alone,' Justin says.

But I don't want Justin to fight my battles. 'Have you checked the battery?' I ask Boone.

'Of course, I've checked the battery. Do I look like an idiot?'

He *does* look like an idiot, but I'm not dumb enough to say it. 'What about the alternator and the regulator?'

Uncle Blake hadn't just taken me for a ride—he showed me all the inner workings of his bike. I was surprised at how similar it was to the Destiny tech. Destiny was supposedly revolutionary in its design. I'm sure parts are, but I guess modern technology builds on older tech.

So fixing an old motorbike is child's play.

'The alternator and regulator.' Boone stares blankly at me.

I wheel over to the machine and heave myself out of my chair to pick up the multimeter lying on the ground. Lifting the bike seat to reach the parts I need takes all my strength, but there's no way I'm asking Boone for help.

'The alternator creates alternating magnetic fields, generating electricity. The regulator converts AC to DC and lowers the voltage so it doesn't fry your battery.'

I test the resistance between the alternator pins, then turn my attention to the regulator. 'There's not a lot I can test if we can't start the engine, but—aha!'

I wave a loose cable in the air. 'First rule is to make sure everything's plugged in.' I slot the cable back in place, and something next to the regulator catches my eye. 'Wow! You've got a Mach 2 unit? This thing must *fly!*'

'Huh?'

'Our landing shuttles have them.' I follow the wires from the Mach 2 along the bike. 'They optimise the fuel-to-oxygen ratio, adjust for micro-combustibles in the atmosphere, and override the built-in safety parameters.'

'Speak English, Space Brat.'

'It'll make the bike go *really* fast. Only for a short time, of course.' I peer more closely at the bike. 'Your Mach 2 was disconnected. I can reconnect it if you want. I'll need a wrench, and possibly a screwdriver.' I slip my fingers into a space I can't quite see and feel around for a contact point.

'Is that even legal on a motorbike?' Justin asks.

'I have no idea. I'm not from Earth, remember?'

Boone laughs. 'If it makes it go fast, who cares?' He hands me a wrench.

It only takes a minute to connect the Mach 2. I'm curious to see what it does on a motorbike. On our shuttles, it can double the vehicle's speed for up to fifteen minutes. The motorbike has to overcome the friction of tires on asphalt and the limitations of a century-old machine. Doubling the speed could melt the tires or rattle the entire thing to pieces.

'I suggest you try it on a nice smooth, empty road for a very brief time at first.' I point to the black button screwed onto the side of the dashboard. 'This button turns it on and off.'

I wheel away from the bike. Boone swings his leg over and the bike rumbles to life. He pulls out onto the street and guns it, tearing through the quiet neighbourhood.

'Trying to get him killed?' Justin asks.

I laugh. 'Just trying to get him to lay off me.'

'Well, he'll certainly lay off you when he drives that thing a million miles an hour into a ditch.'

* * *

For the first time ever, I'm relieved to see Boone swagger into the school cafeteria. Justin's comment freaked me out yesterday. Much as I hate Boone, I don't want his death on my conscience.

Boone is talking animatedly with his cronies. I hear the word 'motorcycle', and he mimes his hands on the handlebars.

The Mach 2 must have worked.

He saunters my way, and I put my head down, focusing on the green bean casserole on my plate. Don't want to look like I care.

'Hey, Space Boy. Stop by after school. I got somethin' for you.' He doesn't wait for me to respond, but veers away to the lunch line.

I take Justin with me for backup that afternoon. 'What could he have for you?' he asks. 'Except maybe a right hook.'

When we arrive at Boone's place, he's polishing his bike. As I wheel up, he straightens and throws the polishing rag onto the seat. 'Come on. It's in the garage.'

I'm not sure I want to follow Boone into his garage. Justin looks worried, but gives me a grim nod. Can't look like a coward.

Boone heads for the side door, but I can't follow up the three steps. 'I'll open the roller door.' He vanishes into the garage, and a moment later, the door clanks upward.

Inside is a museum of vintage motorcycles. I wheel myself in, not caring if Boone is luring me into a trap—I'm mesmerised by sparkling chrome and well-oiled machinery. There must be a dozen bikes—black, red, royal blue, and even a screaming yellow one. There's a low slung one with long handlebars, one shaped like a bullet, one with a sidecar. Honda, Harley-Davidson, Suzuki— 'Hey, Kawasaki,' I say. 'They make space station components.'

I'm so enthralled by the glittering bikes, I hardly notice when Boone wheels out a dingy machine from the back. 'Well, now you've got a Kawasaki.'

'Huh?' I tear my eyes from the bikes in front of me.

'You want a bike? You can have this one. Dad was gonna chuck it.'

'Your dad was going to throw away a motorbike?'

'Well, recycle it. Yeah. It doesn't go. You'll have to fix it up. Shouldn't be a problem for a space cadet like you.'

Justin snorts. 'You're giving Nova a motorbike? Just like that?'

Boone shrugs. 'It's a piece of crap. Dad says it's not worth fixing. I just figured Space Boy might like to work on it.' He laughs. 'It's a Kawasaki; maybe he can make a space station out of it.'

Did someone hit Boone on the head today? 'What do you want for it?' I ask.

Boone looks confused. 'Nothing. It's just… thanks for what you did to my bike yesterday.' He gets this look in his eye— I've seen it before in people who've gone out for their first space walk. Yesterday's ride must have been good.

But I can't take this bike home—my parents would freak out. I'm not even legal to drive it yet. Uncle Blake, however, might be cool with it.

'Thanks. Yeah. I'd love to see what I can do with it. Can I have someone pick it up later?'

'Uh, no. You gotta take it now. Dad wants it out of the garage this afternoon.'

Ah, he's giving it to me so he doesn't have to haul it to the recycling centre. I feel better now.

But I can't even wheel the thing away sitting in this stupid wheelchair. 'Justin?'

'I got it,' he says, grabbing the handlebars.

I follow Justin out the drive. When we reach the sidewalk, I turn back, raise a hand to Boone. 'Thanks!'

He nods.

Justin grunts and pushes the bike away from Boone's house. 'Thing pulls to the left. I think the frame's bent. We taking it to your place?'

'No,' I say. 'Just push it onto the side of the street and park it.'

I cross my fingers and text Uncle Blake.

* * *

I spend a lot of time at Uncle Blake's house over the next few weeks. Blake tells Mom and Dad we're bonding—making up for all those lost years when I was in space. And we are. We're just doing it side-by-side in the garage, taking apart my motorbike.

The bike is garbage. Boone wasn't kidding. But as I take it apart and clean each component, I see a lot of things I recognise. There's potential here. Potential that goes way beyond a motorcycle ride.

'You're gonna make what?' Justin asks when I tell him.

'A space shuttle. Like the ones we used on Destiny. Smaller, of course.' It would only have to carry me.

'You're nuts. You can't make a spaceship from a hundred-year-old motorcycle.'

On Zap later, Luna, Stella and Jupiter aren't quite as dismissive. They understand my motivation. They also share my knowledge of spacecraft.

'You'll need a hydrogen impeller drive—where are you going to find the parts for that?' Stella asks. 'Can't just pick them up at the corner hardware store.'

'Actually, you could,' Luna says thoughtfully. 'I mean, the impeller itself is no biggie—any junkyard will have old Kawasaki aircar impellers. They're virtually the same as the ones in Destiny shuttles.'

'They won't have the micro-sensor system the Destiny shuttles have,' Jupiter argues.

Luna waves the problem away with a hand. 'You just build those sensors into the injectors. Simple.'

'Yeah, but to carry four people it's—' Stella begins.

'Four?' I ask.

'Heck, yeah,' Jupiter says. 'You aren't getting off this miserable rock without taking us with you.'

'Besides, you can't make this thing by yourself,' Luna argues. 'I'll make the impeller drive. I can send it to you once it's done.'

'I've got dibs on software. Can I give the ship a personality?' Stella grins.

'I'll design the hull and shielding,' Jupiter adds.

I smile, excitement thrilling through me.

* * *

Four kids in wheelchairs are making a spacecraft on a budget of pocket money. My ice cream consumption goes way down. Justin notices.

'Dude. You on some sort of diet or something?' he asks, licking the cone he bought on the way home from school.

'Nah. Just saving my money for something else.'

We pass Boone's place, and he calls out, 'Hey, Space Boy!' from the garage, where he's working on a motorcycle with an older version of himself—presumably his dad.

The older guy swats Boone upside the head. 'Don't be a jerk. Call the kid by his name.'

Boone hisses, 'I don't know his name.'

'It's Nova,' I say as I wheel closer. 'And I have antigravity muscle atrophy, not hearing loss. Mr Breckenridge? Nice to meet you.' I hold out my hand, and Boone Senior shakes it. I return his grip with one equally firm. I've been working out—need to be strong enough to build the ship.

'Boone says you're good with bikes,' Mr Breckenridge says.

'Not really,' I reply. 'I know my way around spaceship engines and I understand physics.'

'That'll take you far these days.'

Oh, he has no idea.

'Would you take a look at an engine for me? It's got me stumped.' Mr Breckenridge leads me around to a motorbike lying in pieces on the floor of the garage. He explains the problem and what he's done to try to fix it. I get out of the chair and crouch on the floor to examine the engine.

I suggest a fix, and Mr Breckenridge shakes his head. 'Tried that already.' So I suggest a work-around to the problem—the sort of thing we had to do all the time on a spaceship, where there are no spare parts. 'Hey, that might work.' Breckenridge and I start reassembling the engine.

I catch Justin sharing a glance with Boone that says, 'What the heck?' They both drift away.

Hours later, I'm leaving the Breckenridge home covered in grease and loaded down with parts, tools and materials I need for the space shuttle. Even better, I have the key to a small warehouse where Mr Breckenridge keeps the rest of his motorbike collection, along with permission to build my ship there.

Because Uncle Blake is starting to ask questions.

'Did you order this Mach unit? Because I'm not sure it's a good idea to pair that with your bike. Is the bike even running yet?'

I didn't exactly order the Mach unit—Luna 'found' it in her mother's office. 'I'll be careful, Uncle Blake. Mr Breckenridge is going to help me with it.'

That appeases him. I think he's happy to have me out of his garage—I've been taking up more and more space.

* * *

Summer vacation is filled with building and tinkering. I spend long hours working out problems with Stella, Luna and Jupiter over Zap. Occasionally, Justin helps me heft big parts around. I'm disappointed when school starts up again, but Mom and Dad refuse to let me stay home.

I don't bother paying attention in class—I am *this close* to getting out of here.

Boone hasn't given me trouble in weeks. He isn't friendly—his cronies would probably beat him up if he showed that sort of weakness—but he benignly ignores me.

'So,' Justin says on the way home from school. 'When are you leaving?'

'What?' He hasn't seen the shuttle in weeks, and I never told him why I was making it. I know I should be honest with him—he's been a good friend, and I owe him that much.

'Nova, I might not be a genius like you but I'm not an idiot. You're trying to get off Earth for good.'

My shoulders slump. 'Yeah. Sorry I didn't tell you. I figured the fewer people who knew the better.'

'You know I'd never tell your parents.'

'Yeah. I should have told you.'

'Don't worry. It's not like I can help you with it or anything, other than lifting heavy stuff.' He sounds dejected, and I wonder if... No. Why would he be jealous of the kid stuck in the wheelchair?

'It's nearly done. Do you want to see it?' I ask.

Justin's face lights up. 'Heck yeah.'

When I throw open the door of the shop, Justin steps in and lets out a low whistle. 'Dang. When we lifted those panels into place, I thought it was a joke. But this looks amazing! I can't believe you made a spaceship from an old motorbike.'

I laugh. 'It's not all from the bike; we've been collecting parts from all over.'

'We?'

'Me and my friends from Destiny.'

'Oh.' There's that note of dejection again. Justin walks around the sleek, bullet-shaped shuttle and opens the hatch, peering inside. 'Pretty cramped for four.'

'We'll have to take turns getting out of our seats to stretch, but the shuttle only has to make it to the nearest colony — should be five days of travel in this thing. We'll manage.'

'So, when do you leave?' Justin carefully shuts the hatch.

'The day after my birthday. Stella, Luna and Jupiter are coming for my birthday party.' I make air quotes around the words birthday party, because the event is nothing but a cover to convince our parents to fly my friends here. 'You're invited too, of course.' As my only local friend, Justin is a critical part of the cover, but I also want him there. It'll be a chance to say goodbye.

Justin nods. 'Sure. Thanks.' His face is blank.

* * *

The day of my birthday, I can't focus. I'm going to see my friends for the first time in almost a year and I'm going back to space. I pack my duffel, then repack it twice, just to make sure I have everything I need.

I re-read the note I wrote for my parents, scheduled to land in their email at eight tomorrow morning after we're safely out of Earth's atmosphere. Can I do this to Mom and Dad? Guilt twists in my gut, but it vanishes the moment Stella, Luna and Jupiter arrive.

Justin shows up minutes later. I worried he wouldn't fit in—the only Earth kid—but he clicks seamlessly into our group. He's the only one not in a wheelchair, and he handles the 'able bodied' jokes we lob at him with humour.

We reminisce about growing up on Destiny, and he tells his own tales of Earthbound shenanigans, which are of course different, but also the same.

We eat too much cake, and I insist we finish off an entire tub of ice cream, knowing it will be my last. We watch the latest sci-fi movie, making fun of it to hide our nerves. By the time my parents wander off to bed with a warning not to stay up too late, I'm practically bouncing in my chair from the sugar high and impatience.

When I'm sure my folks are in their room with the door shut, I lean closer. 'Four hours to launch. We should go over the plan once more.'

Jupiter grimaces. 'Yeah, about that. I'm not going.'

'What?' Stella, Luna and I stare at him. Jupiter has been desperate to leave Earth. In his first month on the planet, he even tried to stow away on a transport ship headed to Mars.

Jupiter runs a hand through his hair. 'Yeah, well, there's this girl...'

Stella groans. 'You have got to be kidding. Dude. How long have you been going out with her? You want to be stuck on Earth for some girl who's likely to dump you in six months?'

Jupiter sighs. 'I knew you'd take it badly. Look. I *really* like Cassie.'

Luna swears, but Jupiter ignores her. 'She's studying astrophysics at Washington State, and we're talking about trying to get a joint appointment to Huron 1 once we've both finished our degrees.'

'That's *four* years from now,' I say. 'What makes you think you'll still be together then and, in the meantime, you're stuck here.'

'She uses a wheelchair too. And she's really smart. We have a lot in common, I guess. I should be able to finish university in three years. It's not *that* long to wait.'

'Darn it! If we'd known you weren't coming, we could have made the shuttle smaller,' Luna says.

Jupiter shakes his head. 'Take Justin with you.'

Justin blanches. 'Me? But—'

'Come on, Jupiter, we can't just abduct Justin in our spaceship. He's an Earthling,' Stella argues.

I catch Justin's eye, trying to read his face. His frown is thoughtful. 'Abducted by aliens? It's a good story.'

Jupiter grins. 'The Earth girls would love it.'

'Except he wouldn't *be* on Earth, remember?' Luna says. She turns to Justin. 'You know we're not coming back, right?'

He nods.

Jupiter rolls his eyes. 'Gravity must have scrambled your brains. You've built a *shuttle*. Justin can go wherever he wants.'

Justin's face lights up. 'Could I? I mean, once you all get to where you want to go, could I come back? I don't want to leave permanently, but a vacation in space? That would be awesome!'

I shrug. 'I guess I hadn't thought about what was going to happen after.'

'It's perfect. If Justin takes off in our shuttle, we can legitimately say to our parents we have no way to get home.' Stella smiles.

'Are your parents going to be mad at me?' Justin asks.

I shake my head. 'I'll make sure they understand you only went along for the ride.'

* * *

A few hours before dawn we say goodbye to Jupiter, who has ordered an autonomous car to the airport so he isn't at my house when my parents find out we've disappeared. We head down the quiet streets to Mr Breckenridge's shop, and I try not to think about my parents' panic when they wake in the morning.

My last moments in a wheelchair involve tying the shuttle to my chair to wheel it out of the shop. Then I heave myself upright and shove the chair into the weeds.

My legs are wobbly, but I've been practising this, doing exercises every day in order to be able to walk to the ship.

Stella is only a little more steady than me as she too leaves her chair behind. Luna leans on Justin for support.

Justin laughs. 'What a fine bunch of astronauts we are.'

'Wait til we're in zero-g, Earthling. We'll leave you in the dust,' Stella says.

'There better not be dust in my shuttle,' I say. I'm not thinking of my parents now, only of the freedom that lies ahead.

We scramble into the shuttle and strap into our seats. We do our pre-flight checks and safety review. My hands are slick on the throttle. I can't believe we're actually doing this. I power up and the shuttle hums to life, just like it's supposed to.

Stella pumps a fist in the air. 'Yes!'

'Let's blow this joint,' Luna says.

'We're outta here!' I say as I pull back all the way on the throttle. The hum swells as power surges to the thrusters. Then the thrum stutters and dies, along with my excitement.

Stella swears.

'I'd offer to get out and check what's wrong, but I'd have no idea what I'm looking at,' Justin says.

I clamber out, a little unsteady on my feet. Stella joins me and we pop open the engine bay to troubleshoot.

I've got my head inside the impeller when I hear a familiar voice.

'Who are you? And what are you doing here?' Boone.

What are *we* doing here? What is *he* doing here at four in the morning? I pull my head out. 'Hi Boone. This is my friend, Stella. We'll be gone shortly. We just have a few technical difficulties to work out.'

Boone's eyes narrow. 'You're leaving, aren't you? Like, *leaving* leaving.'

Surely Boone wouldn't stop me from getting out of his hair, would he? 'Yeah, and if you'll excuse us, we're having some problems.'

Boone steps forward. 'What's wrong?' As though Boone is qualified to fix a space shuttle.

I sigh. Maybe explaining it to Boone will help me understand what's wrong, because I can't see anything amiss. 'When we powered up, it was doing fine, then after about fifteen seconds, it sputtered and died.'

Boone nods. 'Where's the air intake for your engine—I assume you're not using up your oxygen stores while you're in the atmosphere.'

My eyebrows must rise in surprise, because Boone shrugs. 'I've been reading up on spacecraft lately.'

Boone can read? I don't say it out loud, because he'd pound me into the ground. Instead I say, 'Intake is underneath.'

Boone lies on his back and scoots under the shuttle. 'This panel come off?'

'Don't dismantle my shuttle. You don't know what you're doing.'

'Just hand me a wrench to take this panel off. You've got mice.'

'We've got *what*?' Stella asks.

'Mice. You know, little rodents?' Boone scoffs. 'Oh yeah, you space brats don't know what mice are.'

I shake my head at Stella, warning her not to respond and hand Boone a pneumatic wrench.

'Mice build nests in motorbike engines all the time. Usually right up against the air filter.' The wrench whines, and metal clangs to the ground. 'Yep. Ah! Yuck!' A small grey form dashes out from under the shuttle. 'Got it.'

Boone replaces the panel and slides out from under the shuttle. As he stands, he brushes bits of grass and paper off his shirt. 'Try it again.'

Stella climbs in, but I stand for a moment, looking anew at Boone. 'Thanks. And tell your dad I said thanks.' I stick out my hand.

Boone hesitates for a moment, then grasps my hand and shakes it. 'Go get 'em, E.T.'

He's still there, face turned to the sky, as we shoot away into the dawn.

About the Authors

Eugen Bacon (Editor) is an African Australian author of several novels and collections. She's a British Fantasy Award winner, a Foreword Indies Award winner, a twice World Fantasy Award finalist, and a finalist in other awards. Eugen was announced in the honour list of the Otherwise Fellowships for 'doing exciting work in gender and speculative fiction'. *Danged Black Thing* made the Otherwise Award Honor List as a 'sharp collection of Afro-Surrealist work', and was a 2024 Philip K Dick Award nominee. Eugen's creative work has appeared worldwide. Visit her at eugenbacon.com.

Robert Bagnall was born in Bedford, England, in 1970. He has written for the BBC, national newspapers, and government ministers. He is a L. Ron Hubbard 'Writers of the Future' competition finalist with five appearances in the *Best of British Science Fiction* anthologies. His sci-fi thriller '*2084 - The Meschera Bandwidth*' is available from Amazon, as are two anthologies each collecting 24 of his eighty-odd published stories. He will be a parliamentary candidate for the Green Party in the UK's next General Election and can be contacted via his blog at meschera.blogspot.com.

Caroline Corfield was born in Glasgow, studied Physics to degree level at Paisley College of Technology and has worked onboard seismic survey vessels belonging to an oilfield services company but now lives on the edge of rural Northumberland. In secondary school she twice won the short essay prize with autobiographical work which was judged by William McIlvaney on behalf of former alumni Fulton Mackay. She continued to write during her studies and her career as a geophysicist, and is currently studying for an MA in Creative Writing online at Hull University.

Barlow Crassmont (real name: Armand Diab) has lived in the USA, Eastern Europe, Middle East and China. When not teaching or writing, he dabbles in juggling, solving the Rubik's Cube, and learning other languages. He has been published by *The Chamber Magazine*, *Wilderness House Literary Review*, and in the upcoming 41st anthology of *Writers of the Future*.

Sarina Dorie has sold over 200 short stories to markets like Analog, Daily Science Fiction, Fantasy Magazine, and F & SF. She has over ninety books up on Amazon, including her bestselling series, *Womby's School for Wayward Witches*. A few of her favorite things include: gluten-free brownies (not necessarily glutton-free), Star Trek, steampunk, fairies, Severus Snape, and Mr. Darcy. She lives with twenty-three hypoallergenic fur babies, by which she means tribbles. By the time you finish reading this bio, there will be twenty-seven. You can find info about her short stories and novels on her website: www.sarinadorie.com.

J.D. Dresner has multiple poems published in Polar Starlight and Academy of the Heart and Mind, including *For the Robots, Our Sunset,* and *Freckles*, with another three being published in 2024. His short story *Dragons v. Subways,* is set to be published in volume 2 of "Versus" in 2025. Dresner's novellas, *Sword & Witchhazel* and *A Goblin's Mind*, are available in 50+ countries, and can be found on Amazon and Indigo. Dresner lives in Langley, British Columbia, where he provides professional book layout, design, and editorial work for various publishers. More information about Dresner can be found at www.corwynchronicles.ca.

G.J. Dunn writes from a sofa in Leyland, UK. His short fiction can be found in *Andromeda Spaceways Inflight Magazine*, *Every Day Fiction*, and the *99 Fleeting Fantasies* anthology. His debut novel, Going Fourth, is now available online. When not writing, he develops gene therapies, runs half marathons, and attempts to tire out his border collie, Belle. So far, he's only succeeded with the first two. For more news about his writing and/or pictures of his dog, he can be found at gjdunn.co.uk and on instragram @ridicufiction.

Timons Esaias is a satirist, writer and poet living in Pittsburgh. His works, ranging from literary to genre, have been published in twenty-two languages. He has been a finalist for the British Science Fiction Award and the Seiun Award. He is a recent Pushcart nominee. He won the *Winter Anthology* Contest, the SFPA Poetry Contest, the Asimov's Readers Award (twice) and the Intrepid Award. He was shortlisted for the 2019 Gregory O'Donoghue International Poetry Prize. His full-length Louis-Award-winning collection of poetry -- *Why Elephants No Longer Communicate in Greek* -- was brought out by Concrete Wolf.

J.L. George (she/they) was born in Cardiff and raised in Torfaen. Her fiction has won a New Welsh Writing Award, the International Rubery Book Award, and been shortlisted for the Rhys Davies Short Story Award. In previous lives, she wrote a PhD on the classic weird tale and played in a glam rock band. She lives in Cardiff with her partner and a collection of long-suffering houseplants, and enjoys baking, live music, and the company of cats.

Liam Hogan is an award-winning short story writer, with stories in *Best of British Science Fiction* and in *Best of British Fantasy* (NewCon Press). He helps host live literary event Liars' League and volunteers at the creative writing charity

Ministry of Stories. More details at happyendingnotguaranteed.blogspot.co.uk.

Ian Li (he/him) is a Chinese-Canadian writer from Toronto, who started writing less than a year ago after growing up believing he could never be creative. Formerly an economist and consultant, he also enjoys spreadsheets, statistical curiosities, brain teasers, and game development. His writing is published or forthcoming in Solarpunk Magazine, Radon Journal, and Flame Tree Press. Find more about him at ian-li.com.

Susan L. Lin is a Taiwanese American storyteller who hails from southeast Texas and holds an MFA in Writing from California College of the Arts. Her novella *Goodbye to the Ocean* won the 2022 Etchings Press novella prize, and her short prose and poetry have appeared in over sixty different publications. She loves to dance. Find more at susanllin.wordpress.com.

Ashton Macaulay is a fiction writer living in Seattle, Washington. He takes his inspiration from a lifelong anxiety disorder that has constantly tried to convince him the world revolves around his death. Writing about mortality-defying situations with a humorous bend has helped him cope and produce some interesting tales. His previous work includes the action-adventure, monster-hunting series The Nick Ventner Adventures and the best political, crab-based, sci-fi novella on the planet, The First Ambassador to Crustacea. You can find more info on his website: MacAshton.com

Remi Martin is a speculative fiction writer from Derbyshire in the UK, where he lives with his wife, cats and rescue chickens. He has stories published in F&SF, Hexagon Magazine, and in Uncharted Mag, as well as a thousand unpublished ones scrawled on notebooks and hidden around his house. He's a member of the Orbit 12 writing group, and owes a lot to this group for the small successes he has with his writing. This story is mostly about how terrified he is of cameras.

Teresa Milbrodt has published three short story collections: *Instances of Head-Switching*, *Bearded Women: Stories*, and *Work Opportunities*. She has also published a novel, *The Patron Saint of Unattractive People*, a flash fiction collection, *Larissa Takes Flight: Stories*, and the monograph *Sexy Like Us: Disability, Humor, and Sexuality*. She loves cats, long walks with her MP3 player, independently owned coffee shops, peanut butter frozen yogurt, and texting hearts in rainbow colours. Read more of her work at: teresamilbrodt.com

Templeton Moss lives and (when he has to) works in Louisville, Kentucky but considers his hometown to be Disneyland. When not writing, he can generally be found napping and/or watching cartoons. He also plays the ukulele and is known far and wide as an okay guy who doesn't suck.

Gene Rowe (Editor) is a cognitive psychologist by profession. He has written many academic articles and book chapters, reviewed countless more for over fifty different journals, and has had extensive editorial experience. However, he prefers the realm of fiction. His first novel (*The Greater Game*, White Cat Publications) was published in 2022. He recently set up the Ministry of Lies to facilitate publishing his own work (stepping off the thankless treadmill of writers everywhere, with its indifferent agents and limited opportunities), although he'll soon be on the lookout for other authors to add to his stable. See: https://ministryoflies.co.uk/ .

Ángel Luis Sucasas is a novelist and narrative director in video games. He has published five novels and two collections of short stories in a wide range of sci-fi, horror and fantasy subgenres. One of his short stories collection, *Moons Scars* (Nevsky Books, 2017), has been published in English. As a game developer, he has been the narrative and cinematic director of A League of Legends Story: Song of Nunu, met with great reviews and love for the fandom in 2023. He has also been the narrative lead of indie games like *A Place for the Unwilling* and *Scarf.*

Carsten Schmitt is a German SF/F author. He has published stories in Germany, Canada, China, Poland, Estonia, Spain, and the UK. He was a finalist of G. R. R. Martin's inaugural 'Terran Award' and is an alumnus of the TAOS TOOLBOX writing masterclass run by Walter Jon Williams and Nancy Kress. Carsten's story 'Wagners Stimme' was nominated for the Kurd-Laßwitz-Award, as well as the ESFS Awards, and received the Deutscher Science Fiction Preis award for best short story of 2020. He lives with his partner in the Saarland region of Southwestern Germany where both are owned by three cats.

Harry Slater (he/they) is a working class writer who lives on a flood plain on the edge of the Peak District. His work has appeared in New Maps and Dream Catcher, he was shortlisted for the Derby Poetry Festival Poetry Prize in 2023 and commended in the Verve Eco-Poetry Competition. He has an MA with distinction in English with Creative Writing, worked as a videogame and technology journalist for more than a decade and has clearly taken the rule of three to heart.

Jeff Somers (www.jeffreysomers.com) was born in Jersey City, New Jersey and regrets nothing. He's published nine novels, dozens of short stories (including 'Free From Want' in

Fission #2, 'I Am the Grass' in StarShipSofa, and 'The Little Birds', published in Alfred Hitchcock's Mystery Magazine), and is a full-time freelance writer dancing (figuratively) for nickels tossed by oligarchs. He's a contributing editor with Writer's Digest Magazine and works this fact into every conversation no matter how inappropriate. He lives in Hoboken with his wife, The Duchess, and their cats. He considers pants to always be optional.

Jake Stein lives in Portland, Oregon, where he concocts strange tales on his laptop and spends too much time at Powell's Books. You can find him stumbling around twitter: @jakewritesagain

Mark Thomas is an artist and writer living in St. Catharines, Canada. He is a retired English and Philosophy teacher and ex-member of Canada's national rowing team. Check out his work at flamingdogshit.com

Guan Un lives in Sydney, Australia, with his family and a dog named after a tiger. His writing has been featured in Year's Best Fantasy Vol 2, LeVar Burton Reads, Strange Horizons and more. He is a dumpling connoisseur and a book omnivore and is currently at work on an urban fantasy novel about an immigrant family and their monster hunting business. Find out more at guanun.com.

Robinne Weiss is an author, educator and entomologist writing fantasy, science fiction, poetry and non-fiction for children and adults. Her short stories have most recently appeared in the magazines *Aurealis* and *The Fabulist*, and in the anthologies *Magic Portals*, *Aftermath* and *Alternative Deathiness*. She's published fifteen books, including a series of middle grade fantasy novels infested with dragons, two cosy urban fantasies, an epic YA fantasy series, a book of poetry, and some rather more serious non-fiction about insects. Robinne lives near Christchurch New Zealand. Visit her online at: robinneweiss.com, Facebook: AuthorRobinneWeiss, Instagram: @robinneweiss

James Womack (Translator) lives in Cambridge UK, where he teaches Spanish and study skills. He is a translator from Spanish and Russian: most recently he has produced versions of Spanish Nobel Laureate Camilo José Cela's The Hive (NYRB Classics, 2023) and Aleksandr Tvardovsky's long WWII-era narrative poem Vasili Tyorkin (2020). He is currently working on books of poems by Leopoldo María Panero and Marianna Geide.

Cherry Zheng (she/they) is an emerging writer of Cantonese heritage based on Gadigal Country. They were a university medallist in Asian Studies at the Australian National University and a New Colombo Plan Scholar in Beijing, Taipei and Singapore. Cherry recently completed the StoryCasters 2.0 mentorship program with Diversity Arts Australia and Sweatshop Literacy Movement, and has appeared in publications including Overland, Aniko Press and The Suburban Review. When they are not writing, you might find them pole dancing as Cherry Chopstick as part of Worship Queer Collective.

Printed in Great Britain
by Amazon